UNFORGIVING

*Recent Titles by Nick Oldham
from Severn House*

BACKLASH
SUBSTANTIAL THREAT
DEAD HEAT
BIG CITY JACKS
PSYCHO ALLEY
CRITICAL THREAT
CRUNCH TIME
THE NOTHING JOB
SEIZURE
HIDDEN WITNESS
FACING JUSTICE
INSTINCT
FIGHTING FOR THE DEAD
BAD TIDINGS
LOW PROFILE
EDGE
UNFORGIVING

UNFORGIVING

Nick Oldham

Severn House Large Print
London & New York

This first large print edition published 2016
in Great Britain and the USA by
SEVERN HOUSE PUBLISHERS LTD of
19 Cedar Road, Sutton, Surrey, England, SM2 5DA.
First world regular print edition published 2015 by
Severn House Publishers Ltd.

British Library Cataloguing in Publication Data
A CIP catalogue record for this title is available from the British Library.

ISBN-13: 9780727894380

Severn House Publishers support the Forest Stewardship Council™
[FSC™], the leading international forest certification organisation. All
our titles that are printed on FSC certified paper carry the FSC logo.

MIX
Paper from
responsible sources
FSC® C013056

Typeset by Palimpsest Book Production Ltd.,
Falkirk, Stirlingshire, Scotland.
Printed and bound in Great Britain by
T J International, Padstow, Cornwall.

This one is for my family – you know who you are.

One

It looked as though there was going to be trouble at the Swan's Neck.

Initially, it was a nothing job.

The landlord of the only pub in Thornwell, a tiny village tucked away in the furthest reaches of Lancashire Constabulary's Northern Division, had phoned in on the treble-nine to the police to say he was having problems with a customer by the name of Spencer Bartle. Bartle was drunk, refusing to leave the premises, and had threatened the landlord whose name was McCready.

In her eighteen months as a special constable, Laura Marshall had never even heard of the Swan's Neck, known locally as the 'Sneck', or the landlord McCready, but she did know Spencer Bartle. He was a young man, early twenties, came from farming stock with the physical build to match. He had a reputation as an evil drunkard, with a predilection for assaulting young women as he walked past them. He worked in a small abattoir which he owned. He usually spent his days dispatching livestock, covered in blood and guts, and when things were not going well for him, he gravitated quickly to drink and violence.

Bartle often stalked the streets of Lancaster city centre in search of trouble, and Laura had been present twice when he was arrested. On both occasions it had taken half a dozen cops to overpower him, like ants bringing down a dung beetle. In fact he had been arrested earlier that week for violent conduct and was currently on bail, though Laura had not been there to witness the arrest on that instance.

His family, she had been told, was equally barmy and unhinged, but she had never met any of them.

When the call came over the radio, Laura, the only patrol free to attend the pub, said she would make her way – she knew, more or less, how to get to Thornwell – but it would take about fifteen minutes or more to get there from the city centre. Her sergeant called her up, warning her to take care and to tell her he was also en-route as back-up, maybe ten minutes behind her.

It was, in police parlance, a bread and butter incident.

On that Friday night, police across the country were dealing with hundreds of similar ones. A drunk. A pub fight. Nothing remotely special, although it was sometimes the routine jobs that turned out to be the most deadly.

Nevertheless, as routine as it was, Laura Marshall was excited. So far, on virtually every incident she had attended as a special constable – an unpaid, volunteer cop, sometimes cruelly referred to as 'Hobby-Bobbies' by 'real' cops – she had been accompanied by another special or regular constable.

Tonight she was out and about alone. She had recently passed a driving assessment giving her authority to drive basic police cars, and because the regulars were so short-staffed that

2

evening the patrol sergeant had reluctantly lobbed a set of car keys at her for the first time with a slightly patronizing warning not to get into 'the shit'.

She promised she wouldn't.

She knew the geography of the area reasonably well, but was assisted by an on-board GPS. She drove out into the wilds, heading east away from Lancaster, passing through the picturesque village of Kendleton, along the narrow, winding, unlit country roads. Just for fun she flicked on the blue light for a few seconds to check out the effect on the hedgerows. Blue light, black shadows, a bit spooky.

Then the road dipped and she was in Thornwell, nothing more than a tiny cluster of houses and a pub set around a Y-junction that formed a neat village green with a tiny stream burbling through its centre, a tributary of the River Lune. Not even one shop, though there was a small village hall and the pub, of course.

The Swan's Neck had a cobbled car park in front and a larger, unmade gravel one at the rear. Three cars were drawn up, and there was no obvious sign of trouble. This was confirmed when Laura's Personal Radio chirped up and comms told her that the landlord had phoned in again to say that Bartle had left the premises and peace had returned.

Laura parked up outside the pub. 'I'll show my face,' she radioed in. A moment later she heard her sergeant calling up to say he was diverting to another job.

If she was honest, Laura was relieved that

3

Bartle had gone – although she hadn't seen him or anyone else as she'd driven into Thornwell – but she knew he had a bad habit of returning to the scenes of his crimes. She recalled a number of city centre incidents where he'd been ejected from licensed premises only to roll back later, even more drunk and violent, and wreak havoc. But if he'd gone, he'd gone, and she was glad of it because the prospect of wrestling with him was not appealing.

A few regulars were gathered around the main bar inside the pub; a few others sat around at tables. All eyes swivelled to Laura as she entered, adjusting her hat and uniform. She had grown comfortable with the interest now, the looks, the leers from men, sometimes out-and-out hatred. It came with the territory of wearing a uniform: people gawped.

She nodded comfortably and went to the end of the bar. The man she assumed was McCready, the landlord, was pulling a slow pint. He nodded amicably at her, finished his task – Guinness with a shamrock on top – then came to her, wiping his hands on a cloth.

'Mr McCready?'

'Aye, that'd be me . . . I phoned to say he'd gone.'

'I know – but I was almost here, so I came to check you were really OK.'

'I'm OK,' he confirmed.

'Spencer Bartle?'

'The one and only.'

'Drunk?'

'As a skunk . . . Take it you know him, love?'

4

'I've met him in town a few times. What's he been up to?'

'Fighting drunk . . . don't know why . . . but he stopped short of becoming a handful.'

'Where did he get drunk?' Laura asked.

A little cloud of guilt crossed the landlord's face.

She said, 'Here I take it?' It was a prim, school-ma'am type of question-cum-statement. McCready's little gesture, a slight deflation of the shoulders, confirmed her suspicion.

'I thought he'd be OK . . . I thought wrong. Him and drink don't mix well.' McCready sighed. 'He broke four glasses, a table and a stool, then stormed out and put his elbow through the back door window on the way out. But he'll pay up. Might be short of a shilling up here—' McCready tapped his temple – 'but he isn't short of brass . . . blood and muck.'

'Where will he have gone?'

'Home, probably, or maybe getting a taxi to take him into town,' McCready said, meaning Lancaster.

'But you don't think he'll be back here?'

McCready shook his head at the question.

'D'you want to make a complaint about the criminal damage?' Laura asked him.

McCready shook his head again and said, 'It's nowt. I just wanted him out; now he's gone, and he'll pay up. He needs to keep on my good side because this is the only watering hole around here he isn't barred from.'

'OK,' Laura said. 'If you change your mind, let me know.' She handed him one of her contact cards, which he wedged behind the till.

'Will do . . . Want a drink while you're out in the sticks, love? On the house?'

Laura froze him with the expression she had been perfecting over the last year and a half, and his facial reaction confirmed he had got the message. Nothing to do with the offer of a drink on duty, just his reference to her as 'love'.

'I'll pass, thanks.'

Outside it was chilly but clear. Laura stood and shivered for a few seconds before getting back into the Vauxhall Astra, thinking again about this being the first job she had attended solo. OK, so it hadn't been much of anything, run of the mill, but she'd been alone and had dealt with it confidently.

From the angle at which she had parked the Astra out front it was easier for her to drive forwards and spin it around in the rear car park behind the pub, do a wide, leisurely circle on the empty, unlit area, feeling and hearing the satisfying scrunch of the tyres on the gravel.

As the headlights arced past a line of bushes forming the perimeter of the car park, a huge, ape-like figure of a man appeared in the beam. His arms were long, dangling at his side, something in his right hand. He was maybe ten feet in front of the car.

Laura's stomach jerked. She wasn't expecting the apparition, and for a fleeting moment of shock, her mind did not compute what her eyes were seeing. Then she slammed the brake on, the car rocking on its suspension – and Laura found herself with Spencer Bartle in front of the car, framed in the windscreen.

In that instant she realized the job she thought she had dealt with efficiently was only just beginning.

He looked immense: his shoulders hunched, his head tilted forwards, his eyes glowering at her from underneath his thick mono-brow, the vehicle beam bathing the contours of his face in light and shade, accentuating his bulbous eyes.

Slowly, he raised his right hand and showed her what he was holding – a crowbar, a foot long solid metal rod with one curved end and a prying tip at the other.

The two were in eye to eye contact, and a yelp jumped from Laura's lips. She fumbled to slot the gear lever into reverse, somehow not depressing the clutch far enough in, making a terrible grating noise as the cogs failed to mesh.

Bartle stepped quickly to his left, and then with one long stride he was alongside the driver's door.

Laura twisted and slapped her left hand down on the door-lock button – which wasn't there. Though the Astra was a battered cop runabout car, it was a newish model, and all the doors were locked centrally either from the ignition fob or from the button on the dashboard, thereby eliminating a need for a press-down button on the door itself. But a succession of cheap old cars and her unfamiliarity with this one had conditioned Laura to reach for a button that wasn't there, a realization that momentarily stunned her.

Bartle was bent over at the door, staring in, but he didn't wrench it open.

He drew back his right hand as Laura still

desperately fought to force the gear lever into a reverse that suddenly did not seem to exist. She was consumed by a terror that also blinded her to the fact she should have slammed it into first and shot ahead now that Bartle was at the side of the car. But she was trapped in a terrible moment, her eyes widening as Bartle raised his right hand across his body, then backhanded the curved end of the crowbar hard against the driver's door window. The glass smashed spectacularly, crumbling instantly, falling out of the door frame like a sheet of snow sliding off a roof.

Bartle dropped the crowbar, then reached through the opening with both hands. He grabbed Laura, his boots crunching on the broken glass as he manoeuvred himself. His thick, strong fingers gripped her blouson jacket, and she screamed as she cowered, yet tried to fight him off. He seemed immune to her slaps. His stench, an overpowering blend of booze, sweat, cigarettes and cheap deodorant, shrouded and invaded her nostrils. Then he let go with his right hand, but bunched it into a huge fist and slammed the half-brick sized hand into the side of her face so incredibly hard that her face distorted, her jaw broke and any fight she had inside her went with a moan and a hiss of breath as her brain ceased to function.

She did not even realize that Bartle then dragged her head first through the broken window, her slim frame sliding easily through the space. He dumped her face down on the gritty surface of the car park. Her hat came off her head and rolled across the ground like a huge coin, coming to rest under the bushes at the edge of the car park.

Laura's senses returned with a rush. Too quickly. Her mind was like a whirlpool. She tried to force herself up and try to find the emergency button on her PR which, if activated, would sound an alarm in the comms room, inform the radio operator who was calling and remain live for twenty seconds so that the cop in trouble had time to transmit hands-free. She groped for the button but could not seem to find it.

Bartle straddled her then dropped the whole weight of his body on to her shoulder blades, crushing her back down and trapping her arms underneath her. He took hold of the tennis-ball sized hair bun at the back of her head, held it tight and slowly twisted her head around so her left cheek was crushed against the ground and on the tiny chunks of glass from the broken window.

She felt something hard, cold and circular being pressed into the side of her head, just slightly forward of her right ear.

In that instant, she knew exactly what it was.

The muzzle of a captive bolt gun, the device used to stun animals prior to slaughter.

Two

Three months later

Unlike the others, PC Jake Niven didn't mind the waiting. He saw it simply as a slice of the cake. You trained. The job came in. You were briefed. You prepared. If you were lucky it was fast moving and instant, all blur and rush. If not, you waited. But somewhere along the line there was always some waiting. Sometimes it was short; sometimes – more often than not – it dragged. And sometimes it came to nothing: you packed up and went home without even breaking sweat. And how often did that happen? Many, many times.

So there was no point in doing anything other than dealing with it.

Jake Niven didn't whinge, just accepted the waiting game.

If nothing else it gave him time for introspection, but he tried not to delve too deeply into his own psyche, or his personal situation. That could be unsettling. Instead, he wrestled with more practical problems: dealing with that bastard of a third hole at Lytham, by improving his golf swing, or maybe visualizing the walk he'd planned over the Trough of Bowland.

Interesting, simple things. Not difficult ones like the precarious nature of his relationships, or

10

how he might just be kidding himself about keeping his head above the water line.

Far better to re-imagine the golf stroke that was eluding him.

'Here.'

Jake blinked out of his reverie and looked at Dave Morton, his partner on the team that day – that night, to be precise. Morton was a twitchy waiter, one of those who could never settle and always had to be doing something, which was OK unless the whole team happened to be crushed together in the back of a battered Ford Transit van, which they were. Six fully kitted-out fire-arms cops, three teams of two, three down either side of the van, facing each other along the narrow, arse-numbing bench seats fitted in the back of the van.

Without uniform or kit, it would have been a snug fit. In kit it was a tight squeeze and very uncomfortable. Overalls, boots, ballistic vests and hats, each officer with a Glock 17 holstered at their side, each with a Heckler and Koch MP5 machine pistol slung diagonally across their chests. Each also had a Taser gun, plus all the usual accoutrements: rigid handcuffs, CS canister, extendable baton, radio, torch. All with hard edges, nothing comfortable. And six people cramped up in the back of a Transit had a certain 'whiffy-hum' to it, even if one of them was female.

Morton was sitting directly opposite Jake, both of them by the back doors of the van. When – *if* – it happened, they would be the first two to pile out of the doors.

11

'Here,' Morton said again. He was holding a paper cup towards Jake, steaming chicken cup-a-soup in it, a smell that didn't necessarily gel well with the body odours within the confines of the vehicle. He had poured it from his flask.

Jake took it with a nod of gratitude, even though four hours into this operation he was bursting to pee.

It tasted remarkably good. He took a few sips of the hot liquid and passed it on to the officer sitting alongside him, catching her eye fleetingly in a shaft of light from the nearby street lamp. She took it from him and glanced guiltily across at Dave Morton, catching his eye, too.

In that instant Jake realized that his friend knew.

Morton had observed the seemingly innocent cup handover carefully and seen the eye contact between Jake and the policewoman, whose name was Kirsten Lee. Morton sat back and tilted his head knowingly, looking down his nose with smug disapproval at Jake as if everything had just slotted into place, made sense.

Jake cursed inwardly, but just arched his eyebrows at Morton, then looked out through the one-way window in the van door to the world outside, thinking: How the hell does he know?

Shit.

With a gloved hand, Jake wiped the window which constantly steamed over, despite the over-worked air-con unit in the van that fought a losing battle to keep the atmosphere fresh.

From the window Jake was looking northwards along Clifton Drive, towards the South Shore area of Blackpool. Even though it was dark he could still make out the Meccano-like structure of the huge roller-coaster ride, the Big One, on the Pleasure Beach. Its red aircraft warning-light rotated brightly on its apex, the highest point where the ride paused before plummeting spectacularly, almost instantly reaching a speed of eighty miles per hour.

The van was parked on the roadside, actually facing the direction of St Annes, the more genteel resort to the south of Blackpool. Across to Jake's right was Blackpool airport; to his left were the Starr Hills sand dunes, and beyond them the black Irish Sea.

There had been very little radio traffic for the last hour over the encrypted and dedicated channel being used for this operation. The target, under surveillance, had been seen to enter a flat in South Shore about ninety minutes earlier, and the expectation – hope – was that he would leave and make his way back to a flat in St Annes he was supposed to be hiding out in. The route he chose would, with any luck, take him right past the Transit van in which the six heavily armed cops sat.

But he seemed to have settled in for the night.

Not that Jake was concerned.

If the target didn't reappear, then they would go for him at the flat at dawn. Ideally, they wanted to take him en-route whilst he was on the move, which made it easier to isolate him – hence the firearms van plus two unmarked and two liveried police cars parked discreetly nearby. They wanted him on the move so that they could control

13

everything, not holed up in a flat, which could get very messy.

Whatever, they were going to get him that night. That much had been decided.

The guy was wanted for murder, was known to carry and use firearms, and he was going to be nailed at some time in the next few hours. Jake hoped that he would be the one to come face-to-face with the bastard, just to see him shit himself when an MP5 was shoved up his nostrils.

Jake inhaled and exhaled, taking in a shot of fresh air from the gap between the ill-fitting van doors that shouldn't have been there, but was.

He thought about the target.

He was a low level drug dealer, the kind of person who seemed to be the target of many similar police operations. The difference with this lad – and he was only a kid, eighteen years old – was that he'd gone into 'turf expansion' mode and fallen out with another gang and the guns had been drawn. If he'd murdered a member of a rival gang, that would have been one thing. But he had killed someone in the crossfire: a completely innocent boy of twelve who had strayed into a wild-west shoot-out by mistake and taken a bullet in the head.

The police had been ruthless in their pursuit, led by a Senior Investigating Officer (SIO) called Henry Christie. After causing serious disruption to a lot of the drugs trade in Blackpool, they had identified the killer, and there was no way he was going to keep his liberty.

Jake had been annoyed by the claim that the young victim had been in the wrong place at the wrong time. That made him fume because the youngster had been exactly where he had every right to be and should have been able to go about his activity without fear of having his head blown off.

It was the gang member with the gun who had been in the wrong place.

Jake found he was grating his teeth.

'Here.'

This time Dave Morton was proffering a tube of polo mints. Jake took them, flipped one out with his thumb and passed them on to the next firearms officer along. This time, no eye contact with her. But Jake could not help but be pressed up tight to her, thigh to thigh.

His eyes caught Morton's again. On this occasion there was no expression of knowledge in them – just anger.

Jake looked out of the van window again, along the deserted road, and sucked on his mint before manoeuvring it with his tongue to sit wedged between his back teeth and cheek to see how long he could keep it there without chewing it or it dissolving. His record was twenty minutes. The team record was thirty-two minutes, held by Morton.

A voice over the radio cut into Jake's thoughts: 'Alpha Two to patrols on Operation Amethyst.' Alpha Two was the call sign of DCI Rik Dean, the on-the-ground commander for tonight. He was second in command to the Gold commander – Detective Superintendent Christie – who was monitoring the operation from the communications room at Blackpool police station. Jake knew that Alpha Two had been working with the surveillance branch to pinpoint the target and was presently sitting in eyeball contact with the target's current location, the flat in South Shore. Alpha Two went on, 'Target emerging from flat . . . A car has drawn up to pick him up . . . not the vehicle he arrived in, which is still parked up; this one is a Ford Mondeo, registered number . . .'

A shuffle of excitement went through the firearms team in the van. Suddenly, they all came to life, as though roused from hibernation. Weapons were touched. Bottoms twitched. Breaths were taken. Heartbeats were controlled. Glances exchanged, throats went dry and, to a person, each needed to pee. Prayers, possibly, were silently said.

They listened to the DCI's commentary.

'I'm confirming it is the target, Wayne Oxford, and he is getting to the Mondeo driven by an unknown male . . . Mondeo presently stationary on Boscombe Road; the men inside are talking . . . Target sitting in front passenger seat . . .'

Jake knew that Boscombe Road was one of the maze of streets that made up South Shore. It ran east–west, and its main junction was with Lytham Road. The assumption being made, based on information received, was that once the target left the address, he would turn right on to Lytham Road and eventually travel along Clifton Drive and head for the flat in St Annes he was believed to be holing up in. It was a fair assumption to make, but nonetheless an assumption. If he travelled in that direction, everything was geared up

16

to net him. If he went in another direction – which villains often had a nasty habit of doing – the operation would become more fluid. *Fluid*, Jake thought cynically. That was the word Henry Christie had used at the briefing. *Just like every other police op, then.*

The DCI's voice came over the air again: 'He's still in the car, talking.'

Jake ran his right hand along the full length of the MP5 strapped across his chest, then allowed the tip of his right forefinger to rest on the trigger guard. Nice weapon, easy to use. Reliable and deadly. He had never used it in anger, but he had pointed it for real at a lot of people, including a kid on a pedal bike armed with a BB gun. He was as sure as he could be that if the time came to fire, he would do so and live with the consequences, emotionally and legally.

Nothing happened for another five minutes, fuelling the tension in the van.

Jake glanced at Morton and saw he was looking back, thoughtful and accusing. Jake returned the look, causing Morton to drop his eyes and purse his lips.

'Target on the move, repeat, target on the move . . . in the Mondeo, two males on board, unidentified driver, the front-seat passenger is our target,' DCI Dean said over the radio, his voice now controlled and cool. In charge. It was exactly the kind of voice you wanted to hear. 'East along Boscombe Road towards Lytham Road . . . All lights on vehicle working.'

The tension in the van ratcheted up a notch as the team began to prepare mentally and physically, focusing tightly on what might lie ahead.

'Now at the junction with Lytham Road,' the DCI informed them.

Jake wondered exactly where the DCI was located. He knew the target was surveillance conscious; travelling in the early hours of the night gave him an advantage and the police a problem. Even in a place like Blackpool, which had a twenty-four-hour culture, traffic on the roads at that time of day was light. A sensitive crim would very easily spot a tail and maybe take evasive action. That was why, whatever happened, the police would have to move stunningly quickly on Wayne Oxford.

'Turning right on to Lytham Road,' Rik Dean said, then repeated the information.

'Alpha Four, confirming eyeball,' another mobile unit piped up.

'Over to you, Alpha Four,' Dean said, handing over the tailing baton to this next unit who were clearly positioned somewhere on, or just off, Lytham Road, ready to take the reins from the DCI.

'Roger that,' Alpha Four clipped. 'He's on Lytham Road, heading south towards Squires Gate Lane and the airport.'

He was heading in the right direction. Jake shifted on the bench seat, stretched his legs and rotated his ankles, getting the blood flowing and purging the stiffness from his joints. He swallowed, set himself for the task to come.

'He's turned left on to Highfield Road,' Alpha Four said. 'I cannot follow or he'll make me out. Alpha Two, instructions?'

'Shit,' Jake mouthed. Highfield Road also ran east–west, meaning that Oxford was now heading inland.

'Alpha One interrupting.' This was the voice of Detective Superintendent Christie from the comms room. Jake knew that Christie would be utilizing audio/visual feeds in the control room and would know the exact location of every cop on the operation.

'Go ahead, Alpha One,' Dean said.

'Let's just sit tight here,' Christie said. 'Alpha Four, see if you can get on to Squires Gate Lane and position yourself there. Let's stick with our intel. It may be that he's just being careful, and he'll simply do a few twists and turns to check his rear and, if he's happy, he'll head home.'

Christie's voice was calm and confident. Jake knew the guy – not well – and that he was well respected by the troops and knew his job.

'Alpha Two, roger.'

'Alpha Four, roger also.'

So they were going to let Oxford have a bit of rope and pray the intelligence was good. Jake was happy enough with that.

The radio transmissions then ended.

In his mind's eye, Jake visualized Oxford driving through the streets of South Shore, left, right, stopping, waiting, checking, moving on, trying to flush out a tail if there was one. He also imagined Christie sitting away from the scene of the action, tense but warm in comms and probably sweating as he watched the monitors and listened in. Jake grinned. He was probably cacking himself that he'd made the wrong

19

decision and that a 'most wanted' man would just disappear into thin air.

'Target now on Squires Gate Lane.' The silence was broken by Alpha Four. 'Heading towards the seafront.' Squires Gate Lane ran, again, east–west, in front of Blackpool airport, and its most westerly junction was with Clifton Drive.

'He's coming, guys,' one of the firearms team said.

Alpha Four: 'Now Squires Gate Lane, junction with Clifton Drive. Left-hand lane, stationary at the lights, which are on red. Units ready to respond?'

There was a raft of affirmatives from everyone.

If Oxford turned left, this was going to be quick and decisive.

'Lights still on red . . . changing . . . He's turning left now!'

The van in which Jake and the firearms team were sitting was perhaps four hundred metres south of the junction, parked on the road alongside the remnants of a holiday camp, now almost completely bulldozed and demolished to be replaced by a housing development.

Jake knew this was where it was all going to get a bit blurred.

His left hand gripped the inner handle for the left door. His right clamped the MP5 to his chest.

Morton held the opposite door.

'He's passed the junction with New Road,' Alpha Four shouted. 'All patrols – go, go, go!'

Jake was amazed how well it all went – up to the point where Oxford opened his door and fled like a whippet.

Two liveried police cars seemed to emerge from nowhere, like demons from a cave, all blue, red and white lights. One was suddenly in front of the Mondeo, one alongside. The two unmarked cars were just as fast, both slotting in behind it, giving it no choice but to pull into the side of the road. That this manoeuvre was completed so quickly and effectively was testament to the expert driving skills of the traffic officers, and they stopped the Mondeo, as planned in the briefing, just metres short of the firearms team van.

As soon as Jake and Morton saw what was happening, they piled out almost before the rolling roadblock had come to a complete halt.

But Wayne Oxford was no slouch either. He must have been living on pins, and his senses and reactions were heightened by his fugitive lifestyle. He threw open his door and, without even a glance, sprinted, vaulting a low wall and running into the remains of the holiday camp.

'He's running,' Jake said, transmitting via his PR with the microphone taped to his throat. 'Into Pontins.'

Jake ran, Morton thundering behind him, into the holiday camp, which now consisted of the shells of derelict, two-storey chalets, windows smashed, doors kicked off hinges; some of the blocks had been completely demolished and were now just mounds of rubble and hard-core, while others still stood, but vandalized. The whole area was unlit and consequently dangerous underfoot.

21

Oxford had disappeared into this wasteland. He had moved quickly.

'Shit,' Jake breathed, clambering clumsily over the low perimeter wall, weighed down by his kit, followed by Morton. He saw a shadow move. 'There,' he gasped, changed direction and ran, already sweating underneath all the equipment.

They reached the corner of a still-standing chalet and slammed their backs up against the prefabricated wall, which wobbled precariously like a badly built stage set. Their MP5s were ready, safety catches off.

'I'm sure he went this way,' Jake said, glancing at Morton, who nodded agreement. Then they heard footsteps crunching.

Jake swung away from the wall, weapon ready, and looked along the chalet, seeing Oxford sprint along the front and out of sight. Jake heard footsteps on stairs.

'This way.'

He trotted to the corner of the building, then pivoted out in a combat stance, ready to fire if necessary.

No sign of Oxford.

At the front of the chalet were the remains of the staircase that ran from the centre of the block and split at the top to give access to the flats on the first floor.

Jake signalled to Morton with a finger. *Up there.* He was sure Oxford had gone up the steps and taken refuge in one of the rooms. Jake caught his breath. 'I think we've got him,' he said over the radio and began to call in other officers to surround the block. As they were getting into position, another cop saw a black shape flit behind one of the broken windows, confirming that Oxford was up there – trapped in a holiday chalet. Most people's nightmare.

From that moment on it was the kind of waiting game they all enjoyed. Oxford was going nowhere; the police were going nowhere. The detective superintendent arrived on the scene within fifteen minutes, and after a short but tense negotiation, Oxford emerged from his hiding place in a wardrobe, hands aloft. Jake talked him down on to his knees, then face down on the floor, where he handcuffed him, heaved him upright and marched him to a waiting police van.

A killer had been caught without too much drama. Good result.

The team reconvened at police headquarters following Henry Christie's mercifully brief – but glowing – debrief at Blackpool nick. A more detailed one would follow in due course. Their weapons were returned to the armoury in the firing range at the training centre, and then, all exhausted, they turned down the offer of a brew and headed for their cars.

Dave Morton loped up behind Jake as he was about to get into his motor. 'Hey, pal.'

Jake's mouth twisted sardonically. The tone of Morton's voice alerted him to what was coming. Jake stood upright and turned to his colleague, instantly struck by the change of personal perspective. Morton had suddenly become a colleague, relegated from friend.

Morton sidled up, close. A space invasion. His face was serious.

'Unwritten rule,' he said, and Jake swallowed. 'You're a fool, Jake, and it'll all end badly.'

Jake turned away, as if to get into the car. Morton grabbed his shoulder, but Jake shrugged it off. 'What?' he demanded, his eyes blazing.

'You know,' Morton said, stressing both words with deliberation.

'Know what?' Jake realized this was a stupid game, but wasn't going to relent.

'I'm not going to spell it out . . . Unwritten rule, OK?'

'So . . . if it's an unwritten rule, then I can't fucking break it, can I?' Jake shook his head sadly, as if Morton was the one in the wrong, got into his car and screeched away across the tarmac whilst Morton watched him disappear.

Jake knocked quietly. Four times with the tip of his forefinger. Then took a step back and waited. His heart pounded, his mouth was dry; it was almost the same sense of anticipation he'd felt in the back of the van, waiting for the target to put in an appearance.

He heard soft footsteps.

She hadn't had time to change, was still in full battledress, although she had removed her boots and replaced them with big fluffy slippers, a ridiculous combination. She had on her ballistic vest and utility belt, attached to which were her handcuffs, baton, CS canister holder – now empty, as the canister itself had been logged back into the system – PR harness and torch ring.

24

Jake grinned at the slippers.

'Something funny?'

'Just you,' he said, now feeling an extra rush that he definitely hadn't felt in the back of the van, even if he had been sitting next to this woman. As exciting as it was chasing armed villains, it never gave him an erection.

'Come in.'

Hc cdged past, chest to chest, into the hallway of the tiny flat. She pushed the door closed, and they were face-to-face, inches apart.

Jake gasped, moved his face forwards and brushed his lips against hers. His intention had been to do this softly and slowly. Explore, touch, take time, experience everything in slow motion. Run his lips down her long neck – but as they clashed together, all those good intentions shot out of the window. The first few seconds were gentle, but then all those hours of pent-up frustration, having been in such close proximity to each other and unable to do anything about it, made them want to burst, and the frustration was unleashed.

It all happened there and then in that hallway. Their overalls were ripped off as their mouths mashed and ground together, each greedily removing the other's garments and equipment, thick leather belts thudding heavily on the floor, clothes torn off and flung away until they were both naked. Jake raised her on to him, her legs wrapped tightly around his waist, and he slid deep into her, thrusting and banging against the wall. Then, thus engaged, he carried her the few steps to the bedroom, most of which was taken up by an enormous king sized bed. They fell on to the duvet, Jake above her, pinning her arms above her head and moving his hips in a circular motion, using the full length of his hard cock to probe slowly then quickly, then deeply, pelvis to pelvis.

Then she took charge, flipping him on to his back, straddling him and arching backwards so he had to stretch to reach her breasts. But he was deep inside her, and she rose and fell with a wonderful rhythm as he grew even harder, feeling her own waves of pleasure course out from her sex. Jake held her bottom with one hand and ran his other all over her, and then he was unable to hold himself any longer.

He came with juddering, uncontrolled spasms as she fell forwards on to him, her soft breasts pushed into his chest, holding his head between the palms of her hands, tearing at his lips with her teeth. As he finished, she climaxed, but slowed it all down, moaning with delight as she sagged on to him, exhausted.

'Oh God, I wish you could stay,' she whispered.

'So do I, Kirst, so do I.'

'You could, you know.'

To that he did not reply. He knew he could not and that he would be leaving within the next ten minutes.

He had a home to go to.

And a family.

And a wife.

And at that moment, it was destroying him.

He left, as he knew he would. Kirsten lay in bed, watching him collect his clothing from the hallway and then re-dress himself whilst sitting on the edge of the bed. In silence. She watched him crossly, her eyes stone cold.

He could not find anything to say, and he left without a word or a kiss.

Outside, morning had arrived full on, and as he emerged into daylight he was very unsettled. He knew he could not maintain this. Something would have to give.

He had parked three streets away and made it to his car, all the while with the unpleasant sensation that he was being watched by a hundred pairs of eyes, all of them knowing his guilty secret.

He actually saw no one and tried to scoff at his paranoia, but could not shake it off. It was always with him these days and came with the territory of being a cheat.

But he was right about one thing. A hundred pairs of eyes were not watching him.

Just the one pair.

Three

Jake Niven dithered just a few seconds before sliding his key into the front door of his house. He took a deep breath to brace himself. Already, he could hear his wife, Anna, screeching at the kids.

The house was in Bispham, just to the north of Blackpool, on a small estate that was about ten years old. Detached, three-bedroomed, it was the second home he and Anna had owned. The first had been a very modest terraced house – still in Bispham – and they had traded up for this modern one five years ago. Even though it was detached and had an extra bedroom and a garden, it still felt more cramped than the first home. But it was nearer to the sea, and a couple of minutes on foot got Jake running along the cliff tops overlooking the magnificent beach below.

He swallowed and inserted the key, shaking off his paranoia and fixing a smile to his face, then stepping into the hallway and announcing his arrival home.

He was met by his son, Danny, hurtling down the stairs half-dressed in school uniform, shirt and tie askew, last minute as ever. He managed to stop himself from colliding with Jake, gave him a lopsided glance and rushed through the lounge towards the kitchen shouting, 'Will you stop yelling, Mum?'

Jake dropped his kit bag in the hall and took another breath, not noticing that his daughter Emma was standing halfway down the stairs, looking curiously at him.

'You all right, Dad?'

Jake suddenly switched back on, annoyed at himself for being caught off guard. 'Hey, honey . . . just tired, that's all. Been a long, long night.'

Emma came down the last few steps and gave him a hug.

'How are you, babe?' he asked, his chin on her shoulder. She was just fourteen, quite tall, and was definitely becoming a woman, but would always be his little babe, even if she was a bit of a tomboy and well into her karate classes.

She drew away and looked quizzically at him. 'I'm good, Dad.' Her hazel eyes narrowed. They were almost Asian in shape, and Jake realized that in the very near future, boys would be drooling over them. They were killer eyes.

'What's up?' He had seen her expression.

'Um . . . nothing . . . just . . .' she floundered.

'What?'

'You smell odd. Like you, but not like you. Sweet, or something.'

Jake's guts did a three-sixty degree turnaround. This kid, he thought, is too observant for her own good – or mine. She had picked up another scent on him.

'A night in the back of a van, coupled with the quick wash before I left HQ,' he lied quickly. He gave her his best quirky-dad grin and poked her shoulder gently. 'You had your breakfast yet?'

29

'No,' she said, smiling. 'Running late—' The sound of her mother's voice cut her off.

'Emma!'

'Better get moving . . . she's on the warpath again.' She pecked Jake's cheek and followed the path her brother had taken – lounge, then kitchen.

Jake cursed under his breath as he peeled off his windcheater and slung it over the end of a radiator, then removed his boots. They came off easily because he hadn't laced them up. Then he followed the wake of the kids.

'Hi, hi,' he said brightly, entering the kitchen and planting a kiss on Anna's cheek. She was busy slapping tuna and mayo on to bread, making sandwiches for school lunches. She half returned the kiss with a twitch of her lips and said, 'How are you?'

'Good. And a result,' he said and jabbed a fist into the air. 'Cops, one, crims, nil.'

'Long night, though?'

'Too bloody long,' he said, wondering suspiciously if it was a cynical question based on suspicion. 'But the baddie turned up and we nailed him.'

'What time?' Anna's eyes flickered to the kitchen clock on the wall above the work surface she was busy at.

Jake screwed up his face. 'What time what?'

'Did he turn up . . .? The bad guy.'

Jake glanced at the clock and did some quick mental calculations. He added three-quarters of an hour to the time that Wayne Oxford was actually arrested and said this to Anna. She nodded. For a moment Jake thought she was going to

30

challenge this, but she didn't. For the third time in as many hours, his mouth freeze-dried instantly. She slammed a slice of bread on top of another and, selecting a very sharp knife from the block, she cut the sandwich in half, then stacked it into a lunch box.

He watched the process, transfixed for a moment, before turning to put the kettle on, shouldering Danny playfully out of the way. His son was eighteen months older than Emma and was growing just as fast. He was getting tall and broadening out across the chest and shoulders. A few tufts of bum-fluff were appearing on his jawline, proudly displayed for the moment. So far the father/son relationship had not deteriorated into a generation war, but Jake could sense battle lines being drawn. Some minor skirmishes had happened, and there was a slight, but ever increasing distance between them.

'I'll run 'em both to school,' Jake volunteered as he poured boiling water on to a tea bag.

Usually, the children caught separate buses to their schools, both hating the morning trudge to the bus stop in any weather. A lift from a parent was always a treat.

'But you've been working all night,' Anna protested.

'I'll do it,' Jake said patiently, 'then I'll get my head down.'

'Cheers, Dad,' Danny said, gesturing his thanks by raising his cereal bowl.

Anna shot Jake a look of disdain. She belonged to the school of thought that it was good for them to have to make their own way. One of life's little lessons. She loved them both like crazy, but didn't mollycoddle them and was always slightly miffed when Jake took them or picked them up.

'Dad, you are a star,' Emma said and slotted two pieces of bread into the toaster. Now there was a bit of time to relax.

Danny edged out of the kitchen into the front room and dropped on to the settee, glad of the respite. He now had a ten minute window to chillax. He put on the TV – CBBC – and started watching *Tracy Beaker*, which just happened to be on at that time.

'All I have to do today is sleep,' Jake said defensively.

'And pick us *up* from school,' Emma chirped hopefully.

'Maybe that, too, babe.'

With his mug of tea, Jake sat with Danny watching TV, whilst Anna finished up in the kitchen. When the children were ready, he did the school run.

By the time he returned, Anna had gone. She worked mornings at a local builder's yard where she organized the office and dealt with that day's orders and deliveries. Three hours a day, ten pounds an hour, five days a week. Not a lot, but important money that helped ensure the family got away a couple of times a year to the sun.

Jake was relieved to find the house empty, though he was surprised Anna had gone so early. She usually did 9.30 a.m. to 12.30 p.m. and didn't leave home until 9.15 a.m.

He took a long shower, soaping off every trace

of the night, then climbed into the unmade bed and was instantly asleep.

Anna went into work early in order to leave early, her employers being fairly flexible on that score. As long as the work was done, they were happy. She therefore left at 12.15 p.m. and drove south along the seafront at Blackpool, past the remnants of Pontins holiday camp, the scene (although she did not know this) of Wayne Oxford's arrest at gunpoint a few hours before. Clifton Drive angled slightly inland, but when she turned right on to Todmorden Road, then left on to North Promenade at St Annes, she was back on the shore. She drove past the boating lake and miniature golf course, then pulled on to the car park next to the Beach Terrace Café, went in and claimed a table.

She didn't have long to wait.

She had spent a little time looking unfocused out across the sand dunes to the Irish Sea, which was a long way out. When she looked around she saw her friend Jackie Powers threading her way through the tightly arranged tables. Anna rose; they embraced and kissed each other's cheeks. Very old friends now, sixteen years' standing. Both women were now in their mid-thirties.

Anna ordered them both a soup and sandwich and a coffee, then returned to the table where she sat nervously and surveyed her friend. 'You're looking good.'

Jackie grinned ironically. 'Sixteen years of shifts does this to a woman.' She tilted her head

33

and framed her face between her hands. Underneath her jacket she was wearing her police uniform, minus tie and epaulettes. These items would be going on when she reported for duty at three. Jackie looked at Anna, paused, then returned the compliment, but didn't mean it.

Anna Niven, née Andsell, had been one of the most stunning looking young women that Jackie – no slouch in the looks department herself – had ever seen. They had met, both at the age of nineteen, when they joined the police at the same time, went through initial training together, and then even got the same initial posting to the same location: Blackpool Central. Which was good, as both girls were Blackpool born and bred.

Jackie recalled those early times with fondness. Both of them had spent a lot of effort fending off advances from testosterone-fuelled young male cops. The difference between them was that Jackie had succumbed to more advances than she would ever have admitted to, while Anna had fallen under the spell of just the one: the young, cocksure recruit called Jake Niven. They had fallen madly in love with each other, and as soon as they'd completed their probationary period, they'd married, settled, and Anna had got pregnant.

Jackie had had her doubts, citing that both were too young, but as it transpired, it seemed to be a match made somewhere near heaven.

On the other hand, Jackie had been through two disastrous marriages – both to cops – and was now resolutely single and loving it.

As Jackie critically eyed her friend in the café that day, for the first time she saw a woman who was approaching middle age too quickly. Pale, tired looking, even haunted; bags under her eyes, hair scraped back, an expression of hopelessness on her face and a quickly spreading frame. Behind that veneer, though, she also saw the same extraordinary looking lady she had once been. Jackie was convinced that Anna could have been a supermodel, but all she'd wanted was a good husband and family. Nothing wrong in that.

The two ladies hadn't seen each other for a few months, and they caught up with each other's news. Jackie was having problems with her current boyfriend, and Anna spoke of the day-to-day drudgery that was her life.

Finally, they finished eating and were sipping their coffees.

Outside it started to rain heavily, large spats of icy water covering the windows and blurring the view of the sand dunes.

Jackie had never had the capacity to see the follies in her own relationships – until they went sour – but she was an expert at spotting the creaky signs in other people's. She leaned back in her chair and regarded her friend, who avoided her gaze by dropping her eyes. Something knotted tight in the pit of Jackie's stomach as she said, 'So now, tell me, lovely, what's up? Spit it out.'

Anna stared into her coffee, which was the colour of tarmac, not denying anything. She stared into it for a long time before raising her face. 'How do you know if your husband's cheating on you?'

That response did not faze Jackie. She quipped instantly back, 'Y'mean short of finding him in bed with some floozy?'

Four

I think we've got him.'

They were words of gold to Henry Christie's rather ragged ears. At least, his left ear was ragged, having been partially shot off about six months earlier by a shotgun wielded by one of the most violent individuals Henry had ever had the misfortune to encounter in his long police career. The blast of the gun had basically skimmed the left side of his face, and the few pellets that didn't embed themselves in his cheek had nicked his ear. Although he'd undergone plastic surgery since then, the shape of the ear remained like a cog in a gearbox. The pellets wedged in his face had been surgically removed, and the scars were almost healed now, though they were still clearly visible, like raised flecks of silver on his skin. Henry knew they would never completely disappear. Scars for life. Badges of rank . . . badges of pain.

When he heard the words spoken by PC Jake Niven over the radio, Henry had been sitting in the comms room at Blackpool nick from where he commanded the operation – Amethyst – to follow and arrest Wayne Oxford, a young thug wanted for the murder of an innocent kid on the Shoreside estate in Blackpool a few weeks earlier.

The death had come as the result of an ambush

by Oxford, who had been lying in wait for a deadly rival in a nasty turf war over who could deal drugs on the estate. Unfortunately, a completely innocent boy had been caught in the crossfire and shot fatally in the head.

Identifying Oxford as the killer had been the easy part for Henry, who was the Senior Investigating Officer (SIO) in the case.

Catching him had proved more difficult.

Henry's murder squad had been faced with a stone wall of people out to protect Oxford, some of whom had now marked their cards for Henry and would later face obstruction charges. Henry had leaned on a lot of Blackpool's lowlifes during the manhunt – and his shotgun ravaged face, he discovered much to his delight, came in very useful when intimidating some of the little shits whose cages he was rattling. It was as a result of pinning one up against a wall and squeezing a set of testicles that he'd got strained word that Oxford might be found that very night in a fleapit flat in South Shore and also that he was supposed to be bedding down in another flat in St Annes. The in-pain snitch had only known the address of the first property.

Hence Henry's quickly assembled surveillance and firearms operation, which had proved a success until Oxford bolted from the car, leaving a terrified, but ultimately innocent driver behind the wheel of the Mondeo.

Henry had not been keen to learn that Oxford had gone to ground in a derelict holiday chalet. That wasn't supposed to happen.

But it had, and a short while after the radio

message from Niven, Henry was on the scene in his bulletproof vest, speaking to Oxford through a loud hailer. The best part was that because of the location, no members of the public were put at risk, and if necessary the police could have starved Oxford out without breaking too much sweat. This was a fact Henry had been at pains to point out to the felon. If he wanted a siege, he could have one.

Oxford had given himself up without a fight twenty minutes after Henry had turned up on the plot.

It had been a great pleasure for Henry to watch the firearms officer make the actual arrest and truss him up without violence.

Once booked into custody at Blackpool nick, Oxford's clothing was seized for forensic examination, swabs were taken from his hands for gunshot residue (although Henry knew this was more an academic exercise than anything because the killing had been weeks ago and anything useful to link him to the scene would be long gone). Then, with Oxford dressed in a paper suit and elasticated paper slippers, and accompanied by the duty solicitor, Henry began to interview him on tape and video with DCI Rik Dean as 'second jockey'.

It was a 'no comment' discussion, which did not bother Henry too much. This was only the initial phase of what was likely to be a long process of battering Oxford – legally – into submission.

There was, however, one thing Henry did need from Oxford, and that was his current address, because the detective believed a thorough search of it would prove very useful. Oxford had refused to divulge any address when booked into the system and continued to say 'no comment' when asked for one during the interview.

That first, no response interview lasted forty minutes. At that juncture, Henry leaned back and surveyed the prisoner through cold eyes and gave a knowing, but slight nod of the head.

'I just want you to know,' Henry told him over steepled fingers, 'I intend to convict you for this offence, and you will be going to prison for a very long time . . . Innocent lad shot dead, involved in gang warfare . . . Not Crown Court judges' favourite offences . . .'

Oxford raised his smug face and smiled. 'No comment.'

It was one of those smiles Henry would have dearly liked to knock off his face. He could tell that Oxford knew this.

There was a tap on the interview room door, which had the effect of breaking the deadlock in the staring competition between the two men.

Rik Dean leaned forward and spoke like the voice-over man on a reality TV show. 'For the benefit of the tape, someone has knocked on the door.'

Henry pushed himself up stiffly, walked to the door and opened it. In the corridor outside stood the custody sergeant, PS Broome.

'Boss . . . thought you might want to see this.'

Henry stepped out of the interview room and closed the door.

'For the benefit of the tape, Detective

Superintendent Christie has now left the room,' Rik Dean said with a smirk.

'What is it, John?' Henry asked the sergeant, just as a wave of nauseous exhaustion swept through his entire being. Henry swayed slightly and put a hand out to the wall to steady himself. Suddenly, his brain was woozy, and he took a deep breath.

'You OK, boss?' Broome had noticed Henry's change of demeanour – and colour. His face had run to a very pale grey with just a tinge of blue.

'Yeah, yeah.' Henry's equilibrium came back as suddenly as it had left him. He knew he was very close to burn-out and, if he was honest with himself, should have been tucked up in bed with a hot-bottomed landlady. The last few months had been a hard push, but he'd been determined not to slacken up. 'What've you got there?'

Broome held up a wallet. Henry recognized it as belonging to Wayne Oxford, taken from him when he'd been searched at the custody desk. It had contained almost £600 in Bank of England notes, 200 euros and a couple of debit cards, all of which were entered in the prisoner's property list on the back of the custody record then seized as evidence. 'I've had a proper look through this and found *this* in one of the pockets.' It was a piece of folded paper, which Broome unfolded and showed to Henry. There was an address scribbled on it. 'I don't know if you need it, but I thought you might . . . Obviously, he wasn't for telling where he lived, which I always think is a bit sus.'

Henry took and read it: an address in St Annes,

and obviously a flat. Henry narrowed his eyes and said thanks. He re-entered the interview room.

'For the purposes of the tape, Superintendent Christie has now re-entered the interview room,' Rik Dean told the microphone.

Henry sat and played teasingly with the piece of paper which, spread out, was about the size of half a Post-it note. He spun it around, turned it over, all the while keeping his eyes firmly on Oxford, wanting to judge his reaction. Then he sniffed and placed the paper on the table between them, address facing upwards. 'Is this where you live?'

Oxford had a very scrawny neck with a very prominent Adam's apple, which rose and fell in his throat like a spiny lizard moving under a blanket. Henry heard him emit a little gasp.

'No comment,' he said tightly.

Henry now allowed himself a grin and a subtle wink. 'As we speak, authorization is being sought for permission to search this address, which I firmly believe is yours, Mr Wayne Oxford.'

Oxford's head spun to his solicitor. 'I want to make a phone call,' he said.

Henry almost laughed now. 'That will be denied,' he said with certainty.

The solicitor stepped in. 'On what grounds?'

'That he will use a phone call to alert others involved in this serious crime.'

The solicitor shrugged, then gave Oxford a helpless look. Oxford's own face crumpled before he snatched the piece of paper from the table and stuffed it into his mouth and began to devour it.

With an amused look, Henry let him do it. He had brawled with prisoners in the past who had tried to eat incriminating documents, and it had never been pretty. He'd been bitten on too many occasions trying to force open someone's mouth. One man had even wolfed down a fraudulent car insurance certificate and an MOT certificate.

The process of mashing it up was difficult.

Ever one to help, Henry offered, 'You want some water with that?'

Oxford's jaws chomped as he tried to digest it. Eventually, it went down.

Henry sighed patronizingly. 'What was the point of that?'

'No comment.'

Five minutes later Oxford was pushed into a cell, and five minutes after that, armed with the appropriate written authorization to search, Henry and Rik Dean, together with two constables they had managed to round up, were on their way to the address on the paper.

Rik was driving his own car, with Henry slumped untidily in the passenger seat; the two PCs were in a police car behind.

'How are you feeling?' Rik asked.

'Pretty shit, but let's not go there, eh?' He'd had enough of deep contemplation, the hand wringing, the guilt. All he wanted to do now was his job – put a killer behind bars.

It did not take long to reach St Annes. Rik turned right off Clifton Drive North on to Todmorden Road, then left on to North Promenade. On the right now was the seafront, effectively hidden by the height of the sand dunes, beyond which was the vast expanse of the beach at North Hollow, popular with sand yachters and kite flyers. On the left were properties: some high-class detached houses, then some apartment blocks tucked in amongst them. A few of these were also good quality, but the one Rik drew up outside, Salter's Bank View, could have been transported and dumped on to the Shoreside council estate and not looked out of place, other than for its height. Six storeys tall, a sixties throwback, made of pebble-dashed concrete and steel. Ungainly, unpleasant and slightly rotting.

Henry squinted at it for a moment, then climbed out of the car as the two PCs pulled in behind and alighted from their patrol car. All four men made towards the ground floor entrance, which led into a badly lit hallway, where they came face-to-face with a locked door. On the wall next to this was a set of buzzers and intercoms.

Henry rattled the door, hoping it wasn't locked. It was, so he was reduced to deploying the old cop trick of pressing each of the buzzers and waiting for some response. Whilst waiting he glanced down the nameplates next to each button. Most were empty, and Wayne Oxford's name wasn't there, anyway. Not that Henry had expected it to be.

He sighed and repeated the task with the buttons, looking over his shoulder at the three patient cops behind him.

'Usually works,' he said apologetically.

'If it doesn't I've got a door ram in the boot,' one of the constables said helpfully.

'Good,' Henry said.

A groggy female voice came tinnily through one of the intercoms. 'That you, babe?'

'Yeah,' Henry said back.

'Been waiting all night,' the woman said.

'Me, too,' Henry responded in his best sultry voice, arching his eyebrows at his colleagues.

There was a click on the intercom, then a buzzing sound as the door was released.

Rik grabbed the door, and the cops were in and heading up the concrete steps to flat twenty-one, assuming it would be found on the second floor. On that landing, Henry caught his breath before moving along to number twenty-one, which was at the far end. They moved relatively silently, then stopped. Rik and Henry were side by side at the door, the uniformed officers just behind, slightly fanned out.

Henry could see that the door, although pushed to, was open, just resting on the jamb. He pulled out his warrant card and warily pushed the door.

It opened straight into a living room, in the centre of which was a young woman, maybe early twenties, dressed in only a bra and panties.

This detail wasn't the important one to Henry, though. What was, was the fact she was holding a big, heavy looking, black revolver in her right hand, supported by her left, and it was pointed directly at the centre of his chest.

Henry ducked instinctively to his right as the woman yanked back the trigger. Behind him, he was aware of the other three cops diving in all directions.

Henry cowered, seeing the hammer draw back

then slam forwards into a bullet in one of the six cylinders. He flinched as the firing pin landed with a dull click and nothing came out of the business end of the handgun.

Henry saw the look of horror and confusion on the woman's face as she realized the gun had misfired. Henry jumped up quickly – the stiffness and tiredness in his body replaced by an instant surge of adrenalin that was like jet fuel to his system. He lunged towards her, horrified as she did perhaps the most idiotic thing that a person who was inexperienced in handling guns, and confused by something that should have happened but hadn't, could do. She turned the gun towards herself, brow furrowed, and looked down the barrel.

At that exact moment, as her right eye focused down the black hole, the gun fired with a tremendous bang.

Even though the noise was loud within the confines of the flat, Henry still actually heard the sickening, squelchy 'thuck' as the bullet entered her eye at a sideways angle and, as everything slowed down in that instant, Henry clearly saw the slug exit out of the side of her head just by her right ear, taking bone and brain with it in a devastating wound.

She spun from the momentum, dropped the gun, then fell on to her hands and knees, her shattered head lolling briefly between her arms, blood gushing, before she rolled sideways, dead.

At that point, Henry had only moved two steps. He stopped.

The other three crowded behind him, shocked.

Henry stood there, stunned, then took two more steps towards her, watched her body spasm, then stop moving.

'Hell,' he said, easing himself down on to his haunches, his mouth open. His knees cracked hollowly. With his first and second fingers he touched her warm neck to feel for a pulse, knowing it was pointless because she could never have survived that. He knew dead when he saw it.

'What the fuck!' Rik Dean said behind him.

'Shit,' Henry said, withdrawing his fingers: no pulse.

'Why did she—' Rik began, then stopped, realizing he was about to ask a futile question.

Henry sighed, feeling his energy drain out again. 'Ambulance, police surgeon, CSI,' he said, twisting his head to look over his shoulder at the white-faced, stunned to silence PCs. 'And body removers . . . You guys OK?'

Both nodded, though they were dumbstruck.

'Do it then, eh?' he encouraged them. 'But just check there's no one else here, first.' Henry pushed himself up and looked at Rik, who grinned lopsidedly.

'That was meant for you,' he informed Henry.

'I know. Hopefully, it would have missed, though – and hit you instead.'

Rik nodded sagely. 'Fancy looking down the fucking barrel.'

Henry regarded the dead woman's head, then tore his eyes away and took a few moments to study the flat. They were standing in the living room, off which was a kitchen and bathroom; to his left was a short hallway leading to what he guessed were two bedrooms. His eyes returned from their wandering and settled on the Formica-topped dining table pushed up to one corner of the living room. Four guns were displayed on this, side by side. Two handguns, two machine pistols together with boxes of ammunition and spare magazines.

Wayne Oxford slouched down low in the uncomfortable plastic chair, scowling through mean eyes across the table at Henry Christie. He was still displaying a challenging, cocky veneer, but when Henry's eyes bore into his, Oxford's withdrew from their line and he looked away.

They were in the same interview room as before, and the same duty solicitor was sitting alongside his client, looking decidedly weary, having been called back in just as he was about to bed down. He had made representations about Oxford's right to have eight hours' uninterrupted rest, and Henry promised that, by all means, once he had finished this interview, Oxford could get his head down.

Henry sighed, thinking he was probably the most tired man in the room.

He forced a tight smile at Oxford. 'Now then,' he said. The tape and camera were running, the preliminaries were out of the way – the introductions, caution. He glanced fleetingly at Rik Dean sitting alongside, and then said, 'We've searched your flat, Wayne.'

Oxford tried to give the impression of impassivity, but he fidgeted at the news.

'We found some very interesting items.'

Nothing from Oxford.

'Due to their nature I cannot, unfortunately, place these items down in front of you just yet. However, because of the magic that is digital photography I can show you some photos of these items.'

On the table in front of Henry was a brown A4 envelope. He opened the flap with deliberate slowness and took out five sheets of paper, laying them face down so that Oxford could not see the photographs on them. Henry thought it was rather like having a fixed deck of cards, because he had staked them in a particular order which he hoped would be effective.

'These shots were taken by a crime scene investigator, and I've printed them off, just so you can see them and maybe comment. Or not. Up to you.'

Oxford's mouth twitched.

'Each of these items was found in your flat, Wayne.' Henry slowly turned the first one, the photograph of a machine pistol. It got not even a word from Oxford. Henry did the same with the next three photographs until he had four laid out alongside each other, just as they had been on the table in the flat.

Henry put his finger on one at a time. 'A Škorpion machine pistol . . . a Makarov nine millimetre semi-automatic pistol . . . a Heckler & Koch MP-five machine pistol . . . and a revolver of indeterminate manufacture, but point forty-five calibre. All of these weapons had ammunition with them.' He raised his eyes. 'Do you wish to comment, Wayne?'

Although his nostrils flared, he was more or less impassive. He said nothing, just continued with his defiant stare.

Henry slowly turned over the fifth sheet, which was a photograph of the weapon the young woman had fired into her own face by mistake. This was a black four-inch barrelled .38 revolver, similar to something Smith & Wesson made, though the manufacturer of this one was, like the other handgun in the flat, unknown at this stage. It was actually not a large gun, but when Henry had first seen it in the girl's hand, pointed at him, it had seemed so much bigger, probably because of the heightened tension of the moment. The bullet that had killed the innocent boy on Shoreside had also been a .38. Henry was convinced that the weapon he was showing to Oxford was the one that had killed him.

'I want you to look very carefully at this particular weapon, Wayne.'

Oxford gave it a fleeting glance.

'I think this is the gun you used to kill twelve-year-old Jamie Turner on Shoreside. I'm certain your fingerprints will be found on it and that ballistics will be able to match the bullet taken from the dead boy's body to this gun. That is my belief.'

Oxford blinked.

'Anything to say, Wayne?'

'No comment.'

Henry nodded, changed tack unexpectedly. 'What's your girlfriend's name?'

Oxford shrugged.

'I happen to know she is called Sophie Leader.

50

She's eighteen years old and was at the address we found in your wallet. Papers in the flat say that Sophie is the occupier and rents it.' Henry raised his eyebrows, getting a little weary now of the non-verbal exchanges because, despite knowing that scientific studies would tell him that over seventy per cent of communication is unspoken, non-verbals don't mean anything in a court of law. Only words were of any use.

Ominously, Henry tapped the photograph of the gun with his fingertip. It had been taken in situ on the floor of the flat where the girl had dropped it after killing herself. 'This gun has now killed at least two people and may well be linked to other serious crimes . . . In fact, I'd stake my life on that. Time will tell, but I reckon it has killed an innocent boy and someone else equally innocent.'

Oxford screwed up his nose. 'What the fuck are you on about?' he snarled, and Henry smiled inwardly because more often than not when a 'no comment' interview is broken, it rarely reverts to being that again. The thin end of the wedge had been kicked into place.

'What sort of ammunition do you use?' Henry asked. 'Commercially produced or manufactured in someone's shed . . .? Actually, don't answer that because I already know. The victim on the estate was killed by a home-made bullet. Forensics have already told me that . . . So, the thing about ammunition like this – and I speak from bitter experience on this point – is that it can be a bit temperamental, if you get my drift?'

'You're talking bollocks,' he said sourly.

'Did you ever let Sophie mess with the guns in the flat?'

'I don't know what you're on about. You're, like, an idiot, blabbing on.'

'How long have you been going out with her?'

'And that's your business?'

'Did you love her?'

'And, again, what business is that of yours?'

'Listen very carefully to that question again, Wayne.' Henry leaned forwards and emphasized the first word. '*Did* you love her. Not *do* you love her.'

'You're talking through your arse, cop . . . Not my girl, don't know her.'

'OK, OK,' Henry said, sitting back. His fingers delved into the envelope again and pulled out some more photographs. 'These items were found in the flat,' he said irritably, 'so I don't want any more ridiculous denials.' He turned a few over for Wayne to take a look at, pushed them towards the prisoner. 'A provisional driving licence in your name, but with a different address. A photo of you and Sophie Leader, which was on the fireplace; looks like it was taken on Blackpool prom. A debit card with your name on it. Do not continue to lie to me, Wayne.'

'I fucking crashed there now and again, that's all,' he conceded. 'I don't have an address, OK? I'm no fixed abode. It's her place, not mine.'

'And the guns?'

He clamped his mouth shut.

'A proper little arsenal. Tooling up for something?' Henry speculated. 'Gang war? Robbery? What?'

'None of the above,' Oxford responded glibly. 'I don't know anything about the guns, OK?'

Henry narrowed his eyes. 'Nothing whatsoever?'

'Fuck. All.'

'Never touched them, then?'

Oxford wilted. Henry pointed at him. 'Because if you have, your fingerprints and DNA will be all over them.'

'I want my eight hours.' Oxford faked a yawn and stretched his arms.

'OK . . . but just a couple more things before your beauty sleep. Sophie Leader – your girl-friend, yeah?'

No response.

'Again, listen to this question carefully: *did* you love her?'

Oxford breathed down his nose irascibly.

'Did you let her handle the guns?'

'Just fuck off, eh?' Oxford shifted uncomfortably in his chair.

'Let me tell you what happened when I went to your flat, Wayne. I knocked on the front door, went in, and there was Sophie, pointing this revolver at me.' Henry tapped the photo again.

'Good.' Oxford half-smiled.

'Then she fired at me. She must have realized, perhaps, it wasn't you coming up to see her, though we will never know exactly why.'

He chuckled. 'Even fucking better.'

'But it didn't go off because it was loaded with shit ammo.'

'Shame.'

'Well, to be accurate, it didn't go off immediately.'

'What d'you mean?'

'Not until Sophie looked down the barrel to see what was wrong. *Then* it went off!'

Oxford stared with incomprehension at Henry, who reached into the envelope to pull out the last of the photographs. He drew it out slowly, face down. 'This is what I meant by this revolver having killed two innocent people, Wayne. It killed Jamie Turner first . . . but when Sophie fired at me, the gun didn't go off, and then she looked down the barrel.'

Henry turned the photograph over, a painfully slow reveal. 'Look at this photograph, Wayne.'

Oxford tried not to drop his gaze, but the lure of confusion and curiosity he was feeling drew his eyes surely down as Henry rotated the photograph so it was the right way up for him to see.

'That is what I meant when I asked: did you love her? Because now she's dead, and that gun of yours killed her because you loaded it with home-made, unpredictable, dangerous ammunition.' Henry's eyes bored into Oxford's. 'Think about it . . . Think about it hard when you're having your sleep . . . Interview concluded.'

Five

'You wanted to speak to me.'

'I'll talk to you – but you have to protect me.'
Wayne Oxford's face was puffed red and swollen
from his crying and blubbering. His eyes were
raw, and his nose dripped snot. It was twenty
minutes since Henry had left him to ponder the
fate of his girlfriend and his own future, which
looked very bleak at that point.

Henry settled back into the chair opposite
Oxford in the interview room, and Rik sat alongside him, both drinking coffee. For a moment
Henry said nothing, just regarded the distressed
prisoner and his somnolent solicitor, who had not
even made it home this time before being
summoned back to see his client.

'I'm assuming the protection thing refers to the
guns?' Henry asked.

Oxford nodded.

'Well, first things first, Wayne . . . at the
moment those guns are secondary to what's going
on here because even though I'm no firearms
expert I'm pretty sure that the ones on your dining
room table were not used to kill Jamie Turner.
Here, now, this minute, the one I'm interested in
is the one Sophie killed herself with.'

'You make it sound like she deliberately killed
herself,' Oxford said, snorting through his tears.

Henry ignored him. 'The thing is, you've been

55

arrested on suspicion of murdering that young man. That is my first priority here, and when I'm happy that issue has been resolved, then I'll start looking at the other things – such as the other guns, such as your involvement in gangs and drug dealing and turf wars – but Jamie Turner's murder is my first priority.'

Rik Dean leaned forward earnestly. 'Did you kill Jamie Turner?'

Oxford rolled his jaw and raised his eyes to Rik. 'Yes . . . but I didn't mean to . . . He was in the way, wrong place, wrong time . . . collateral damage.' Oxford shrugged.

'You intended to murder someone, though?'

'Yeah, but not him, not the lad.'

'What gun did you use?'

'A point thirty-eight . . . probably the one Sophie . . . had . . . killed herself with.'

Henry Christie's bottom twitched, his invisible sign that told him he was now mining gold.

Oxford blinked rapidly and lowered his face, then glanced sideways at his solicitor, who said, 'My client will now tell you everything you need to know about Jamie Turner's death. He will admit everything.' Oxford nodded in agreement as the brief spoke. 'And as much as I understand you need to deal with that as a matter of priority, he also needs to tell you something about the other weapons in the flat.'

'OK,' Henry said cautiously, suspecting some kind of bargaining chip was about to be dealt. 'But I will make no promises about anything else until I hear what they are. If he is completely truthful, I will make it clear to a court that he

56

cooperated with the police investigation into Turner's death fully.'

'And the other weapons will not be mentioned?' the solicitor added hopefully.

Henry gave him his best sardonic look. 'Put the information on the table and we'll discuss it. I have to know what I'm dealing with before I make any decision.'

Solicitor and client exchanged another glance, and the brief gave him an almost imperceptible nod.

Oxford looked at Henry. 'The guns aren't mine . . . except the one Sophie had,' he mumbled, then looked up in a panic. 'Please switch off the tape and the camera. What I'm going to tell you now, I don't want it recorded anywhere.'

Henry reached across to the tape machine and switched it off. 'Happy now?'

Oxford nodded. 'Like I said, the guns aren't mine . . . I'm holding them for someone.' He exhaled with a juddering breath.

Henry and Rik waited, unable to remove the cynical expressions from their faces.

'I'll get fucking killed for this,' Oxford said desperately.

Henry still said nothing. It was down to the prisoner to fill the silence.

'I'm holding them for Fraser Worthington, and he's coming for them tonight,' he blurted. 'And I'll deliver him on a plate to you if you protect me and reduce my charge to manslaughter.'

The mention of that name made Henry's ring-piece twitch like mad.

* * *

Henry and Rik retreated to the corridor outside the interview room where they had a hushed conversation.

'What do you think?' Rik asked.

Henry rubbed his eyes and willed his brain to keep working. 'What do you think the chances are that Worthington knows chummy in there has been arrested?'

Rik thought it through. 'At this moment in time—' he checked his watch, seeing the time was nearing eleven a.m. – 'maybe not . . . but the press are already sniffing around about Sophie's death, so if that gets out . . . dunno.' He shrugged.

'It would spook him if he heard that, but if we could keep a lid on it . . .' Henry pondered out loud. 'And, hopefully, none of Oxford's mates know he's been arrested yet; just gone off the radar for a few hours . . .'

The two detectives looked at each other.

'Fraser Worthington's a big fish,' Rik said. 'Nasty man.'

'Yeah,' said Henry, fighting to keep his brain on track, 'and if he is alarmed in any way, he won't come anywhere near the guns, because that's how guys like him operate . . . Something not right, they go to ground.'

'Correct.'

'But if he thinks all is right with the world, he turns up, Wayne hands him the guns and we step in and nab him.' Henry's eyes narrowed.

'Which would depend on a lot of factors, not least of which is Oxford's full cooperation, and he's clearly shit-scared of Worthington.'

'But what holds more fear – a life sentence for murder, or a lesser one for manslaughter? That's why he's trying to bargain with us.'

'Are you seriously thinking of charging him with manslaughter instead of murder?' Rik asked.

Henry frowned doubtfully. 'Based on what we have now, what's the realistic chance of securing a murder conviction against Oxford?'

'Pretty bloody good, I'd say.'

'I think so, too.' Henry started to waver. 'And the prospect of explaining the decision to Jamie's parents to charge him with manslaughter instead of murder is not something I feel I could justify. They don't give a shit about us catching Fraser Worthington. All they want is justice for their boy . . . and so do I, come to that,' Henry conceded. 'Oxford deserves to be convicted of murder, and if we can prove it, then we should . . . Missing the chance to nail a scumbag like Worthington might hurt us, but it's the lesser of two evils – although there could be another way to nail him.'

He sighed long and hard through his nose and rubbed his temples as it all rolled through his mind. He had endured a great deal of pain and heartache from Jamie Turner's family over the last few weeks and had made a lot of promises about catching and putting his killer away for good – promises he was determined to keep. Losing the chance of taking down a big-time armed robber like Worthington was way down on the scales of justice if he was honest with himself.

Henry was screwed up about it, though. It was

59

such a good opportunity, a great double whammy. He sniffed.

'Well?' Rik asked impatiently.

'We're going to have to work around this somehow.' He jerked his head, indicating that Rik should follow him back into the interview room.

With his fingers interlaced on the table in front of him, Henry looked deeply into Wayne Oxford's bloodshot eyes.

'Wayne, we've had a chat, and to be frank with you I'm going to have to charge you with murder.' He shrugged. 'That's a given, I'm afraid. If the charge gets reduced to manslaughter when it reaches court, then so be it, name of the game, that's not my call.' Henry pulled his hands apart and leaned on the table. 'You see, you're a cold blooded killer, and my job is to catch people like you.'

'B–but,' Oxford blabbered, casting desperate looks at the solicitor.

'No buts.'

'What about the other guns? I told you, they aren't mine!'

'I know, but I have to deal with that separately – the punishment for your illegal possession of a number of dangerous prohibited weapons and ammunition will be huge, and that, together with a conviction for murder, will see you in prison for many years to come,' Henry said cruelly. 'And if I'm honest, I don't really see you dropping Worthington in it when it comes to the crunch, because I'll bet you're more scared of him than you are of me, and if you do grass on him, you'll probably get knifed to death in some prison showers two years down the line.'

'But I've already told you – *they're his guns!*' he protested.

'Mm, you have. But in your possession.'

'And he's coming to collect them tonight.'

'That, too,' Henry said.

Oxford slumped back in his chair, flabbergasted.

'And clearly I have to act on that information,' Henry said with a half-smile.

'Fuck you,' Oxford said as he worked it through. 'I want to make a phone call.'

'I'll bet you do,' Henry said.

It felt to Jake like he had to drag himself physically out of his slumber. It was such a real effort to wake up that by the time he reached for his mobile phone, which he'd left next to the bed, it had stopped ringing. He'd been lying face down in the pillow, and now he wedged himself up on his elbows, swallowing back dribble, and glanced at the offending device on the bedside cabinet, on to which a text then landed.

Jake's face drooped forward. He could feel his features sagging loosely, tugged by gravity. He swallowed, twisted over and swiped up the phone, tabbing through to read the message.

It was from work and read, 'BRIEFING HQ 4PM. U OK 4 THIS? FULL KIT.'

Jake flopped back on to the soft pillow, seeing it was only now 1.30 p.m. He'd hoped to have the day off . . . That was, he would tell Anna that he'd hoped to have the day off, but secretly he was glad of the text. At that moment he could not get enough of work, but he would never admit it and would always complain to Anna about the hours he worked. However, he would have liked a bit more sleep.

He texted back: 'YES.' This, he knew, would land on the Operations Inspector's phone.

He placed his phone back down and listened for any signs of occupation in the house. He could hear rain lashing down, as it seemed to do every day now, but nothing else. Rolling out of bed, he glanced through the curtains and saw that Anna's car was not on the drive. She wasn't back from work yet.

He swore and went into the shower room.

Jackie had to get into work and left Anna in the café, where she sat alone for the next hour, her mind churning, going through all the combinations: the clues, the facts, the figures, the guesses.

To be honest, there was very little to go on.

Since becoming a firearms officer ten years ago, then getting on to the Armed Response Unit, Jake had often worked long hours. Financially, that had been good, especially with a fat mortgage and two fast-growing kids. Anna had returned to work after Daniel had been born, but had quickly gone on to part-time working, something that had just been brought in by the force as the organization felt the pressure of equality and discrimination legislation. That had been just about manageable, but when Emma entered the equation Anna had decided to quit the cops to devote all her time to the children, despite the financial hardship of just one wage.

So long hours had been the norm for some time for Jake.

It was just the other things, particularly over the last few months.

The lack of sex was one. The complete lack of sex, actually. There had been times over the years when the frequency of making love had diminished, but it had always returned with a vengeance. Recently, there had been no comeback.

Regular late finishes were another factor. Not solid chunks of overtime, but short blocks, coming home late for no reason and it not showing up in his salary.

Jake's vague distance was also a worry, along with his newly discovered passion for golf: spending five hours out of the house on a rest day wasn't unusual now.

Anna sighed, wondering if she was just being oversensitive. She knew she was grouchy, always felt tired, always felt like it was she who sorted the kids; she knew she rarely 'scrubbed up' for Jake (although that was a two-way street – he just slobbed around the house), and maybe she had become unattractive to him.

Maybe nothing was going on. And yet . . . She swigged down her coffee. It had gone extremely cold.

'Where have you been?' Jake demanded.

'Met up with Jackie for lunch.'

They had come face-to-face in the hallway. Jake had been fastening his boots whilst sitting on the bottom step when Anna came through the door.

'I think, "Where are you going?" is the question to be asked,' she countered. 'I thought you had the day off.'

'I know, I know,' he bleated. He finished tying the boots, stood up and grabbed his windcheater from the radiator. 'Been called in for a briefing at four.'

'What about?'

'No idea. You know the score. Sorry and everything . . . it's just my job.' He rubbed his forefinger and thumb together, meaning money. 'Can't turn it down, can I?'

Anna's face set like granite. Then she realized how she must be coming across to him and forced a different expression on it. One of disappointment. 'I thought we could have had a curry tonight.'

'Yeah, me too.' He touched her shoulder. 'I'll let you know what's happening as soon as I know. Whether it's a job, or what,' he promised. He brushed his lips against her cheek and shoved past, going out through the front door without a backward glance.

'Jake,' she called meekly – but the door had slammed and he was gone.

She sat down on the same step he had been on and clasped her hands together on her lap, just as her face collapsed and the tears came.

Jake couldn't wait to get on the mobile and was fiddling with it as soon as the car moved away from the house. Kirsten's number wasn't kept in the phone's memory, so each time he called her he did it from scratch, then deleted all traces after

64

the call was complete, including time elapsed. He drove with his right hand, his left dealing with the phone, using his thumb to negotiate the numbers, glancing up at the road ahead and back continually, even letting go of the steering wheel and holding it between his thighs at some points.

He had just the vaguest moment of disquiet when he thought about how deceitful he was being, but then tossed that away. Because there was no doubt about it, Jake had fallen out of love with his wife and was madly in love with Kirsten, and he didn't give a flying fuck about anything or anyone else. He was certain he could manage it.

He wedged the phone between his right shoulder and ear, waited for the connection.

Anna looked down accusingly at her mobile phone. *'The number you have dialled is busy,'* the cold electronic voice of the operator told her. *'Please hang up and call again.'*

She thumbed the end call button with disgust and threw the phone down the hall against the front door. It bounced and clattered on the laminate flooring, bursting open, the back, battery and front of it scattered in three different directions.

'It's me.'
  'I know.' Kirsten sounded sleepy.
  'You up?'
  'Sorta.'
  'You been called in?'
  'Yeah.'

'See you there, then.'

'Un-huh.'

'Thanks for this morning. It was fantastic.'

'Uh – yeah, it was.'

'I love you – you know that, don't you?'

'Yeah, yeah,' she said absently.

Jake waited. Nothing came. 'See you there, then.'

Anna reconstructed the phone and switched it back on, then went into the tiny lean-to conservatory at the rear of the house, opening the back door. The rain had stopped, and the atmosphere smelled fresh and vibrant.

She slid her hand behind one of the cushions on the cane-backed sofa and found the pack of cigarettes hidden there. She flipped open the lid and put a cigarette between her lips, lighting it with the throwaway lighter kept in the already half-smoked packet. She took a deep lungful of smoke, went to the door and exhaled into the air.

She leaned there, not certain what she was even thinking.

Then her phone rang.

'Hi sweetie, how are you?' It was Jackie.

'Still doing OK,' Anna lied.

'Hon, you asked me to look at something?'

Anna's whole being tensed up. 'Yes.'

Afterwards, Anna went back into the kitchen and looked at the wall-clock for a very long time, remembering her exchange with Jake that morning about arrest times. With each tick and each sway of the pendulum she felt like a knife was being pushed further and further into her heart. And she knew, right there and then, that she wanted, more than anything else in the world, to die.

Six

First of all, big apologies for this.' Henry was standing next to the interactive whiteboard at the front of the classroom situated at one end of the long, narrow building that was the main firing range at the Police Training Centre, Hutton, four miles south of Preston. The classroom was at the back of and separated from the firing range itself and was used to teach theory and some basic fire-arms handling to participants attending the various firearms courses held at the venue. The whole facility was as up-to-date as any in the country.

Jake Niven thought Henry looked downright exhausted. His face was pale, his eyes set deep and black in their sockets. Each time he moved, pain carved lines in his shotgun-scarred features.

Jake knew a bit about Henry, but hadn't come across him often.

He knew that maybe a year earlier Henry had come face-to-face with a deranged female who'd produced a handgun and tried to gun down the detective. One bullet had gone into his shoulder, and it was only misfiring, defective, home-produced ammunition that had saved his life, because on the second shot the gun had not gone off. The woman had subsequently been killed in a hail of bullets after a no-win siege with French police when she had been found holed up in a grotty flat in Marseille.

Jake also knew that much more recently – hence the still-prominent scarring on Henry's face and ear – he had come up against a shotgun wielding nut job, and though Henry had survived the attack, that particular night had ended tragically. The offender, one Charlie Wilder, was now on remand, awaiting a Crown Court trial.

Jake had no idea what had happened in the intervening hours since he'd last seen Henry after Oxford had been arrested, but he guessed something significant, hence the firearms team being called back in and now being briefed.

Jake thought it a bit ironic when Henry said, 'I know you all must be shattered . . . and once again, thanks for last night. It was a brilliant operation and arrest.' Henry pressed a wireless clicker in his hand, and an image appeared on the whiteboard. It was a mugshot of Wayne Oxford. 'You all know this fella,' he said, wincing as he turned sideways to glance at the screen.

Jake felt the leg of the firearms officer sitting alongside him press against his outer thigh. The classroom furniture had been arranged 'boardroom' style – basically, all the individual tables pushed together in the centre of the room to form a large rectangle. The firearms team were seated on three sides, leaving the open end where Henry, Rik Dean and the whiteboard were situated. As unintentionally as they could make it seem, Jake was next to Kirsten, close and touching. Jake kept his eyes firmly on Henry and the board, but was aware in his peripheral vision that Kirsten had peeped at him.

He grinned until he caught sight of Dave

69

Morton's eyes. He was sitting directly opposite, scowling unkindly.

Jake's gaze lingered for a second, then focused back on Henry.

'We've been working all day on this guy, with little success at first – until we discovered his address and went to search it.' Henry paused theatrically. 'Then something very unpleasant happened when we entered the property . . . Oxford's girlfriend accidentally shot herself . . . dead.'

The firearms team muttered with surprise and shock.

'It's all been referred to the IPCC, but we are blameless, thankfully,' Henry explained. 'But that's not the real reason you're here . . . The reason is that, firstly, we discovered a little arsenal of weapons at the address.' Henry clicked the remote in his hand and a new photo appeared on the board: the four guns from the flat laid out side by side. The image drew one or two appreciative gasps and whistles from the audience of firearms experts. Then he brought in another photo – this time of the revolver that Sophie Leader had killed herself with. He explained what had happened and drew more responses from them, mostly uncomplimentary. Then he went on, 'As much as interviewing Oxford was like pulling teeth initially, once he learned of his girlfriend's death, his grief opened him up wide.'

'Sang like a canary,' Rik interjected.

'Whatever,' Henry said, frowning at him. 'Point is – and this is where you guys come in – Oxford admitted he was holding the guns for a third

70

party.' Seeing the 'yeah, right' body language from a few of the sceptical officers, Henry held up his hand. 'Yes, I know he would say that to save his own skin, but in this case I believe him.' He did another little dramatic pause. 'He told us he was keeping the weapons for this guy.' He pressed the remote and a new face appeared on screen. 'One Fraser Worthington, a man who I can best describe as a gangster.'

A few of Jake's colleagues muttered under their breath, but Jake just frowned. The name and face meant nothing to him, which irked him somewhat.

The face on the screen was a mugshot of Worthington taken about ten years earlier. It showed a sallow, spotty-faced youth, front view and profile, glowering challengingly at the camera. The freshness of his teenage features was tempered by a swollen, ugly looking black eye, an injury not elaborated on by Henry, though clearly there was a story to tell.

'Fraser Aldous Worthington,' Henry announced grandly, 'to give him his full title. And as old as the photo is, this wasn't even the beginning of his criminal career. He has convictions from the age of ten onwards, mainly assault and robbery. He likes hitting people and stealing their money and valuables. Nothing has changed in the inter-vening years, except the scale of his ruthlessness and his deeds – and the fact that he's got a lot more savvy and difficult to catch.'

Henry pressed the remote. Worthington's photo pixelated out and was replaced by another – this time a slightly grainy black and white one, but

71

more recent. It showed a casually, but well-dressed man walking along a shopping street, which Jake recognized immediately as Clifton Street in Lytham. He also recognized the man as being the older version of Worthington. Henry clicked through a series of similar images – Worthington strolling along, apparently nonchalantly, maybe window shopping or, as every cop in that room believed, casing business premises.

'Taken six months ago,' Henry explained. 'Part of a surveillance operation run by our surveillance branch and the Serious and Organized Crime Unit.' He paused and readjusted his stance with another painful wince as he moved his head and shoulders. He cleared his throat. 'OK, so for those of you who don't know, since that original mugshot was taken ten years ago, Worthington has streamlined his activities and become a prolific armed robber. An old-fashioned crime these days, but still highly profitable, if risky. He is connected with various trusted associates and tends to work in short bursts, then fades into obscurity, usually keeping his head down in Spain or Northern Cyprus. When the money he's made runs out, he comes back for more, keeps under the radar, does a few well-planned jobs – then he's gone again.

'Although we can't prove it, we suspect he committed six high-value armed robberies across the region last year. Two shops, two betting offices, one cash-in-transit and a jeweller's. But no arrests. Two people bludgeoned with baseball bats; one security guard shot in the leg, the lower part of which had to be amputated. Just short of a million in cash and a quarter of a mill in gems – split between four.'

Jake squirmed at the thought of so much money.

'We think his brother Arlow fences the jewels . . . They go in fast, hard and well-drilled,' Henry emphasized, 'and are clearly not reticent about using force or firing their weapons.'

'So what's the significance of that photo, boss?' one of the team piped up, pointing to the whiteboard.

'I'll come to that in a minute . . . I just wanted to impress on you what dangerous people you might be coming across in the near future. The actual tactics they employ are something you as a team will be scrutinizing very closely, very soon. Imminently, actually.'

Something inside made Henry crease up – a jolt of pain. 'Excuse me, just need to take a seat for a second . . . getting old and creaky . . . so apologies if anyone can't quite see me clearly, but I'll keep my voice up.' Henry eased himself into a chair, and Jake saw the relief flood on his face and really felt for the guy. Never having been shot, Jake could only guess at the lingering pain.

'Why's he never been locked up?' someone asked.

'He has . . . but, as we all know, knowing someone has committed an offence is different than proving it in court,' Henry answered, then went on. 'The significance of these surveillance photos is we believe Worthington is doing a bit of reconnoitring. This photo was taken about four

73

months *after* the series of crimes I've just mentioned to you. In that gap, we think Worthington and his crew were sunning themselves in the Med and we just got lucky when he turned up back in this country and got this photo, after which he shook off the surveillance team and disappeared. Which is something else you need to know – he is very surveillance conscious – it's part of how he operates – but, so far, nothing has come of this stroll, no jobs that could be attributed to him.'

Henry smiled grimly. 'Because of this morning's arrest we have accidentally stumbled across the person who has been holding some weapons for Worthington, plus' – Henry's face brightened up – 'we have also found a possible address for him, which is now under surveillance, although we're not sure if he is actually in it. But, from what we gleaned from Wayne Oxford, we're pretty sure Worthington's somewhere back on the plot, and this time we aim to keep a tight rein on him and catch him in the act.'

Jake raised his hand. Henry nodded at him.

'How will this morning's arrest affect him, though?' Jake asked. 'Surely, he'll be spooked by it – especially if the guns are now in our hands . . . It's not as though we can hide the fact we have them, is it? We can't exactly lure him in.'

'No, probably not,' Henry admitted, 'and there is a big chance he'll be spooked, though we have tried to keep the arrest under wraps as much as possible . . . but that doesn't mean we shouldn't run an op against him. There are a lot of imponderables, but if he has planned some jobs and they need to go ahead, then he will probably be able to source weapons from elsewhere, and if he learns Oxford has been arrested, he'll hope that he doesn't blab to us – even though he has. Under normal circumstances, Oxford wouldn't have said a word to us, but because his girlfriend managed to shoot herself, he opened up. I bet right now he's regretting it.'

'So what's the plan?' someone else chirped up.

Henry shrugged painfully. 'Hopefully, to keep tabs on Worthington, and if he pulls a job we'll – you'll – be on to him like a hawk on a rabbit.'

'All a bit vague, isn't it?' Kirsten said crossly. 'What was the word? Imponderable?' She was in the queue at the training-centre dining room with the rest of the firearms team, tray in hand, waiting to choose her food. Unusually, the meal was being paid for out of the Force Major Investigation Team's budget, Henry Christie's department. It was unusual because in these tight-fisted financial times it was rare for the cost of any meal to be subsidized. She went on, mimicking Henry, 'They don't know this, they don't know that.' Then she added, under her breath, 'Boring old fart.'

Jake was alongside her in the slow-moving queue, which consisted of others who were on training courses at the centre. Patiently, he said, 'That's how it goes . . . ambiguity.'

'Chances are it'll come to nothing,' she moaned.

Jake noticed she did a lot of moaning and had been doing so ever since Henry had finished his briefing, following which the team had been given a tactical briefing from a Serious and Organized Crime Unit detective inspector and their own firearms inspector based on what was known about how Worthington's gang operated and what weapons they were likely to use. Plans were still being formulated as to how the operation was going to pan out and, yes, it was all a bit vague, but that came with the nature of the job.

Even though Jake realized Kirsten was tired, her negativity was beginning to grate on him a little, and he couldn't be bothered to continue the conversation because he, too, was feeling tetchy and weary. The last thing they needed was a lovers' tiff in the dinner queue. He took a deep breath, pointed to the minced meat and onion pie and chips and smiled sweetly at the dinner lady who was dishing out the food. She responded by smacking an extra-large portion on to his plate, to which he added mushy peas and a dollop of gravy. Real stodge, but genuinely tasty.

Kirsten was ahead of him as they left the servery and turned into the dining area. He was so rankled by her that he did not really want to sit next to her, but knew he would have to. Sometimes she just annoyed the living crap out of him, but he could not resist her even though he had an unpleasant premonition that their liaison would end disastrously. For not only were they breaking the 'unwritten rule' that you didn't shag a team colleague because of the terrible implications – not just about skewing judgements on an operation, but also team dynamics – but he was also committing adultery.

But that was how it went when your head was up your arse.

As it happened, Kirsten, perhaps sensing Jake's irritability, sat next to another team member. With relief, Jake sat down heavily on an adjacent table and dragged his plate off the tray, propping up the tray next to his chair leg. He began eating his meal, feeling the energy buzz from the hot food as it seeped down his throat into his stomach. Under the right conditions, 'county pie', chips and gravy could be the best food in the world.

He glanced sideways as Dave Morton slid in alongside him and arranged his own plate. Jake eyed him with weary suspicion and gave an inner sigh, but Morton concentrated on getting himself comfortable, then launched into his food whilst Jake continued to mull over his relationship with Kirsten.

He supposed it wasn't any different from any other man cheating on his wife.

It sucked you in.

It became horribly irresistible.

The sex was amazing, the stolen companionship terrific.

The way he could talk to Kirsten in a manner he could not even begin to talk to Anna. Talk about his true feelings, his hopes, his expectations. So yes, surface-wise, it seemed so right. But the gnawing, deep-down feeling was that he was conning himself. He thought he had the wherewithal to handle anything that came from it, even the fallout, because a big part of him wanted to believe that Kirsten was his future, not Anna. The kids would be there, for sure. He loved them to bits. But he and Anna, or so he tried to convince himself, had become used, shoddy goods. They seemed to have lost all means of communication. Two people trapped in a going nowhere marriage, and this affair (more self-convincing here, or delusion, possibly) could be the catalyst needed to finally rip them apart and fire each of them off into different orbits, from which they could begin again, separately.

For the moment, Jake wanted to keep a lid on it because it was all so complicated. And he wasn't completely certain of Kirsten's intentions. Sometimes she hinted about the future; other times she just laughed it all off.

'What?' Jake had heard Dave Morton whisper something that had interrupted his train of thought.

Morton's head hung over his meal. He was speaking downwards into his food, making it hard to hear. 'I said, unwritten rule . . . You're breaking it, pal.'

A chill replaced the heat generated by the food in Jake's guts. 'What are you on about?' he asked Morton.

'You got careless.'

Jake waited.

'It was like following a fucking three year old.'

'What the fuck . . .?' Jake hissed.

'I saw you go in, saw you come out.' Morton's head turned with agonizing slowness, like a demon. His eyes locked malevolently on Jake's. 'This morning. Some debrief, huh?'

'You sick fucker.'

The expression on Morton's face remained

constant. 'You drop her now, or I'll blow the whistle long and hard – and it will end in tears.'

Jake's grip tightened on his cutlery. He was about to respond, possibly by plunging his fork into Morton's eye. Instead, he looked sharply away and placed the implements across his plate, which he picked up and put back on his tray. He took it to the self-stack station and stalked out of the room.

Fraser Aldous Worthington peeked through the gap in the curtain. From what little he could see, there was nothing untoward, but that did not necessarily mean the cops weren't there. He knew they had got a lot better – more subtle, more sneaky – at surveillance than ever, so the fact he couldn't see them did not make him relax. He always assumed they would be there because that was the only attitude he could take – especially on the brink of pulling a job.

He let the drape fall back into place and turned and nodded to the woman sitting near to the TV. She nodded back, and he dropped a fifty-pound note on to her lap, pecked her cheek and stepped out of the first-floor walkway outside her flat, closing the door behind him.

He paused here, too, inhaling the air of the early evening.

Again, nothing seemed problematic, so he trotted down the outer staircase and went to the crumpled but very clean Alfa 164 parked at the end of the cul-de-sac, still seeing nothing out of place.

He slid into the car and fired up the engine,

which ran sweetly, then reversed out of the parking space, trying to work out the logistics a surveillance team might be up against in this location, and where such a team might be hiding and watching from.

If they were there, they would be struggling to secrete themselves in the immediate vicinity because they would stand out and be rumbled by the locals, who were skilled at identifying cops, even hidden ones.

Skelmersdale, Lancashire's newest town, situated on the Merseyside border, designed and built in the 1960s, was an exciting social experiment, but had become a law-abiding citizen's nightmare. Its geography and structure, on paper so very appealing, with its low rise housing, cul-de-sacs, underpasses and dead ends, was hard enough to police just on a day-by-day basis and was virtually impossible for any form of surveillance: anything remotely out of place was spotted almost instantly, word spread, and sometimes violence was used on interlopers.

But no word had spread, nothing had made its way to Worthington's ears – and he had paid good brass to half a dozen kids to keep their eyes open for him. He had to assume, therefore, that if the watchers were there, they were off the plot and waiting for him to make a move.

Such was life.

He drove slowly out of the cul-de-sac on Digmoor council estate and headed along the A577 through Up Holland, taking his time, hoping to draw out and expose any followers. He saw nothing nor anyone to arouse his

80

suspicions. He drove across the M6 bridge at Orrell, then swung a left to take him to the motorway junction, where he looped right around and picked up the northbound carriageway of the motorway.

The Alfa, which belonged to his mother, was a good, unspectacular workhorse, a throwaway car he did not give a shit about. It responded well enough to his foot on the accelerator as he peeled on to the motorway. He took the vehicle up to seventy-five mph and cruised, constantly checking his mirrors, then started to do a bit of lane-skipping, cutting across and back from the slow lane to the fast, accelerating and slowing down. But not dangerously because the last thing he wanted was to cause or get involved in an accident. He watched the changing pattern of vehicles behind him and those overtaking him, concentrating hard to ID a vehicle or series of vehicles manoeuvring behind or passing and following from the front.

He was unable to spot anything.

As he approached the Junction 28 exit he was in the outside lane as he passed the 300-metre marker. This was the Leyland turn-off, and he was travelling at seventy-five mph. After a quick check of his mirrors, he veered across to his left over three lanes and rattled over the hatch markings at the top of the exit slip-road, which he tore down towards the traffic lights where the road met the B5256 Leyland Way. Turning left would have taken him towards Leyland. The lights were on red, and he stopped in the outer lane, knowing that if he went right, then immediately dog-legged left, he would be on the entry slip-road for the M6 North again.

This is what he did, but as he turned on to the slip road, he stopped on the hard shoulder, flicked on the hazard warning-lights and climbed out of the car, pulling the bonnet release catch as he did. He edged to the front of the car, raised the bonnet and stood there, apparently gazing at the engine. In reality he was watching every car that came past him.

It was just another very basic anti-surveillance tactic. He knew if he was being followed, a good team would not be thrown by this, but at least it would screw them about. If they were not so good, the chances were that they'd still be on the motorway, banging their heads on the steering wheels, or maybe stopping and pretending to have broken down, in which case they would be very spottable. Whatever the result, this simple ruse would cock them up no end.

He slammed the bonnet down, jumped back in and set off back on to the motorway.

He saw no sign of followers . . . so possibly they were not there after all.

But he would never let down his guard.

Less than ten minutes later he pulled off the M6 at Junction 31A, the signpost on the gantry pointing to Longridge and Preston North. On the exit slip-road, he filtered into the right lane to follow the Preston signs, dropping down first on to Longsands Lane and then on to Eastway, the B6241, a road that circled the outer rim of Preston itself. He travelled east, then cut up to the ASDA superstore, where he stopped in the car park as near to the entrance as possible and sat for a patient ten minutes to watch all traffic coming in.

A fully liveried police car did drive on, a youngish female officer at the wheel. Nothing for Worthington to concern himself with.

Although never completely satisfied, Worthington pulled a black, fur lined trapper hat on to his head that covered his ears, got out of the Alfa, leaving the ignition key tucked under the driver's seat, and strolled into the super-market, picking up a hand basket. He sauntered around doing a form of window shopping, no intention of buying anything.

Several times he passed a young man doing much the same, mooching up and down the aisles: a man dressed in a motorcycle outfit with full leathers and carrying a full face helmet over his arm. They never looked directly at each other.

Ten minutes after entering the shop, Worthington went into the gents toilets close to the store exit. As he entered, a cubicle door opened and the man who had been previously kitted out as a motorcyclist emerged, now dressed in clothing similar to Worthington's.

Without a word they slid past each other – Worthington into the cubicle, the man out of it. Worthington took off his trapper hat and gave it to the man, who pulled it on and left the toilets as Worthington closed the door.

In the cubicle, neatly stacked, were the motor-cycle leathers the man had been wearing, including boots and the helmet. A few minutes later Worthington was in the outfit. He packed his trainers and jeans into a plastic bag, then eased up the zip of the jacket and his transformation was virtually complete.

When he came out of the toilets he was already fitting the helmet whilst walking out of the store. He made his way to the motorcycle parking area and mounted a Yamaha 650cc, firing it up with the key that had been left in the leather jacket for him. He stuffed the bag containing his trainers and jeans into one of the panniers, easing the bike off its stand. He drove slowly out of the car park, and as he did so, he glanced at the place where he had left the Alfa. It was gone.

He smirked.

It was on its way back to Skelmersdale, with someone who looked very similar to him at the wheel.

It was just another undercurrent, almost nothing. Another minor bit of teeth-grating, but suddenly Jake realized he wasn't remotely keen on Kirsten smoking. She was one of the few officers on the team who did. Not to excess, though. She enjoyed a ciggy after a meal and after sex, something Jake had initially found endearing – and they'd laughed once or twice at the old joke about smoking after sex – but it soon got to be another irritant, especially as Jake loved to keep fit and healthy and smoking went against his grain.

Now he did not like it at all.

He and Kirsten were standing by the outer wall of the firing range, overlooking the training-centre sports pitches.

Jake paced like a wild cat, almost growling as he walked up and down.

Kirsten leaned casually against the breeze-block wall, one leg drawn up, observing Jake's reaction whilst emitting smoke into the cool evening air.

'Bastard actually followed me – can you believe it?' Jake demanded. He shot another look at her, and she took another drag. 'Followed me to your pad.' Seeing the smoke come out of her mouth and nostrils was the moment he realized he did not like the smoking at all.

'Ever thought he might be jealous?'

Jake shook his head forcefully. 'Nah – he keeps mithering about the unwritten rule.'

'What? The unwritten rule that says two people can't fall in love?'

That stopped Jake in his tracks. He was about to respond because the word 'love' had never really been used by her before.

Before he could say anything, though, she went on quickly, 'Or the unwritten rule that he's the only one allowed to do it?'

'What do you mean?' Jake frowned, feeling a bit simple, but then feeling something else, something physical: a tightening of his gut, a fire raging in his chest.

'He tried it on with me.'

The blood drained from Jake's face. 'What happened?' His voice was ice cold.

'Oh nothing, nothing.' Her eyes avoided his. She took a last drag of the cigarette, flicked it down and crushed it whilst exhaling.

'I said, what happened, Kirst? *What happened?*'

Her nostrils flared, and she looked up to the sky. 'He followed me home after that robbery op in Preston. You were on your sniper course. We were all pretty hyped up, buzzing because we'd had to draw weapons. I had to fend him off . . . I'm not saying anything more.'

'Did he touch you?'

'I got free.'

'So he held you? Bastard.' Jake thumped the side of his fist on the wall.

'And he warned me not to say anything if I wanted to stay on the team.'

Jake stared incredulously at her. 'He what?'

'You know the score. He's a big influence on the team. The old lag,' she said witheringly. 'He could easily turn everyone against me, even though he's only a PC. He's got the sarge in the palm of his hand.'

'I'm not having that,' Jake declared, spinning away.

Kirsten grabbed his arm. 'No! Do nothing, otherwise it'll mess us up, too.' She clutched his biceps, would not release him. 'Do nothing,' she pleaded, 'or we're screwed, and it'll all blow up in our faces. You know what they're like. He's bitter and vindictive, and he'd love to split us up.'

The rage inside Jake slammed from side to side across his chest, but as he stood there, with Kirsten still gripping his arm, it began to ebb. He breathed steadily again as he looked into her eyes, thinking how beautiful she was, even in her overalls, her hair pulled back in a bun, no make-up, no jewellery, ready for action as a firearms team member.

'You . . . you,' he said croakily, 'mentioned love.'

'Oh that,' she said with a dismissive wave, instantly deflating him. She let go of his arm. 'Don't take that too seriously. We both know it's about screwing, don't we?'

'Do we?' he began, but was interrupted by another team member poking his head around the corner of the building and calling:

'Come on, guys. Some sort of game on.'

Henry walked back into the classroom at the firing range in which sat Jake, Kirsten, Dave Morton and PC Rob Brown, the latter being the firearms officer who was Kirsten's partner on the team. These were the only team members to have been summoned back.

Henry sat, surveyed the officers quickly. 'Thanks for coming back; sorry to keep you waiting,' he said, noticing a strangely pissed-off look on the female cop's face. 'I promise you, we won't be much longer now.'

'What's happening, boss?' Jake asked.

'What's happening is that the surveillance team picked up Fraser Worthington in Skem, then followed him north on the M6, where they promptly lost him.'

The officers gave a collective groan.

'I know,' Henry acknowledged, 'but these things happen. He pulled a nifty move at the Leyland junction and caught them napping.' He shrugged, but they could all see he was not pleased.

'So he's up to something?' Dave Morton suggested.

'Maybe, or else doing anti-surveillance manoeuvres is something he does as a matter of course. However . . .' He smiled thinly at the four cops. 'I'd still like to nab him, and as much as it's not ideal, we do have the information that he's due to pick up those guns I mentioned from Wayne Oxford's flat in St Annes. That is assuming he hasn't been tipped off. I'm hoping he'll resurface, knock on the door, and we can arrest him on a "conspiracy to rob" charge . . . or something that will at least prevent him from carrying out anything he might have planned.'

'So what's our job?' Kirsten asked.

'We're going on a stake-out,' Henry revealed, rubbing his hands gleefully together.

Seven

Henry Christie knew for certain he should not be here. He should be retired, drawing his hefty pension and investing a chunk of his big lump-sum pay-out into the Tawny Owl pub, country hotel and restaurant in which he now lived with his wife-to-be, Alison Marsh.

He should not be sitting in a decrepit, blood-stained flat, wearing a bulletproof vest, an earpiece screwed uncomfortably into his jagged left ear, and kitted out with an extendable baton, rigid handcuffs, CS spray and a baseball cap with a chequered band, awaiting the possible arrival of a dangerous individual who enjoyed robbing and hurting people.

Henry knew he should be pulling pints and being 'mine host' with a nose that was becoming bulbous with booze and a waistline spreading from too many frequent visits to the kitchens, while really beginning to understand what the whole business of living was all about.

If things had gone to plan, that is what would have happened, where he would have been – if the previous chief constable, Robert Fanshaw-Bayley, FB, had not died.

Almost three months ago now, on a quiet Saturday morning – three days after FB had been buried, almost two weeks after he had died so tragically on a hillside in East Lancashire

– Henry had been summoned to the office of the man who was acting chief, Bernard Ellison. He was a man Henry did not know particularly well because Ellison had been transferred in from another force to become deputy chief constable, and had then stepped up to the mark to stand in as chief until a new one was appointed. If he played his cards right, Ellison could well become that man.

Though Henry did not know him well, he seemed a decent enough guy, though clearly driven and ambitious, no doubt with a ruthless streak running through him – traits that Henry lacked somewhat in terms of his career, but not when hunting murderers. He might have reached the heady rank of superintendent, but he always knew it was more by luck than judgement.

Ellison had even greeted Henry at the door of his office, which overlooked the sports fields at the front of the main Headquarters building, and graciously welcomed him in.

'Sit, sit, Henry. Coffee?'

Henry sat on the leather Chesterfield sofa – the one that had been a feature of the chief's office for as long as Henry could remember. 'Coffee would be good. Just milk, thanks.'

Ellison poured two mugs from the filter machine on the bureau, added milk and handed one to Henry, sitting alongside him on the sofa like a chum.

'How are you?' Ellison asked.

'OK-ish,' Henry said.

'It was a dreadful experience.' Ellison had been there when the chief's body had been recovered from an old mineshaft by a mountain-rescue team.

'Yup.' Henry nodded, sipped his coffee. The experience had sent Henry hurtling after the person responsible for the death, who he'd ferociously attacked. He'd had to be dragged off him before he killed him – and Henry knew he would have killed him, too.

'What are your plans, Henry? I know you can retire if you so wish.'

'Would you like me to?'

'I didn't mean that . . . I just want to know what your thoughts are. I have to plan your replacement, so it would only be right if you did tell me.'

Henry wilted slightly. 'As unpopular as this may seem, I want to see this through,' he told the chief. 'I know the case has been taken off me for personal reasons, but I'll leave when Charlie Wilder has been convicted and I've answered his accusation of assault if I have to.'

Wilder, the cause of the night of horror that had left too many people dead or badly injured, had complained about Henry assaulting him, which of course had muddied the case against him.

'In fact,' Henry went on, 'I'd love to face his accusation across a courtroom, and he knows it . . . It's just a smokescreen for his defence, and I get it.'

'So you're not worried?'

'Not in the least. I relish it.'

'OK,' Ellison said and sighed, giving Henry a look of doubt.

'So I've decided to stay on in the meantime, then I'll go after Wilder's trial. It would only be right.'

'And in the meantime?'

Henry's mug was almost at his lips. 'What do you mean?'

'You want to stay on as an SIO? I could get you an easy office job to take you through to the end if you like. A cushy six months, or however long the trial takes to come to court.' Ellison tried to make it sound tempting.

'Nah,' Henry said, not taken in.

On his return to the FMIT building on the opposite side of the sports field, Henry had sat down in his office, half expecting that all calls to his number would be diverted to someone else. It was pretty clear to him the acting chief wanted him to go.

That had not happened.

Almost as soon as he'd settled himself, his phone rang, and five minutes later he was in his car speeding towards the M6 to an area in the very north of the county that he was beginning to get to know very well indeed.

And a short while later Henry had been addressing the desolate-faced uniformed chief inspector who was standing anxiously before him in Thornwell's tiny, chilly, village hall. 'Let me get this perfectly straight. This young lass has been sent alone to deal with a disturbance in licensed premises caused by a known, violent troublemaker. When she arrives, the problem is over, she calls in to say so, and then it is *assumed*—' he stressed this word – 'she drives back to Lancaster.'

'Yes, that was the assumption.'

'And yet she wasn't missed until the night shift ended at seven this morning? Am I getting this right?' Henry could feel his insides contracting with anger.

The chief inspector – his name was Collinson – nodded.

'So, somewhere in the region of, say, six hours,' Henry said. 'And nobody missed her. What. The. Fuck?'

Collinson's head twitched as he felt the insertion of a metaphorical 'buck' somewhere deeply unpleasant. He might not have been on duty overnight, but that did not mean he had no responsibility for what had gone on. 'It was very busy out there,' he explained pathetically. 'The town kicked off.'

Henry regarded him fiercely, realizing for the first time how terrifying he must look with his shotgun scars. 'We'll be coming back to that issue,' he promised Collinson ominously, watching the man's Adam's apple rise and fall as he swallowed dryly.

'Yes, sir,' the chief inspector said. Normally, Henry wasn't bothered about being called 'sir', but Collinson decided it would be wise to make an exception in this case.

'Bring me up to speed with what has happened since it was discovered that one of our officers has gone missing.'

Describing what had been done since Laura Marshall's disappearance was slightly easier territory for Collinson.

But then Henry said, 'No, tell you what, tell

93

me again what happened last night, so I have it firmly in my head.'

Collinson inhaled a deep breath. He then explained that Special Constable Marshall had been sent to the Swan's Neck in Thornwell after comms had received a treble-nine from the landlord. It had only been realized that she was missing when the shift was about to parade off at seven a.m. At first it was thought that she might well have just gone off duty earlier without telling anyone (which could have happened, Collinson stressed – special constables were not subject to the same booking on and off scrutiny as regulars and often came and went without patrol sergeants knowing). It was only as the night patrol sergeant was leaving the station that he happened to notice her car was still on the car park and, not really thinking anything untoward at that stage, he popped back in and checked – only to discover the patrol car she'd been using had not been returned either. An early patrol was sent around to her flat in Lancaster, and there was no reply.

Straight away a traffic car was sent to check the route between Lancaster and Thornwell, via Kendleton. These roads were pitch black at night, tight, bendy and dangerous, and sometimes drivers missed a corner or a deer jumped out in front, causing them to swerve off the road. First thoughts were that she too might have crashed, gone off road and into a field or a ditch, maybe into a river. That had to be checked out, but the traffic officer found nothing, and definitely no sign of a missing cop or car.

By this time, the night duty sergeant was having

palpitations, and he rang the chief inspector at home, who turned out and took control.

Henry listened to this again, then checked his watch. Now it was just after eleven a.m. and over eleven hours since Laura had called in to say everything was fine at the Swan's Neck.

'Not happy,' Henry said coldly. 'How can it be possible that . . .?' he began with exasperation, but didn't finish his question. Collinson bit his lip. 'Let's go and see this landlord . . . McCready?' Fuming, he spun and went out of the village hall ahead of Collinson into the still fresh morning.

Henry inhaled as he stepped out and paused to look around the place. Although he now lived in the next village, three miles away, Thornwell was not somewhere he had visited, but it looked a pleasant enough spot. A few ducks and a pair of regal-looking swans floated on the tiny stream that cut through the village. Some residents were out, curious to see the police activity. Henry nodded at a couple of old guys sitting on a bench overlooking the pristine village green, then looked across at the Swan's Neck, the only rival in this area to the Tawny Owl – but a poor one at that.

It was a double-fronted pub, quite substantial, but had an air of neglect, and Henry guessed from what little he had learned of the licensing trade that the place was struggling to keep going. It probably relied on regulars, but that was fatal for survival. The days of sitting back and letting punters come to you and spend had long since disappeared. Now pub owners had to be ruthless and proactive, which is why the Tawny Owl was thriving under his fiancée Alison's stewardship.

95

She never let anything grow under her feet and pursued every channel of business, now even applying for a licence to hold weddings. Nor did it hinder things that she was a bit of a looker, Henry realized. Some guys came in just to ogle her.

Something that could not be said about Bert McCready, the landlord of the Swan's Neck, as Henry discovered a few moments later.

Henry pounded on the double doors, and eventually the grumpy man answered. He was small, rotund and had a mop of hair flattened on his head that was clearly a cheap wig which did not match the colour of his sideburns. A bar towel was flipped over his left shoulder.

He eyed Henry and the chief inspector. 'Already spoken to you guys,' he muttered, opening the doors fully and bolting them back.

'Need to speak again,' Henry informed him. He held out his warrant card and introduced himself. 'I'd like you to tell me about last night.'

McCready jerked his head. Henry and Collinson followed him, entering the pub. Henry inhaled the stench of stale beer, and, yes, there was some damp in that aroma too. The unpleasant niff of an old-fashioned pub. Although Henry did not want to make comparisons, he knew that first impressions counted, and when anyone entered the Tawny Owl they were always greeted by a wonderful aroma of woodsmoke, brewing coffee and good food – all done on purpose. Customers were no longer impressed by having the soles of their shoes sticking to carpet.

McCready sidled behind the bar to put a barrier

between himself and the law. Henry perched one corner of his bottom on a bar stool, his eyes roving slowly around the premises, noticing a swept-up pile of glass by the door and the stacked-up remnants of a table and stool.

'The visit of Spencer Bartle?' Henry asked, nodding at the piles.

'Yep.'

'Tell me.'

McCready's eyes jittered between the two cops. 'Simple. He came in here, drank too much – my fault – started arguing about nothing, got shirty when I asked him to leave, so I called the cops. He'd gone before that policewoman landed. As far as I know she got into her car and drove off. Best idea from me is to check the valleys carefully . . . These roads are treacherous. You've only got to get a deer in front of you or misjudge a bad corner.'

Henry surveyed the man as he spoke. He seemed to be telling the truth, but Henry wasn't impressed for some reason – instinct, maybe. Plus, his mantra when investigating anything was: don't believe a word.

'How long was it between Bartle leaving and the policewoman getting here?'

McCready cogitated. 'A good ten minutes, I'd say.'

Henry nodded, slid off the stool on to his feet. 'Where did he go?'

'Dunno . . . town, maybe.'

'How would he get there?'

'Taxi . . . KountryKabs . . . They run from a unit on the industrial estate up the road. Cabs, coaches, that sort of thing.'

'I've seen their cars. Is there much business round here for them?'

'Not midweek, except for school and hospital contracts, but pretty busy at weekends. No bugger wants to drive into Lancaster for a night out and drive back pissed.'

'OK.' He gave the landlord a thin smile. 'Probably talk again . . . Nah, *definitely*,' he said with significance. He gave the unimpressed man a wave and left the pub trailed by the chief inspector.

Outside, he stopped.

'What d'you think, boss?'

Henry gave Collinson a withering look. 'That she met Spencer Bartle.' He sighed, surveyed the front parking area of the pub, then walked slowly around the perimeter of the building and cast his eyes around the car park at the rear. He began to walk diagonally across, gravel scrunching under his shoes, his eyes roving, seeing nothing out of place. He stopped in the centre of the car park, looking all the while, traversing back and forth until finally he was looking down at his feet.

That was the moment at which he felt very queasy.

Slowly, he eased himself down on to his haunches and peered at the grit under his feet. He reached down and picked up a tiny cube of broken glass between finger and thumb, rolling it, holding it up to the light. He pushed himself upwards again, then turned very slowly, still looking down at the gravel at his feet.

The chief inspector watched him, bemused. 'What is it?'

Henry handed him the tiny chunk of glass, which he looked at on his upturned palm.

Collinson frowned. 'Car glass – that's how it crumbles . . . Broken windscreen, something like that.'

Henry continued to revolve, seeing more of the glass mixed in with the gravel as he became familiar with what he was looking at. As his eyes rose again, he frowned and experienced another of those queasy inner feelings.

He walked slowly towards what he had seen. From a distance it was nothing – just a dark shadow underneath the perimeter hedge that could easily have been a ball of litter. As he got nearer, the shape began to take on some kind of form. Its edges sharpened, and there was a glint of something silvery.

His frown was fixed as, once again, he dropped slowly on to his haunches, knees cracking like a walnut. He reached out to lift the low hanging branches, exposing what had caught his eye, seeing the shape for definite at last. His mouth was dry as he tried to swallow.

He glanced over his shoulder at Collinson, who had followed mutely, but who then, seeing what Henry had seen, said, 'Shit.'

Henry blew out his cheeks. '*Yes, exactly* . . .'

'Sorry, boss?'

Henry's contemplations had been rudely inter-rupted by Jake Niven, who was sitting alongside him in Wayne Oxford's flat in St Annes.

'Eh?' Henry turned to him. 'What do you mean?'

'You said something, boss.'

The two of them had been sitting on the sofa for over an hour, waiting to see if Fraser Worthington would knock on the door. After an initial hushed conversation, the two men had melted into their own private worlds of cogitation. Henry's mind had gone back to the still-missing policewoman, Laura Marshall, a case being treated as murder; Jake had been considering his own over-complicated life.

Henry, his head nodding as he thought back, had blurted the words, 'Yes, exactly,' out of the blue and interrupted Jake's thoughts.

'Did I really say that out loud?' Henry said, wiping his mouth, grinning a little self-consciously at Jake. 'Must be losing it.'

Jake smiled. 'Join the club, boss.' Jake was in his work gear, the navy-blue uniform of a firearms officer, a Glock 17 at his side and an H&K machine pistol propped on the floor.

So far no one had knocked, and Henry was considering calling it quits and coming at Worthington from a different angle, one he had not quite yet worked out. But, whatever, it seemed the man had got wind of Oxford's arrest and tonight was going to be a no-show.

Jake stretched. 'What a tangled web.'

Henry glanced at him, saw a troubled face and was about to ask a 'deep-meaningful' when their radios chirped up, calling for Henry.

'Receiving,' he said, pushing his earpiece a little further in, like a small burrowing insect. It was the operator in comms who had been briefed to monitor and control the little operation Henry had hastily set up following the news that Worthington had slipped the surveillance net.

'Just had a message from Sierra Tango Two,' the operator said, referring to the call sign of one of the surveillance team's mobile units which had previously lost Worthington north on the M6 and were still trying to pick him up again. 'Can I patch him through?'

'Go ahead,' Henry agreed, knowing they were operating on a different radio channel. He winced as a burst of static cracked through his ears and someone asked, 'Superintendent Christie?'

'Yes, go ahead.'

'Sierra Tango Two here, boss,' the surveillance officer said. 'An update for you in relation to our target. His vehicle is now parked in the same position as it was first thing.'

'Does that mean the target is now at that address?'

'It means the car is, but no eyeball to target to confirm ID,' the surveillance officer said.

'OK, received . . . Thanks for that.'

'Further instructions?'

'Stand by on that,' Henry said, thinking it all through. Not least of the components in his calculations were the cost implications of keeping officers on duty. He glanced at Jake, who had heard the transmission. So the surveillance team had lost Worthington, who had apparently gone off the grid but might now have returned home, although that wasn't a certainty. Other than by actually banging on his door to see if he really had returned, which would be counterproductive, it seemed to Henry there was only one practical solution. Worthington's disappearance did worry him, though.

'Sierra Tango Two,' Henry called up, 'sack it for the night, and we'll reconsider the whole thing tomorrow.'

'Understood.'

The patch-through was then disconnected by comms.

Henry shrugged at Jake but said, 'I don't really want to . . .'

'No, nor me.'

'DCI to Superintendent,' Henry's radio called. It was Rik Dean, who at that moment was sitting in his car, slouched very low in the seat, with a view along North Promenade towards the front of the block – Salter's Bank View – in which Oxford's apartment was situated. 'Might be nothing, but a motorcycle has been up and down the prom twice. First time normal speed; second time a slow fly-past. One male on board.'

'Make, number?'

'Can't see . . . He's cruising back down again.'

Rik was parked about 100 metres north of the block, whilst 200 metres the other way was a grubby looking Transit van in the back of which the other three officers involved in the stake-out were waiting – Kirsten Lee, Dave Morton and Rob Brown.

Rik had seen the motorcyclist and thought nothing of it the first time he drove past, heading south, even though the brake light did come on as the bike slowed slightly, going past the block of flats. The bike went on, disappeared, but five minutes later, presumably after having done a loop around, the lights appeared in Rik's rear-view mirror and the bike went by again, this time almost at walking pace. That was when Rik started to pay attention.

The bike rolled slowly past the block, then the surveillance van, which was the point at which Rik alerted Henry.

Once more it disappeared down the prom, then once more came up behind and past Rik again, who had slithered as far down in his seat as was humanly possible without actually being curled up in a foetal position in the footwell, whispering into his radio.

The bike drove slowly past the block and the Transit van again, but this time as Rik craned his neck, his eyeline just above the dashboard, he saw it had stopped about fifty metres beyond the van, a message that he whispered to Henry, adding, 'The rider is still astride the bike.'

'Roger,' Henry said, tensing up next to Jake. 'What's happening now?'

'He's off the bike, lifting it on to its stand . . . He's too far away from me to see a number . . . Any of you guys in the van make it out?' Rik asked the three officers in the van itself. The van was parked with its nose towards Rik, and the three officers were in the back of it.

'Negative,' Kirsten whispered.

'He's walking back towards us,' Rik warned.

The figure walked past the van towards Rik's car, then stopped outside the block of flats and looked up at them. Oxford's flat was at the back of the building.

Inside the van, the three officers were silent

103

and unmoving, hidden from view by a panel that divided the driving cab from the rear compartment where they sat. They could see the rider through a blacked-out window and slats cut into the side of the van.

The rider had not taken his full-face helmet off and so could not be identified.

'Shit,' Rik said.

'What?' Henry demanded, frustrated because he could see absolutely nothing.

'He's now walking very slowly past the van . . . Jeez!'

Rik's latest blasphemy was because the rider had stopped at the van and was trying the driver's door.

It was locked.

'What?' Henry demanded again.

'Just tried the van door,' Rik said. 'Now he's walking back to the bike.'

Rik writhed to get a better view and watched him run the bike off its stand, mount it, start it, engage gear and roll slowly forwards.

'Looks like he's going,' Rik said.

The bike accelerated away, then spun around in the road and roared back towards the officers in the vehicles, stopping alongside the surveillance van.

'He's stopped by the van again,' Rik said, then screamed, 'you guys get down – he's got a gun!'

The motorcyclist had reached under his leather jacket, and even from where Rik sat, he could see the unmistakable shape of a handgun in the biker's right hand – which he pointed at the side of the van.

Rik saw muzzle flashes, heard the sound of the gun being fired as the figure pumped three shots into the side of the van. He tucked the gun away, revved the bike wildly and, with a spectacular, contemptuous wheelie, roared away into the night.

Eight

Henry arrived back at the Tawny Owl just as Alison was gently ejecting the last stragglers from the bar and was about to lock the front doors. He hurled his extremely battered Audi coupé in to the car park, just missing one of the regulars who staggered cheerfully away, none the wiser about his brush with death. He trotted up the front steps where Alison waited, arms folded.

'I'm amazed,' she said.

'By what?'

'That you actually came home. You've been on the go, like, forever,' she accused him, but behind the words was some degree of admiration.

'Things kinda got going, and when it happens you've got to stay on board . . . It's a bit like surfing,' he said, giving the impression that he was actually doing just that. 'When a big one comes, you gotta ride it or drown.' He ducked under an imaginary wave.

Her expression turned cynical. 'Bollocks – now come in,' she said and jerked her head towards the bar, making Henry wonder where the rolling pin was hidden.

'Not before you give me a hug.'

She sighed despairingly, then opened her arms and sank tenderly against his chest as he wrapped his arms around her and nuzzled her neck,

106

inhaling her sweet smell, which, even after working almost as many hours as he had, still lingered tantalizingly.

When they broke apart she said, 'I've saved a portion of chicken and mushroom pie and some new potatoes, just in case.'

'Famished – and hungry too,' he admitted, grinning, so happy to be home.

'The embers are still putting out some heat in the bar . . . Could I serve "sir" his food and drink in there? Then "sir" can tell me about his day?'

'Be rude to refuse,' Henry said, bowing gallantly.

The sex was wild and mad as Jake and Kirsten writhed, thrust and intertwined on her king-sized bed. Jake had never experienced her so desperate – desperate being the only word he could think of to describe how things had been from the moment he had arrived at her flat, just a few minutes after her.

But he knew what was driving her and understood.

She had been as close to death as she could have been when the helmeted biker pumped three rounds into the side of the observation van then raced away. It had been little short of a miracle that not one of the three officers inside had even been hit, let alone killed or seriously wounded, and that was only due to Rik Dean's screeched warning over the radio for them to get down.

If there was one thing a firearms officer did when bullets were flying, it was to react instantly to any instruction that would save their life. All three had crashed on to the floor of the van as three holes appeared in the side at a level where, if they had remained in position, at least one of them would have been shot in the chest. As it was, each bullet entered one side and exited through the opposite.

In the aftermath of the moment, all three had been dithering wrecks, and Kirsten had vomited her fear by the side of the road. She could not wait to get off duty, unable to think about anything else other than getting safe.

Jake had followed her from headquarters, and after he'd found a discreet parking spot he'd entered her flat to find her tipping her second large scotch down her throat, which was immediately retched into the sink.

It was at that point, as she wiped her mouth dry with the back of her hand, Jake had snaked his arms around her and turned her to him, aware that her slim frame was shaking.

'I was so scared,' she admitted.

'I know, I know,' he cooed.

The whole thing between them became primal, and they devoured each other until, not many minutes later, they were lying spent and exhausted, panting for breath, their chests rising and falling.

It was no time to be eating, really, but Henry was dithery and ravenous and needed the energy boost provided by the beautiful pie and a pint of Stella Artois lager, all of which he consumed with gusto at one of the beaten-copper-topped tables in the deserted main bar in front of the dying embers of what had been a roaring fire. The heat still radiated from the hearth, and Henry thought there was nothing to compete with an open fire when it came to warming a human being, body and soul. Something primeval and comforting about it.

When the food was gone he sat back and smiled contentedly at Alison as a little wave of euphoria seeped through him, though its march was halted slightly by the look on her face. 'What?' he asked guiltily.

'Have you done it yet?'

It was the question she asked him on a daily basis.

When Robert Fanshaw-Bayley had died on that terrible night, Henry had made certain promises to Alison concerning leaving the police and cementing their relationship with a wedding ring – or at least a date on which one would be slipped on to the appropriate finger.

Henry drew a deep breath – because they were promises he had yet to keep.

Before he could say anything, Alison said, 'You promised there would be no more nights like this . . . ridiculous hours of work, a complete lack of communication with me. I didn't know if you were coming home or not . . . Ah! Ah! Ah!' She waved a rebuking finger at him before he could cut in and defend himself. Then she sighed. 'I'm not having it, Henry. I'm not one to lay down the law, but you've got to stop this, get out of this horrendous cycle, for both our sakes . . . I want a life with you.'

'I know,' he admitted.

'Does it really matter whether you're in the job

or not when Charlie Wilder comes to court? I mean, really? The case has even been taken from you. And as much as you're in charge of the investigation into the disappearance of that policewoman, surely to God someone else can take it on? And the lad who was shot in Blackpool? You can't let anything go, can you? There will always be something else that comes along, some other excuse to cling on to . . . Let it go.'

'I'm shit at that, but I do know something: you are someone I will not let go.' He saw her face begin to tremble. 'I know that if I keep this up we'll be torn apart, and that is not going to happen because I love you more than – warning, corny line on the horizon – words can say.' He paused. 'As it happens I have arrested the person who killed the young lad . . . It just threw up some other things I needed to follow up. It happens,' he said, shrugging.

'OK,' she said, relenting.

'My eye has caught sight of a bottle of Jack Daniel's behind the bar,' he said cheekily. 'If I pay for it in kind, how about a nightcap, miss?'

Eventually, Kirsten fell asleep. Jake's arm was trapped underneath her shoulders, and he had to extract it carefully if he was not to wake her up. Jake sat on the edge of the bed for a few moments, before getting dressed and letting himself out of the flat.

Outside he stood on the path, listening intently, his eyes also roving the street to see if he was being watched. He felt as though he was, but he knew he was being paranoid and that Dave Morton – his ex-friend – would be at home now, probably deep into a bottle of whisky, because he had been just as shaken as anyone by the shooting. Surely, the last thing on his mind would be to follow Jake to Kirsten's flat again?

The drive home through the deserted streets was tense for Jake, his heart pounding against his sternum. He turned into his avenue in Bispham and killed the car headlights for the last fifty metres before stopping outside his dark house. He let himself in as quietly as he could, knowing each creak of the door – the way it closed, the sound it made – and then he was in the hallway, standing erect, still, listening.

The kids would be in bed, sleeping soundly.

It wasn't them he was worried about.

He slid off his work boots, then climbed the stairs softly, again knowing which ones creaked, where to put his feet to avoid this. When he reached the landing, he paused again, knowing he needed a shower to swill off the day and the musty aroma of the sex he'd just had. He berated himself mentally for not showering at Kirsten's. He had considered it, but had not wanted to wake her either, just as much as he did not want to wake Anna.

Shit.

He knew he could not slide into bed alongside his wife without rousing her, without the light going on.

His face tightened as he thought it through, and he decided to go back downstairs and crash on

111

the settee. When morning came, he'd claim he had not wanted to disturb her.

He turned just as the bedroom door opened, and Anna stood there in her nightie, pain fixed on her face. Her hair was messed up. Not long ago Jake would have found this look as sexy as hell. Now, to him, she just looked a state.

'Anna.'

'Where've you been?'

'On a job. It got out of hand . . . shots fired, but no one hurt,' he explained thinly. 'Mopping up, you know.'

'OK . . . are you coming to bed?'

'Yeah, yeah . . . Look, you go back, tuck in . . . I just need a drink to steady my nerves.'

She nodded, her eyes darting all over him, searching him out. 'I'll go back then.' She reversed into the bedroom and closed the door softly.

Jake exhaled before going down to find a bottle of whisky.

Alison and Henry's love-making was long and slow, no rush until the last moments as they came together. Alison held Henry's face gently between the palms of her hands, their eyes interlocked as the sensation grew and became almost unbearable, until finally Alison ground herself deeply on to him. They both came in a juddering orgasm that, at the end, had them both giggling when Henry rolled off her, and they lay side-by-side facing the ceiling, catching their breaths.

'That was nice, thanks,' Alison said.

'Yeah, not bad . . . Life in the old goat yet.' She punched him gently, and he responded, 'Me being the old goat, that is.'

'Thank you,' she said, pulled up the duvet and within moments was asleep.

Henry was exhausted, and it was only moments later that he, too, was asleep.

The black dream came quickly. Blindness, a flood, a drowning sensation, mud. Being trapped deep underground, lost, the torchlight flickering. Henry ran against the rising water, panic and terror setting in as the level reached his waist. Then the voice next to him, mocking him, telling him he was useless. He flashed the dithering torch into the face of that man, only to see the whole side of his face had been blown away, that his shoulder, too, had been torn off . . . Next, Henry was free and stomping on another man's head, trying to kill him.

Henry jerked upright with a muted scream, then caught his head in his hands, rocking forwards, gasping for air.

'Henry?' He had woken Alison. She sat up, slid her arms around him. 'Not again?' she asked anxiously.

He exhaled, trying to calm himself down. 'Yes.'

'Same one?'

'Same.'

She held him tight, and he lay back in her arms. 'It wasn't your fault he died,' she said.

'I know . . . I know all that . . . I just can't somehow bring myself to believe it isn't. It's like I led him on some idiotic, gung-ho mission into a lion's den.'

'You were not to know what was going to happen.'

He blinked. A tear formed at the edge of his eye. He wiped it furiously away. 'Fuck!'

'Let it go, Henry.'

'Believe me, I'm trying.' He uttered a harsh, snorting laugh.

'What about seeing a counsellor?' Alison suggested tentatively.

He responded with another snort. 'Been there, done that . . . It's like wading through treacle, all that mother-related shite.'

'Think about it, though,' she persisted. 'A good one is worth gold . . . I've been there too.'

Henry looked at her in the half-light, knowing what she had been through. The loss of her soldier husband, stoned to death by Taliban supporters in an Afghan village. 'Yeah, I know.' He folded himself around her, held her, two people trying to make a future and shake off the past.

'By the way,' she whispered, 'you didn't answer my question.'

'No, I didn't.' He snuggled in, feeling the soft contours of her body compressed against his.

'So?'

'I signed it and put it in the correspondence tray before I left work earlier. My "Intention to Retire" report has gone in . . . In just over a month's time I'll be a pensioner.'

Henry physically felt a change come over Alison. Without warning, she flipped him on to his back and straddled him. 'That calls for a celebration,' she said, reached down and slid him inside her before rearing up in a magnificent display and beginning to move to coax him back to life.

'Jeepers,' he responded, 'I should retire more often.'

Nine

Henry could have slept forever, but did not get chance because daily life at the Tawny Owl began just before six a.m. in order to prepare for business. There were six guests in overnight, all wanting cooked breakfasts, and some local residents had also taken to calling in for a Full English too. So whilst he could have lounged in the nice, comfortable bed, he was grateful really that Alison got up so noisily.

He knew it would be another hectic day for himself, too, particularly in the aftermath of the drive-by shooting, which Henry was playing down as far as the media was concerned. In other words – lying. The official line would be that an unknown gunman had fired three random shots into a parked van, reason unknown. With the agreement of the three cops on board, Henry would not reveal that the van was being used for police surveillance and three constables had almost died. At least, not for the moment. He knew he had to play his cards close to his chest whilst deciding what his approach would be regarding Fraser Worthington – and that was only assuming the biker *was* him. Despite the circumstantial evidence, there was nothing to prove it was.

After a long, hot shower – one of the perks of country hotel living: the water was

116

ceaselessly boiling – Henry shaved carefully, making sure his razor did not accidentally slice over any of his facial injuries. He dressed and made his way to the kitchen to find Alison already at work, on the phone to her vegetable wholesaler, whilst at the same time mouthing instructions to the sous chef who came in for the breakfast run.

Another perk of hotel living was having the option of the full breakfast, but he tried not to make too much of a habit of this and had a crispy bacon bap instead . . . with a fried egg, obviously.

Clutching this and a mug of freshly brewed coffee, Henry made his way through the pub and out of the front door, where he inhaled the morning which had yet to dawn properly. A mist hung over the village green and woodland opposite, and occasionally Henry had been fortunate enough to spot a red deer sneaking through the village.

Not this morning.

He walked down the front steps and looked at his car. It had been attacked by a ferocious gang, wielding baseball bats, on the same night FB had died, and Henry had still not been inclined to get it repaired, mess though it was. This was another remnant from that awful night, and he knew he had to get it sorted.

As he inspected the car he heard a lorry approaching from the village. He looked up and saw the shape of a big, square animal transporter chugging unhealthily towards him along the main road, appearing through the apron of mist like a bull elephant. Henry stood back and watched it as he sipped his coffee.

As it came level with him he saw the livery declared the vehicle belonged to Bartle's, and the stock trailer being pulled by the articulated unit was filled with what seemed like hundreds of fully grown pigs, their fat pink snouts pressed between the gaps in the slats in the side of the trailer, grunting and squealing irately.

The driver's face turned to Henry, then jerked away, and the vehicle was gone up the hill and out of the village towards Thornwell.

Henry folded the last portion of his bacon bap into his mouth and washed it down with the coffee, whilst his nostrils flared thoughtfully.

'Hi, sweetheart.'

Alison had appeared behind him. He turned, still thinking, and said, 'Bartle's Animal Transporters, Spencer Bartle at the wheel.'

Alison's face creased, registering her distaste at the name. 'You still think . . .?' she asked.

'I still think,' Henry confirmed. 'I just can't prove.'

For a moment, Jake Niven wasn't sure where he was. He was awake, but his eyes were closed, and he was uncomfortable. He wasn't in his bed, for sure. Then he groaned and remembered. He was on the settee in the living room.

Still not having opened his eyes, he explored his bodily sensations, starting with the horrible thing that was his mouth. Dried up with alcohol and having slept with it sagging open, it tasted disgusting.

Next his head, which ached dully and persistently and poundingly.

His eyes stayed tightly shut.

'You didn't come back up.'

Then his eyes shot open and he sat up, seeing Anna sitting in the armchair across the room, still in her night gear, with her dressing gown tucked primly underneath her legs.

Jake gave a short laugh. 'No . . . Must've fallen asleep . . . Downed a couple of shots of Tullamore Dew, then must've nodded off. Sorry, love.' He rubbed his face, knuckled his gritty eyes, feeling them crunch and squelch.

'You must be tired,' Anna said.

Her tone of voice made him frown warily. 'Yeah, busy couple of days. What time is it?'

'Just after seven. Are you in today?'

'Yeah, back to normal . . . In at eight.'

She rocked slightly as she regarded him through tired eyes.

For the first time Jake noticed she had a piece of paper on her lap, A4 size. 'Are you OK?' he asked.

'Not really.' Her voice was croaky.

'What's that?' He propped himself up and nodded at the paper.

'It's an extract from a custody record, a photocopy.'

'A custody record?'

Anna nodded.

Jake's brain was still muzzy from the alcohol and sleep. 'Why have you got a custody record?'

Her eyes dropped to it. 'It's for a man called Wayne Oxford, and you arrested him in the early hours of yesterday morning.'

Jake's mouth dried up even more, but not with alcohol. This time with fear.

119

'I know about custody records, Jake,' Anna said. 'Used to be a cop, remember? Dim, distant past.'

He said nothing, just stared at her.

'The time of arrest is logged, as is the time of arrival at the nick, and then anything else that happens to the prisoner and who deals with him or her.' She lifted the paper and peered at it. 'Says you arrested Oxford at 2.45 a.m., then arrived at the police station ten minutes later.' She nodded and said, 'Sounds reasonable. You presented him to the custody officer and then . . .' Anna made a show of looking at the sheet and pretending she was not finding what she was looking for. 'And then, you don't have anything else to do with him, Jake, because a prisoner reception team was waiting for him, and once he was booked into the system, that was you done and dusted, and—'

'Whoa,' Jake cut in.

'No – whoa yourself, Jake,' Anna said. 'Even allowing for a quick statement to be written and a debrief and a journey across to HQ, there is no fucking way on this earth you had to come home after eight o'clock in the morning, five hours after the arrest, smelling of fucking bubble bath.'

'Where did you get that from?' he demanded, sitting up and realizing. 'That bloody bitch Jackie Powers . . . She'll be in the shit for this . . .! Data protection.'

'Don't you even mention her name,' Anna said ferociously, 'because if you threaten her with anything—' she swept her hand down like a knife – 'I'll divorce you.' A tear dribbled down her cheek.

'Anna!'

She crumpled up the custody record into a tight ball and threw it at him, making him duck instinctively, then stood up.

'I had lots to do after the arrest,' he defended himself weakly. 'Statements . . .'

'Rubbish! You did nowt,' she said with contempt. With one last look, she turned and left the living room, closing the door softly, and went upstairs.

Jake slumped back on to the settee, covering his face with his hands.

Henry's first port of call that morning was to the incident room he had set up to deal with the disappearance of Laura Marshall, which, following his quick discovery of her police hat and the broken glass (later identified as the same type of glass used for the side windows of Vauxhall Astras) in the rear car-park of the Swan's Neck, had become a murder investigation.

Initially, he had thrown a lot of resources at the incident but had got nowhere fast. Spencer Bartle came under the spotlight, but he was a slippery bastard, and although Henry was convinced he was the prime suspect, he'd got nowhere with it. Knowing someone had committed an offence was one thing; proving it was very much different.

The result was that although resources – and that meant detectives – were still working hard on the case, it was definitely stalling. Henry was beginning to think he would be handing an unsolved case over to someone else when he retired – something he did not like the thought of at all. It didn't help matters that the victim was a serving police officer.

The incident room was at Lancaster police station, and once Henry had managed to squeeze his car into a tiny space in the tiny car park at the station, he made his way to the room which, not to his surprise, was deserted. It was just after seven a.m., and the first arrivals were not due until eight a.m.

The room was on the fourth floor looking out across the cityscape towards Lancaster Castle and the River Lune. Henry wandered slowly around, then closely studied the flip-chart papers blue-tacked to the walls which gave the timeline of the night's events.

The call for assistance at the Swan's Neck from the landlord, McCready, had come in at 11.02 p.m. Comms had called up Laura at 11.04 p.m., and she had responded immediately. Although McCready had phoned back at 11.10 p.m. to say the troublemaker had left the pub, because of the volume of incoming calls to the comms room, it had taken the operator another five minutes to call up Laura to give her the update, so that was 11.15 p.m., but she had not acknowledged that first call. It was assumed that by then she was well on her way to the pub and was probably in a bad reception area on the country roads.

The operator established contact when Laura actually arrived at the pub at 11.21 p.m. when she said she was going to check it out anyway, which is what any good cop would have done. By which time Spencer Bartle had left the pub some eleven minutes earlier.

Laura had gone into the pub and spoken to McCready, and according to him, she had spent about five minutes in the place before leaving, which would have taken the time to about 11.25 p.m.

Neither she, nor her police car had ever been seen since.

Henry looked at the timeline, his fists bunching angrily at the thought that it was many hours later before any of her colleagues had noticed she was missing. 'Duty of care,' Henry said under his breath, knowing the force would suffer greatly for this terrible lapse.

Spencer Bartle had been interviewed. Henry had actually arrested him, but he'd had an alibi. A local taxi firm had picked him up from outside the Swan's Neck at 11.15 p.m. – a taxi he had pre-booked; something the taxi firm confirmed – and driven him to Lancaster. The taxi driver and Bartle said they both remembered passing a police car coming in the opposite direction.

Henry had seen some CCTV footage of Spencer Bartle in Lancaster city centre, though none of it was before 12.30 a.m., just into the following morning. Bartle claimed, and it was supported by the taxi driver, that he had been dropped off in Lancaster at about 11.35 p.m., which meant he could not have had any dealings with Laura.

Bartle was – and remained – Henry's chief suspect, and although the detective tried to keep an open mind about it, he still fancied him for whatever had happened to Laura.

He sighed with frustration and thumped his

123

forehead with the heel of his right hand, determined this one would not beat him.

After a short briefing with the detectives at Lancaster, Henry next travelled to the custody office at Blackpool, where he linked up with Rik Dean, who was overseeing the processing of Wayne Oxford before his appearance at Blackpool Magistrates' Court later that day. The police were going to apply for a 'three day line-down', which meant they could keep him in custody for up to that length of time and interview him further. There was an awful lot to talk to him about. Then he could be put before magistrates again to be remanded in custody to await trial.

Henry parked on the lower level car park and walked through to the custody office, which was, as ever, heaving with prisoners and cops; it was a real sausage machine with over 12,000 prisoners processed every year. He entered the custody reception area and looked at the whiteboard on the wall behind the sergeant's desk and saw that every cell was occupied, some doubled-up. Henry shook his head at the organized chaos that was the custody machine: a place where people who worked in it rarely had any respite and often went home at the end of a shift with a mushed brain and red-raw zombie eyes. Burn-out was quick and cruel in this environment unless you were able to mentally distance yourself from the bedlam.

Four prisoners waited sullenly in the holding cage, another was at the desk being booked in, whilst another, further along the desk, was being charged with something, and yet another was being led away to the cells and another being taken to an interview room.

'Crikey,' Henry said, then spotted Rik Dean emerging from the cell corridor looking pretty fresh and up for it. 'How are we doing?' Henry asked him.

'OK.' Rik had a Manila file in his hand. 'He's due in court later, and now he's shitting himself about Fraser Worthington.'

'In what respect?'

'In the respect that he now regrets even mentioning his name and is terrified of reprisals.'

Henry shrugged. 'He'll be OK for the next three days.'

'Oh yeah – but after that, Risley,' Rik said, naming the remand centre to which Oxford would be taken pending further court appearances. 'Not the safest environment in the world. Something we need to look at.'

'I'm sure we can fix up solitary,' Henry said. 'Have you mentioned anything to him about last night's drive-by?'

'No, but he's been asking if anything happened.'

'Don't tell him the truth. It could be something we might use . . . Not sure how, yet. Has he been charged?'

'No. I'm just preparing the paperwork. CPS has signed off the charges, so we're ready to go.'

Rik charged Wayne Oxford with the murder of Jamie Turner.

Henry observed, keeping his eyes on Oxford, noting any body language. He had been brought

125

up from his cell, listless and tired, but trying to give a tough guy, don't give a shit impression. Henry saw him flinch as Rik read out the words from the charge sheet. Just a minor tic, but it was there. Not many crims truly don't get bothered by it: one of those life-defining moments when the implications of an action, the taking of someone else's life, hits them in the lower gut and the prospect of not seeing true daylight, other than through a wire mesh or bars, for a lot of years sinks in.

Rik invited Oxford to respond to the charge, but he declined.

The custody sergeant, overseeing the ritual like a priest, then told Oxford he was being denied bail (as all prisoners charged with murder were) and would be appearing at court later when the remand in custody to police cells would be applied for.

'We'll take him back to his cell,' Henry offered.

The sergeant eyed him warily, aware that detectives were not averse to pulling a fast one by carrying out illicit interviews in cell corridors or in the cell itself, both of which were definite no-nos. Henry stared him out, and the sergeant relented but said, 'No funny business.'

Henry tried to look affronted, but held back from saying, '*Moi?*'

With Oxford between them, he and Rik steered him back to his cell, letting him go ahead of them into the concrete box.

'How long will I get?' Oxford asked.

'For murder? It's always a life sentence,' Henry informed him.

'What's that mean, though?'

'Hard to say. Play your cards right, maybe ten.'

'Ten years? Out in five, then?'

'No – twenty years, out in ten,' Henry said, correcting his assumption.

He slumped on to the bench miserably. 'If I live that long.'

'You will,' Henry promised him.

'I ratted on Fraser,' he said dully.

'We'll ensure you're safe,' Henry promised. 'And he doesn't know you did.'

'What happened last night?'

'He didn't turn up,' Henry lied. 'The guns are with us now, anyway.'

'Maybe I'll be OK, then.' Oxford looked up. 'Can I see Sophie's body?'

'No, not yet, if ever.'

Oxford lurched across the cell and vomited into the steel toilet.

That morning Jake was back in Division, carrying out his normal duties as an authorized firearms officer (AFO) on the Armed Response Vehicle. He worked from Blackpool police station, covering most of the Fylde region. As with all AFOs he spent every sixth week as part of a firearms team which trained and was on standby at HQ for any major incidents or prearranged operations, but now he was back on his day job. That meant patrolling and responding to routine policing incidents like any other cop, but with the addition of a Glock strapped to his waist and a safe in the Ford Galaxy containing two MP5 machine pistols, a shotgun, stun grenades and other equipment. Another team was at HQ, but in the event of any firearms incident occurring, Jake and whoever his partner was would be the first responders.

He entered the station at 7.45 a.m., his mood bleak from his waking encounter with Anna who, amazingly, he had managed to avoid since their argument. He'd had a long shower, then dallied in the en-suite as he heard her banging around the bedroom, and when he got downstairs she was already gone. It was far too early for her work, and he assumed she had got out of the house to avoid him. The kids were up, getting ready for school, but had not emerged from their bedrooms then. Jake had to be in work for eight a.m., so he'd left them to make their own breakfasts and get to school under their own steam.

He didn't even say goodbye to them because he did not have the courage to look either of them in the eye.

When he walked into the locker room, he found Dave Morton was already there, kitting up. His partner for the day.

They cyed each other cautiously, then Jake said, 'How are you feeling?'

'After being nearly shot to death? Surprised you actually give a shit.'

'That's unfair. You know I do.'

'Yeah, right,' Morton said peevishly.

Jake busied himself with getting ready to turn out, and then they both checked in with the patrol sergeant, who logged them on via the computerized duty-states and updated them on the lack of progress regarding the shooting incident: the biker with the gun had vanished without trace.

After this, Jake told Morton he was going to grab a quick brew from the canteen and asked if Morton wanted to join him.

'Hardly . . . Be in the car in ten minutes.'

Jake nodded and made his way to the lift, which took him up to the canteen. He joined the early breakfast queue whilst churning over the muddle that was his thoughts and trying to contain the feeling of dread in his guts.

He was more afraid now than he ever was in his life, but the question that kept rising to the surface, one he could not push down, was: who had provided Anna with a copy of the custody record? His instinct was to make that person suffer.

The slow moving queue shuffled along.

He'd blamed Jackie Powers, but Dave Morton was an obvious suspect too, now he came to think of it. Morton's feelings about Jake and Kirsten were obvious, but would he do something so sneaky and underhand, something that would potentially wreck a marriage? Certainly, he was furious with Jake, but was it just the green-eyed monster at work, because Jake was sleeping with a much younger woman, the same one who had snubbed his advances? Surely, he wouldn't tell Anna, knowing it would destroy her.

The way Morton was coming across now made Jake think he just might, even though he had known Anna for many years.

Nah, surely not, Jake assured himself.

'Filter coffee to take out, please,' Jake asked when he reached the till. He thanked the lady, took his Styrofoam cup and was moving across to the milk and sugar counter when he heard a familiar chuckle from the far end of the dining room. Stirring in the milk and fitting the lid he walked between the tables until he came to where Jackie Powers was sitting with her back to him, together with a couple of other ladies who worked in the comms room.

Jake stood alongside her, silent, brooding.

The other two ladies glanced at him, and Jackie turned her head to follow their eyeline. Her face broke into a grin. 'Hi, Jake.'

He accused her instantly. 'It was you, wasn't it?'

To Jake, the look on her face was one of feigned innocence. 'What was me?'

'The custody record.'

'Don't know what you mean, my love.'

'Don't you "my love" me,' Jake said softly with an undercurrent. 'Marriage wrecker.'

Jackie drew back at the allegation. 'I don't know what you mean,' she reiterated slowly.

The other two women watched the exchange agog, their mouths actually open.

'I think you do, Jackie.' Jake bent forwards threateningly, unable to prevent himself. In a concurrent thought he knew he was acting out of character, yet could not stop this idiotic display. 'If my marriage is screwed up over your do-good meddling, I'll see you suffer.'

Jackie drew away from him.

'So fuck you, Jackie – a girl's best friend.' He raised his eyebrows and nodded pointedly at her, then stalked out of the canteen, his heart whamming, feeling as though he was enclosed by a swirling, out of focus mess and sure that every single eyeball in the room was fixated on him.

He began to walk down the stairs, but on the first dog-leg twist, Jackie Powers caught up to him and spun him round. His coffee flipped out of his hand over the banister and hurtled down the gap in the steps, crashing five floors down to ground level, where it burst.

Jackie faced him with her eyes blazing. 'You get your facts straight before you start alleging anything,' she growled. 'Your wife suspects you of cheating on her, and from what she told me, she's probably right – but I hope she isn't, Jake. Not for your sake, but for hers and the kids, because she's my friend and I love her.'

'The custody record . . .'

'She asked me, OK? But I didn't. I didn't even look at it, because as much as she's my mate, I won't get involved. I'm on her side, but I won't get in trouble with work by copying confidential documents.' She jabbed him in the chest with her forefinger. It hurt. 'You're barking up the wrong tree, mate, and if you give me hassle, I'll frickin' have you, OK?'

Jake pushed himself off the banister and started to walk down the stairs.

'She loves you, so don't you screw it up!' Jackie called after him.

His face was a red storm as he hurtled down, the air pressure drop making his ears pop as he descended. He pushed his way through to the lower-floor garage where Dave Morton was waiting impatiently for him in the Ford Galaxy. He dropped on to the front passenger seat.

'Where's your coffee?' Morton asked.

'Decided against it . . . C'mon, let's roll.'

The main offices of the Force Major Investigation Team are situated at police headquarters at Hutton, but Henry also had a cramped satellite office at Blackpool nick from which he had a view of the rear of the Sea Life Centre and beyond to Blackpool Tower. He wasn't quite high enough to see the Irish Sea.

After dealing with Wayne Oxford, Henry made his way to this office, which he kept securely locked, mainly because his coffee-making equipment had a habit of going AWOL if he didn't. He filled his filter machine with water from a tap in the nearby toilets, heaped a couple of spoonfuls of ground coffee into it and set it to burble away.

Then he sat at his desk in the cramped accommodation and got his act together for the day ahead.

He had some breathing space with Wayne Oxford, but he intended to touch base with the grieving parents of the young lad Oxford had murdered. At least he would be telling them some good news about the arrest and charge. He wanted to ring them first and make an appointment to see them at their home.

Next he had to pull together a small team to look into the shooting incident from last night. The offender – who Henry assumed was Fraser Worthington (and he knew what assumptions did)

– had got clean away, but Henry wanted to get someone to review any CCTV footage that was available in the vicinity of the incident, rippling out as far as the motorway.

He also needed to do a welfare check on the firearms officers who had been in the surveillance van: see how they were, if they needed counselling. From the conversations he'd had with them at the time, they'd seemed shocked but generally OK, but the implications might have sunk in overnight, and they could all be nervous wrecks now. It was his job to ensure they were OK.

He also had work to do on Sophie Leader's tragic death. A local detective sergeant was dealing with that, but Henry wanted to spend time with him and go to see her family, too.

And on the subject of Fraser Worthington . . . Henry sighed, wondering how best to take that forward.

Clearly, Worthington did not possess the weapons that Oxford had been holding for him, but would that make any difference to any plans he had to kick off a robbing spree? Henry had been brought up to believe that prevention was better than cure, so with that in mind he decided to track Worthington down and arrest him on any airy-fairy pretence he could, which would probably come to nothing, but might just scare him off by leaving him in the certain knowledge that the cops were watching him.

On which note he picked up his desk phone and contacted the surveillance unit for an update. A couple of watchers were back in the vicinity of Worthington's flat in Skem and confirmed that the Alfa was still outside and there had been no sign of a motorbike.

Henry ended that call thoughtfully, after which he called Jamie Turner's parents. There was no reply, so he left a message for them to call him, or he'd just call back later.

He spun on his chair and poured himself a freshly filtered coffee, which tasted very nice. When he spun back, Rik Dean was just entering the room, clutching Wayne Oxford's file, which was expanding quickly.

'Help yourself,' Henry told him, and Rik poured a mug of the steaming brew before plonking himself down on the chair opposite Henry.

Henry regarded Rik – a man he'd known for a long time – thoughtfully. Rik had started off as a PC on the beat, who had been a great thief-taker. Henry had seen this and had nurtured him and got him on to CID, where he was an outstanding detective. However, Rik's subsequent rise through the ranks had been entirely his own doing, as had the fact that he was also due to become Henry's brother-in-law very soon when he married Lisa, Henry's sister. And God help them both, Henry had often thought, as both of them had a history of wicked ways, but their yin and yang seemed to have cancelled this out, and they now seemed a well-suited couple, after some teething troubles. Rik had even shown some interest in getting wed at the Tawny Owl.

Henry declared, 'Fraser Worthington is a cunning bastard.'

134

Rik nodded. 'Which is why he never gets caught.'

'He evades a surveillance team, disappears for a few hours, then reappears – supposedly back at his mum's flat.'

'Although we don't know for sure if he is there.'

'And not being able to confirm that was a mistake on my part – I'm giving myself a mental kick in the arse. I should've got someone to knock on his door.'

'You can't cover all bases . . . and it wouldn't have proved anything if he wasn't there,' Rik said reasonably, sipping his coffee.

Henry touched his shotgun ravaged ear, drawing the tip of his forefinger along the ragged edge, not terribly reassured by Rik's comment. Inside, he was furious with himself. 'Then some biker turns up and shoots holes in the police van . . .'

'Just glad he didn't spot me,' Rik said.

'He would definitely have shot you, that's for sure.' Henry smiled. 'It's got to be Fraser, hasn't it?' Henry sniffed. 'It has to be linked to the weapons. It has to be Fraser,' he repeated.

'Unlikely we'll ever prove it, though. All sorts of things have to slot into place for that to happen: ballistics – I mean, CSI haven't even found the bullets yet; forensics; the bike turning up; admissions of guilt . . .'

'Doesn't mean we don't try though . . . I'm just lucky three cops aren't dead or seriously injured.' Henry exhaled. 'Fuckin' hell, Rik! Close shave, as Wallace would say. At this juncture I think we need some quality time with Fraser so we can whisper into his shell, like—' and here,

Henry touched his ripped ear again, which did bear some resemblance to a clam shell – 'and give him the hard word.'

Henry's mobile phone rang. He answered it. 'Ah, Mrs Turner, thanks so much for returning my call . . .' It was the murdered boy's mother.

Anna Niven was dumbfounded by just how dreadful she was feeling. Occasionally, over the years of her marriage she had wondered what it would be like if Jake ever cheated on her, and in those few and far between moments of contemplation she had thought she would be upset – obviously – but would not feel that everything around her, inside and out, would collapse.

Her whole body had become dithery, a mushy mess. Each and every organ within seemed to have rotted away to jelly. Her heart and lungs were liquid as she tried to comprehend what she believed to be the confirmation of her suspicions.

Her skull pounded; her arms and legs felt as empty as a vacuum. She had lost all her strength, mentally and physically – because she knew it was true.

The trapped look in Jake's eyes was the ultimate giveaway – that, and his instant, defensive demand to know where she had got the custody record from. That she had it would have only mattered if Jake had been innocent, and he would have been justified in complaining.

But she knew he wasn't.

From that moment, after throwing the rolled-up custody record at him, she had got out of the house as quickly as possible, did not want to be anywhere near him, did not even want to set eyes on him. She'd had to run because her brain had become a rushing, white-water torrent.

She left the house before Jake got out of the shower and drove to the seafront, then headed south through Blackpool to St Annes, where she went to the Beach Café again and ordered coffee. She sat at a table with a good view through a dip in the sand dunes to the sea, which seemed a very long way out. Miles.

How could it hurt so much, she wanted to know.

She sat there for a very long time.

Her mobile phone rang. She had expected it to be Jake, but the number was withheld and she almost did not answer. It could be Jake calling from work.

'Hello?'

'Babe . . . it's me, Jackie . . . Are you all right?'

'Why shouldn't I be?'

'Cos I've just had a head-to-head with your very irate hubby in the canteen here at the nick.'

'Shit. What's he said?'

'He accused me over the custody record or something. Called me a marriage wrecker.'

'Fuck . . . I'm so sorry, hon.'

'Are you OK? That's all I'm bothered about.'

'I'm fine . . . It's all gone, y'know?' Anna stood up abruptly and walked out of the café, immediately hit by the buffeting, chill wind channelling through the sand dunes from the sea. With the phone clamped to her ear, she stood with her face into the wind, letting it blow her hard as she told her story to Jackie.

*   *   *

137

For the first two hours of their tour of duty, the two officers did not speak or, where possible, even look at each other.

Jake was churning over the events of the day so far. First his rude awakening with a custody record shoved in his face, then his stupid encounter with Jackie and her response, which had seemed to be the truth. Jackie was the sort who was brutally honest to the point of stupidity, and if she had given the photocopy to Anna, Jake was pretty sure she would have said so and, meta-phorically, shoved it in his face too. Jackie Powers took no prisoners in that respect.

When he'd worked this out, Jake's eyes turned slowly to Dave Morton.

It was good to let it all out to Jackie, even if she had done much the same only recently. She was a good listener, sounding board, and didn't make any rash suggestions, such as 'kick him out', or 'move yourself and the kids out and live with your mum', or 'move in with me'. For all her experiences with men, Jackie knew how impor-tant Anna's marriage was to her, and her advice was to take it one step at a time, keep talking. Only if that failed should she kick the cheating son of a bitch out.

After the conversation Anna got back into her car, feeling slightly more with it, and drove down to Lytham, the quieter, genteel neighbour of St Annes, where she decided to mooch around the shops, get a breakfast and work out a strategy.

It sounded businesslike. In reality, it was frag-mented and hazy.

She parked in the pay and display car park near to the windmill on the seafront and strolled into the town. As she did she started feeling light-headed again. Walking was hard as, once more, her emotions began to shroud her like a kidnapper's mask.

It had been a quiet morning and, unusually, the ARV driven by Morton was not deployed on any jobs. Consequently, their patrolling was more of an aimless drift around, untargeted. Out of the blue, Morton announced that he fancied a drive out to Warton on the Ribble Estuary to park up near British Aerospace and see if any of the European Fighter Jets that were being built and developed there were doing any test flights that morning. There were a few spots on the surrounding country lanes which were good viewing sites for both nerds and the occasional curious folk.

At the moment of that decision, Morton was driving down Squires Gate Lane past Blackpool Airport. At the lights he turned left on to Clifton Drive and went south, passing the demolished holiday camp in which Wayne Oxford had been arrested.

Jake had looked slyly at Morton a few times, slowly building up courage to ask about the custody record.

At the exact moment he chose to accuse him, the comms operator – who happened to be Jackie Powers – urgently called up all patrols.

From that point on, the lives of several people, including Jake and Anna Niven, Wayne Oxford and Fraser Worthington, and Dave Morton and Henry Christie, would never be the same again.

Some would die; others would be forever affected by the events of the next hour.

Ten

'How are we doing, boys?' Fraser Worthington glanced at the three young men in the car – the driver and two back seat passengers – who were all dressed in black overalls, trainers and black belts. On their laps each had a black ski-mask and a firearm. But not the firearms that Worthington had planned to be using that morning. Instead, they were ones sourced from another dealer he'd had to rouse in Manchester in the early hours.

The men nodded, each one ready for action. They knew their jobs, loved what they did and the wealth it brought, and were eagerly anticipating carrying out the first robbery in a series of four which were going to take place over the next week. This one would be easy: just to get the team back into the rhythm of robbery. Bread and butter stuff – in, cause havoc, threaten, terrify, overwhelm, assault, steal, then leave.

Two minutes tops.

Worthington smiled. These guys were the best crew he'd ever worked with, and he was looking forward to this job and the next ones, then getting back to his villa in northern Cyprus and his very voluptuous lady friend.

He faced front again, his eyes narrowing momentarily. There was just that unsettling speck of doubt in his mind, caused by last night's shenanigans. He was ultra-cautious and always trusted his instincts.

He had arranged to pick up the firearms at Oxford's flat at nine p.m., hence the reason for him ditching the Alfa and replacing it with the motorbike and the other safety measures he'd put in place – such as having the Alfa returned to Skem just to put the police off the scent. If, indeed, they had been on it in the first place.

He had killed some time with an old girlfriend in the Cottam area of Preston after the vehicle/clothing swap at ASDA, and she had been well briefed to provide him with an alibi if necessary. After that he had checked with his gang, who were staying in a safe house in Fulwood, prepping. Then he had gone to pick up the guns.

As he had done a slow drive along the promenade past Oxford's flat, he thought he caught sight of some movement in the shadows in a car parked up on the prom, but could not be certain even on the second drive past – but the van definitely did catch his eye.

Outwardly, it appeared to be nothing, just a beat up old Tranny van.

It just did not feel right to him, and if it didn't feel right, it wasn't right.

A shadow in a car; a van on the street.

He could not call Oxford on his mobile. That was a no-no, a definite giveaway if the cops had been watching him, and he was always highly suspicious of using mobile phones when jobs were in the offing, anyway.

All in all, the situation just did not feel good.

So, just for the sheer hell of it, he pumped three

rounds into the side of the van and tore away on the bike. Not long after, having travelled back to Cottam on country roads, he was at his old girlfriend's place. It was from here, using her phone, he discovered that Oxford had been arrested for a murder, and there was always the possibility he had blabbed about the guns which they would have found in his possession.

So his instinct had been correct. Even if the cops were not waiting for him to show up, it would have been foolish to knock on Oxford's door.

Fraser Worthington took no chances.

He then had sex with the girlfriend, so that if he had to prove his whereabouts there would be DNA evidence to back him up, after which, using her car, he went to Manchester and picked up guns from another dealer, which he delivered to his waiting crew in Fulwood, then returned to his girlfriend's house for some sleep.

The four men were now sitting on the car park of the McDonald's restaurant at Dock Bridge on Lytham Road, maybe a couple of miles from their intended target in Lytham itself.

They had been through the drive-thru, and each had ordered a breakfast, obviously hiding their hoods and weapons from the server on the way through. They paid with cash and ate their meals at the far end of the car park.

Then they were ready to roll.

Wayne Oxford had been led from the custody complex in the basement floor of Blackpool nick through the connecting corridor to the holding area beneath Blackpool Magistrates' Court, adjacent to the police station. Just a short walk with his hands cuffed in front of him, eased on his way by the hand of one of the private security guards who now did the escort job that had once been the preserve of police officers.

Oxford was one of half a dozen prisoners making the journey straight from police cells on that day: bail refused, straight to court, do not pass go. The underground holding area was busy with the other five prisoners who had just arrived from the remand centre for their hearings. Oxford, however, was the only one up on a murder charge, so he was placed in a cell by himself to await what would probably be a very short appearance before the bench. Just a case of confirming his ID, then, with no arguments from his solicitor about bail, the bench would send him back into police custody for three days.

Henry Christie rose from his office chair, stretching creakily. He went to one of the narrow windows overlooking Bonny Street, peering north towards the tower, much of which was encased in scaffolding and mist. He was reasonably certain he had got a grip on the complexities and the route through the day ahead.

Wayne Oxford would be back in police cells after his court appearance, and a small team of detectives were now being briefed by Rik Dean to deal with him.

The post-mortem on Sophie Leader was due to take place later that afternoon, and the coroner had been informed of progress in that respect.

A DI from Skelmersdale had been asked to go and knock on Fraser Worthington's mum's front door and to arrest him if he was there.

And, Henry hoped, that was about that. Lots of delegating going on as he tried to keep his distance and let others do the work for a change.

Standing by the window, his mind drifted back to the night the chief constable had died. The images – though everything had been dark, murky, muddy and wet – were still vivid in Henry's mind. So too was the desolate feeling that he had let a man die in a half-flooded quarry shaft, had robbed him of the dignity of dying surrounded by his family. A grubby death, Henry had called it.

He touched his ragged ear and sighed. 'Shit.'

The ring of his mobile phone cut into his thoughts.

The man sat quietly in the public gallery of courtroom number one at Blackpool Magistrates' Court. He had entered the court through the main entrance and, as all members of the public were now obliged, had walked through the metal detector arch, which bleeped accusingly as he stepped through. He rolled his eyes at his stupidity and fished out the key ring which had obviously triggered the alarm.

The private security guard made him empty his pockets, then go back through the scanner, which now stayed silent.

Apologizing profusely, he picked up his keys, entered the building and made his way to the courtroom and took his place in the gallery.

And waited patiently, his eyes constantly scanning the court layout, the distances, the angles, the possibilities, obstructions and people.

Inside himself, he was cold and clinical, not even considering the consequences of what he intended to achieve that morning.

The gang relocated to Lytham and parked on Hastings Place, close to the County Hotel in a line of other cars, nose facing the town centre. Fraser Worthington was the only one of the four who remained cool and laid back, controlling his breathing, his heart rate. The others were agitated, continually moving and fidgeting. The coke they had inhaled into their systems, coupled with the amphets and Lucozade, was making them eager and tense.

Their target premises was on Park Street, the junction for which was about 100 metres ahead of them.

Worthington checked his watch. 'Need for speed,' he said.

Still in his shirtsleeves, Henry scooped up his personal radio from the desk and tore out of his office, interrupting a routine transmission. 'Superintendent Christie interrupting – urgent.'

'Go ahead, sir.'

Henry ignored the lift and flung himself down the stairway, crashing against the wall and banisters as he leapt down the concrete steps three or four at a time.

'Need to get patrols to the magistrates' court . . . Received a report of an armed man either

146

already in court or trying to get in with a view to causing harm to the defendant Wayne Oxford who's up this morning from our cells. Phone the holding cells at court and make sure Oxford isn't brought up. I'm attending on foot from my office,' he finished as he hit the first-floor level of the station and burst out through the doors on to the concourse, on the opposite side of which was the court.

'What is the man armed with, sir?'

'A ceramic kitchen knife . . . Just get patrols en route, more details to follow,' Henry shouted as he sprinted across the gap between cop shop and court house.

'Roger . . . Patrols to acknowledge?' the operator asked.

Henry's arms pumped as he ran perhaps his fastest fifty metres since he was sixteen years old.

Anna Niven, with her head still firmly stuck somewhere metaphorically unpleasant, blundered along Lytham's main shopping street, the blood still beating in her brain, not really concentrating on anything in particular other than the horrible jumble her life had just become. It was purely by accident that she found herself standing outside a small jeweller's shop on Park Street, just off the main street, staring at the window display of new and second-hand jewellery. It was the sort of shop that sold top of the range rings and watches, but also seemed to have a thriving trade-in business too, according to the notices in the window.

Whilst staring at the rings, she started involuntarily to roll the two rings on the third finger of her left hand with her thumb. Her wedding and engagement rings. She looked down at what she was doing, seeing the two most important possessions in her life, bought with love, loyalty and commitment by Jake.

Now worth zilch.

Her eyes misted over, and the corners of her mouth drooped.

She entered the shop with the intention of having both items valued, as she suddenly thought that she might need every penny in the next few weeks, depending on how it all panned out.

She feared the worst, but fixed a smile on to her face as she approached the glass counter and spoke to the nice young lady on the other side of it. She held out her fingers to show her the two rings.

Wayne Oxford stood in the dock, facing the magistrates. He had been brought a fresh set of clothing by his sister and looked smart now, wearing a suit and tie. He also looked weary and red-eyed, but betrayed no emotion to the panel of three and the clerk of the court.

A guard stood to one side of him, just a couple of feet from his shoulder. Oxford was not wearing handcuffs because prisoners appearing in court, unless too dangerous and unpredictable, were allowed that right.

'Is your name Wayne Oxford?' the clerk asked him.

'It is,' he responded.

'And are you of no fixed abode?'

'Correct.'

The man in the public-seating gallery at the side of the court slid the fingers of his right hand up the sleeve of his left arm and grasped the knife.

It was a small paring knife, made from ceramic, and just as sharp as its steel bladed cousin, but because of its composition it could not be picked up by a metal detector.

He began to rise as he withdrew the knife.

He had worked out the angles now – the height, the distance – and was convinced he would succeed. The dock was about two feet higher than floor level, but there was a fancy brass rail surrounding it which he knew would help him reach the prisoner.

His face remained expressionless.

The prosecuting solicitor from the CPS stood up and cleared her throat, about to address the bench and apply for the three-day remand to police cells.

The man walked sideways to the end of the bench seat, and from there he was about twenty feet from the dock.

He visualized his moves, speed and goal.

The paring knife was now in his right hand, almost concealed inside his fist, held down by his thigh.

No one had even glanced at him.

Good. He needed every second of advantage.

His nostrils flared, and then, just as the court-room door flew open, he rushed silently across to the dock, completely focused on his task.

*   *   *

Henry ran across the tiled floor of the court foyer, dismissing the shouts of the security guards, and aimed for the double doors of court number one. He crashed through them and immediately caught sight of the man running across the courtroom, spotting the small, off-white blade of the paring knife in his hand.

Henry screamed a warning, which had no effect whatsoever on anyone.

By the time he reached the corner of the dock, the man had vaulted over the side of it, and as Henry leapt over too, just seconds after, he knew he was too late.

The security guard in the dock was cowering, terrified, in one corner, and the man was straddling Oxford, repeatedly plunging the short, but deadly blade into Oxford's face, neck and chest.

Henry landed unsteadily, going over on his ankle, but he flew at the man, knocking him sideways, wanting to overpower him, wrest the knife from his fingers. Even as he did this he knew he was too late for Wayne Oxford; an arc of dark-red blood spurted high into the air, and Oxford's feet and legs twitched a dramatic dance of death. As Henry pinned the man down – a man with no fight in him any more – the pumping fountain of blood subsided, and Henry knew that Oxford had bled out within seconds.

The attacker lay motionless under Henry's weight, allowing him to peel the knife out of his grip, as a large pool of blood spread quickly across the floor of the dock under Henry's knees. Even so, Henry knew it was his duty to try and save Oxford.

The young lady behind the counter frowned at Anna as she unscrewed the two rings from her finger, leaving a deep, white indentation where they had been. She placed them on the counter top on to a felt mat.

Still frowning, the lady picked them up, then fitted a jeweller's magnifying glass into her eye socket. 'Are you sure about this, Madame?'

'Yes.' Anna's voice quaked.

The woman held the diamond cluster engagement ring up to her eye.

It was at this moment two things happened, almost simultaneously.

The actual owner of the shop opened the security door behind the counter and glanced out, just checking all was OK on the shop floor.

It was.

Until a moment later when a masked Fraser Worthington and two members of his crew burst into the shop.

Worthington was at the head of the three-man team, brandishing a sawn-off shotgun which, as he strode in like a black-clad demon, he fired into the shop ceiling, filling the room with deafening noise, smoke, falling debris, confusion and terror.

Armed with baseball bats, as well as firearms, the other two men – well drilled in the art of armed robbery – smashed the glass fronted counter displays and cabinets and began scooping out the jewellery and watches into ready prepared hessian bags.

The store owner reversed into the relative safety of the back of the shop, closing the heavy security door and smacking the palm of his hand on to the red alarm button, sending an initially silent signal to the alarm company.

Fraser brought down his shotgun and bounced towards the two females in the shop – assistant and customer – screaming, 'On your fucking knees, on your fucking knees,' at them. The words sounded even more horrific for coming out of the mouth slit in the balaclava, and the movement of his lips and teeth looked horrific.

Anna dropped to her knees instantly.

The woman behind the counter hesitated, her terror inducing paralysis. Worthington grabbed her hair in his fist and hauled the slightly built lady bodily over the counter, throwing her violently down next to Anna.

'Oi – there was no need for that,' Anna protested bravely.

Worthington spun and jammed the roughly sawn barrel ends into Anna's cheek, drawing blood. He pushed his masked face only inches from hers and growled, 'Who the fuck asked you, bitch?' As he spoke, spittle from his mouth hit Anna's face, making her cringe. He shoved her away with the muzzle, then rose and shouted, 'No one needs to get hurt here.' He waved the gun in an arc across the shop, stopping abruptly when he saw the manager's face behind the security door window. The man ducked the instant he knew he had been spotted, and Worthington fired the gun at the door, though the pellets did little damage to it.

Anna lay on her side, touching her cheek, feeling warm blood on her fingertips.

* * *

On hearing Henry Christie's dramatic transmission as he raced towards the magistrates' court, Dave Morton slammed the brakes on the ARV and did a U-turn as Jake flicked the switch for the blue lights and two-tone horn.

'I love the sound of a siren in the morning,' Morton said through gritted teeth as he hauled the wheel down and spun the Galaxy around.

Jake called up comms to say they were presently on Clifton Road, Lytham, and therefore their ETA was at least ten minutes. Other officers and mobile patrols had also called up and were on their way.

Clifton Road, Lytham's main shopping street, was a tight thoroughfare, with parked cars either side. It was dangerous to travel along it at speed because of its narrowness and the fact that pedestrians crossed from either side, also.

However, this did not stop Morton from pushing down the accelerator.

Almost as soon as they had passed the junction with Park Street, though, comms called them up specifically. 'Romeo Eight receiving?'

'Go 'head,' Jake said, responding to their call sign, a slightly abbreviated version of the full one, Alpha Romeo Eight.

'Cancel the court, please . . . Silent intruder alarm activated at The Jewel Shop, Park Street, Lytham . . . It's an unusual one, activated by staff on premises.'

'Just passed that,' Morton said.

'Roger,' Jake replied to comms. 'One minute away – any more info?'

'Nothing . . . Just trying to establish contact with the premises now.'

153

'OK.'

Jake turned off the two-tones and hung on tight as Morton flipped the vehicle right into Hastings Place in order to do a full loop around to Market Square, then up to the junction with Park Street.

From that moment on, things happened very quickly.

With the blue lights still flashing, Morton careened on to Park Street, and both officers instantly clocked and categorized the black saloon car parked with two wheels on the pavement outside the jewellers, facing away from them.

'Getaway car,' Jake blurted.

'Yep.'

Morton screeched up behind it and slammed on the brakes as Jake leapt out of the Galaxy just an instant before it stopped, but the car shot away down Park Street without any hesitation, with one person aboard.

Jake shouted in the registration number as he ran to the front door of the jeweller's, adding, 'This looks genuine,' in reference to the robbery.

Morton was not far behind him.

Jake was trying to see what was going on inside the shop, but the decorative etched and misted windows in the door made it difficult to make anything out, so he just went for it. He entered at the exact moment Fraser Worthington grabbed Anna's hair and wrenched her up, holding her in front of him like a shield and jamming the muzzle of the shotgun into her already bleeding face.

'Get fucking back!' he screamed.

Jake stopped, stunned on two levels.

154

Firstly that he had actually run into a robbery in progress, which even when responding to an alarm was unusual. Most were false alarms.

Secondly that his wife was being held as a hostage or human shield, and what the fuck was she doing there in the first place?

Worthington rested the shotgun across Anna's shoulder and aimed it at Jake. The other two robbers ditched their baseball bats and spun to him with their firearms pointed at him.

Morton, moments behind and with his view blocked, stumbled in at Jake's back, crashing into him and causing Jake to stagger forwards. This revealed the tableau to Morton, who reacted by going for his sidearm, the Glock, as Jake went down on to his knees.

One of Worthington's men fired his shotgun at Morton, catching him in the left side of his neck just above the collar line of his ballistic vest. The force of the blow spun him backwards. He pirouetted, clutching his throat, and dropped to his knees as gouts of thick blood cascaded from the terrible wound. He slithered and slumped face down on the tiled floor into a deepening pool of blood, which was pulsing rapidly out from his body.

'We get their fuckin' car,' Worthington shouted, knowing that their own getaway car had left them high and dry.

Jake took all this in: his friend gurgling obscenely as his life blood ebbed out of him; the terrified face of Anna, who was being roughly held by a desperate robber; the other two with bags full of jewels and the guns in their hands.

Anna's eyes pleaded with him.

Worthington dragged her across to Jake. 'You – fuckin' car keys,' he demanded. 'And don't do anything, or I'll blow this bitch's head off.'

'He's got 'em,' Jake said, trying to hold on to Anna's eyeline and somehow convey reassurance to her by staying calm himself – but he saw her head was shaking in terror and also saw the cut in her soft cheek. Jake pointed at Morton. 'But they still might be in the car.'

Worthington jerked his head at the crew member who had shot the cop. He strode over Morton's now still body and out of the shop, whilst Worthington dragged Anna back to the counter in his ferocious grip.

A huge surge of anger gushed through Jake at that moment, which he knew he had to control. Anything rash and stupid would result in more bloodshed. He glanced at the shop assistant cowering by the counter, her head covered by her own hands.

Then, for a moment, the world stopped turning, and Jake could feel his heart slamming dully within his chest, hear the rasping of his breathing from his lungs.

'They're in the car,' a voice shouted behind him, and Jake came back into the real world.

Jake's head flicked around, and he saw the robber that Worthington had sent to check for the key in the Galaxy was back.

Worthington threw Anna aside. She bounced into the counter, screamed in pain, then tripped raggedly as Worthington brought his shotgun around and aimed it squarely at Jake.

'In for a penny,' Worthington said. Even though he was still masked, Jake could see the man's mouth curve into a wicked smile behind the hole in the ski mask, and he knew what was going to happen. They'd killed one cop, so another would make no difference.

Worthington raised the gun.

Jake leapt like a frog and flung himself across the shop as Worthington fired. A glass display cabinet disintegrated behind where Jake had been.

Jake rolled and came up. Worthington had to rack another shell into the chamber, but it didn't want to go smoothly and jammed for just a second too long, giving Jake that extra moment he needed as his incessant, repetitive, firearms training kicked in.

He drew the Glock from its holster at his side, brought it out smoothly, releasing the safety catch with his thumb and aimed it at Worthington, who had managed to slam the reluctant shell into the breach.

Jake fired, double-tapping – 'Ba-bam' – into Worthington's chest.

Worthington dropped the shotgun, took an unsteady step backwards and looked down at his chest, then dropped to his knees before falling face down.

Jake swivelled, bringing the gun around to the robber by the front window, and said, 'Drop your weapon or I'll shoot you.'

Amazingly, the man responded immediately and dropped both his bag of loot and the gun and raised his hands in submission.

Jake then spun to the third one, who was standing by Morton's body.

'You too,' Jake said. 'Drop your weapon.'

'Fuck you,' he yelled back, and brought his shotgun up and fired at Jake, who dropped into a crouch and returned two shots, one of which hit the guy in the shoulder, the other missing completely. The man screamed in shock at being hit, but still attempted to fire again, racking the shotgun.

Jake fired once more, driving a nine mm slug into the guy's upper right arm again, spinning him around, flecking blood everywhere. The robber dropped his gun and fled from the shop.

Jake spun back to the other robber, who was standing there rigid with his arms still raised. He aimed the Glock at his chest and said, 'You, face down, now, otherwise I'll shoot.'

As though electrified, he dropped to his knees, then tipped forwards on to his chest, splaying his arms.

Jake stood in the middle of the shop floor, turning in a slow dream, seeing the body of the lead armed robber, and Dave Morton's unmoving body, blood spreading out from underneath both.

He looked at Anna, sitting there, quivering in terror.

And in the distance he heard the two-tone horns.

Eleven

Jake Niven left the interview room at Blackpool police station just after ten p.m. that night, having endured eight hours of ferocious questioning from a DCI and a DI who had been dredged up from Greater Manchester Police by the Independent Police Complaints Commission (IPCC), the official body responsible for investigating police wrongdoings.

Although Jake had not been formally arrested, he knew that if he had been foolish enough to stand up and try to walk out of the interview, he would have been hauled back by the collar.

It had been better, then, to play along with it than end up tossed into a cell, which was always a distinct possibility in the circumstances – you shoot someone dead, you get locked up.

So, after having had his uniform seized for forensic analysis and his gun taken from him (he was informed by the Superintendent Ops that he was hereby suspended from firearms duties), and after having dressed in a forensic suit and elasticated slippers, he went with it, kept his cool despite the tough questioning, answering truthfully, because that was all he had.

In a nutshell, he and Dave Morton had been sent by comms to an attack alarm, had walked into an armed robbery in progress and had reacted to the situation.

What complicated matters was that he and Morton were AFOs, and Jake had used his weapon, killing one of the robbers (who, Jake was only to learn later, was Fraser Worthington) and critically wounding another . . . and, of course, Dave Morton had received fatal gunshot wounds.

Despite all these complications (and here, Jake knew it would have been much easier all round if neither he nor Morton had been armed and had simply walked into the robbery and then been shot dead by the robbers), Jake was one hundred per cent certain of his position in all this chaos.

As far as he was concerned, it was cut and dried.

He had reacted reasonably and with restraint in a horrible scenario that was not of his making and had used only the right amount of force to resolve it. He was expecting questions to be thrown at him that tried to make him out to be a gung-ho firearms officer who thought he was in a Wild West shoot-out. He realized they were questions that had to be asked in order to try to make him crack and admit to it. But it wasn't true.

Jake held steady.

After six hours of pedalling this nonsense and going over and over things, trying to trip him up, the two detectives from GMP suddenly relaxed, broke into smiles, accepted what Jake said was true and eased up on him.

They did try to make some mileage out of Anna being in the shop, but despite their questioning on that issue they eventually accepted that it was simply a coincidence and Jake didn't even know why she was there.

Two hours after that they were as satisfied as they could be and – magnanimously, it seemed – allowed him to leave, but with the less than subtle warning in his ear that other witnesses would be spoken to, and if their stories did not tally with Jake's recollection of events, he would be dragged back in. He was also warned not to try and make contact with any of these people in the meantime.

When Jake politely pointed out that might be a tad difficult as one of the witnesses was his wife, the DCI revealed that she had been interviewed already by another officer and her story matched his, so it would be OK to talk to her.

'Right,' Jake drawled at this news, unaware that Anna had been spoken to. He only knew she had been whisked to hospital for a check-up, then discharged after treatment and that was it. He had heard nothing further.

'And she's waiting for you out there,' the DI added vaguely, 'with a change of clothing and a suitcase,' he concluded mysteriously.

Exhausted and dehydrated Jake took his leave of the men and made his way through the largely deserted lower ground floor corridors of the nick until he reached the rear of the public enquiry desk with its entrance on Bonny Street.

He sidled out from behind the desk into the public foyer, which was unusually empty with the exception of Anna who sat in the far corner with the mysterious suitcase at her feet and a plastic bag crammed with clothing on her lap.

She stood up uneasily as Jake approached her, looking frail and ill. There were padded dressings on the facial wounds Fraser Worthington had caused by ramming and twisting the harsh end of the shotgun into her skin.

'Anna, babe,' he said and opened his arms.

He expected her to fall into them.

He was wrong.

Instead she stood there, four feet away from him, making no effort.

He let his arms fall limp to his sides. 'How are you?' he asked.

She uttered a short, scornful laugh. 'How do you think?'

'Not great?' he ventured, trying a half-smile. 'Anna,' he began feebly, but found himself unable to find the words to continue.

'Look, Jake . . . I know this has been horrendous . . .' she said, then stopped and looked at the ceiling, on the verge of losing her composure. She pulled herself together. 'I know this has been awful, and I know they'll be after your hide because that's how it is—'

'You pull a gun, you open a door . . .'

'Something like that . . . but I know you'll be OK because you did the right thing, but—' She raised her left hand and twisted off her wedding and engagement rings and held them out for Jake, who let them fall into the palm of his hand, puzzled. 'There's something I can't get over . . . I know all this was terrible and I know you were a hero today . . . but, Jake, you're not a hero to me any more. You were once . . .'

'Why were you there in the shop?'

'A whim.' She shrugged feebly. 'Just seeing how much they'd bring.' She gestured to the rings on the palm of his hand. 'Seeing how much all those years of marriage were worth. As it happens, I didn't get a price.'

'Anna.'

She held up a hand quickly. 'Who is it?' she asked simply.

Jake hesitated.

'No bullshit, Jake. Time for bullshit's well past.'

'Kirsten,' he whispered.

Anna inhaled unsteadily and nodded. She knew of her, but had never met her. 'There's a change of clothing.' She pointed to the supermarket carrier, then at the suitcase. 'And more stuff in there: shaving gear and such like, and more clothes.'

'Anna,' he said, desperation creeping in.

'*No.*' She turned to leave.

Jake stepped quickly in front of her.

'Don't,' she warned him. 'Do not fucking come home, Jake. There's enough in the cases for a few days . . . You can set up with her, can't you? Kirsten.' She almost gagged on the name.

'Anna, I love you.'

'Well you've got a funny way of showing it. Now get out of my way, or I'll knee you in the balls, Jake.'

His mouth clamped shut. He stepped aside and watched her leave the police station, then sat on one of the plastic chairs in the waiting area.

It did not seem very long since Henry Christie had been sitting alone in a pub, staring into a Jack Daniel's, contemplating death.

163

On that occasion he had been an up close witness to a man who had taken his own life, taken the decision to blast his own head off right in front of the stunned Henry. And that had been the gruesome foreword to a night of extreme violence resulting in further deaths and ultimately the demise of Robert Fanshaw-Bayley, the chief constable, a man Henry had known over thirty years.

A night to forget, although Henry knew the ramifications of it could clatter on for years to come.

Neither could he hope to forget it, either.

Once again, Henry was sitting in a pub – this time the Tram and Tower on the outskirts of Blackpool on the housing estate where not too long ago he had owned a house and lived with his wife, Kate. The house was now sold, occupied by another family, Kate now dead, but Henry was back at what had once been his local. He was not here because he was living in the past, but because the pub was in spitting distance of the motorway on his route home and he wanted a drink.

He knew the landlord, Ken, and hadn't seen him for some time, and because he was feeling shitty he thought he would call in, have a chat, throw a pint of Stella down his throat and a JD chaser.

Unbeknownst to Henry, Ken had retired and gone to live in France, according to the new landlord, so Henry had no one to talk to. He ordered his drinks, perched on a stool at the far end of the bar and thought about death and how very fucking unpleasant it was to watch the life ebb out of someone, either quickly or not so quickly.

The man who had blown his brains out in front of Henry had died instantly.

Wayne Oxford had died not so quickly, and Henry had seen the life leave him as he tried to plug the knife wounds with the heel of his hands and failed miserably. As much as Oxford was a bad man, Henry had not wanted him to die, and he had tried to save him – mainly because he did not want the man who had plunged the little knife repeatedly into Oxford's chest to become a murderer.

That man had already suffered enough.

He had lost his one and only son to a home-made bullet fired indiscriminately by Oxford and was grieving so intensely that all his focus had gone on revenge.

Had Henry been thirty seconds earlier he would have prevented the attack, but that time-lag meant that Jamie Turner's father had been able to stab Oxford over twenty times in a frenzy. He was now languishing in a cell on suicide watch, and only a lenient judge would ever set him free.

Henry had been drenched in blood, getting soaked as he tried to save Oxford in the confines of the dock, watched by the uncaring eyes of the killer and the petrified eyes of the security guard peering through his fingers, crying like a baby.

Henry only sat back on his haunches when he knew he had done what he could and that to carry on would be pointless.

He had known anyway, but he'd had to try.

Then he had looked around at the faces of the audience, which had gathered to peer into the dock as though it was some ghastly spectator sport.

He had told the court clerk to seal the courtroom and, once sure that the crime scene was protected, that Mr Turner had been led away into custody, and that CSI were on their way, plus a police surgeon, Henry had then walked back to the police station in his blood-sodden clothing. He had gone to his car to retrieve the spare set of clothes he always carried, then went to the shower room and had a long, burning-hot shower, scrubbing the blood out of his short hair, off his skin, from under his fingernails. He spent a long time in the shower before getting into his fresh gear and bagging up the blood-soiled set for forensics.

On his return to his office he learned about the shooting at the jewellery shop in Lytham, but there was no way he could even think about getting involved in that because of what had happened in court. Rik Dean was given that job.

He sat in his office for a very long time after that before gathering up the courage to telephone Jamie Turner's mother, the woman who had called and alerted him that her husband had gone off to court armed with a ceramic knife and murderous intentions.

Calling her back had been a tough one.

After that he kept an ear out to the situation at the jeweller's, but he had to concentrate on what had happened in court which was a 'fucking

166

mess', as the Divisional Commander succinctly described it.

At 9.15 p.m. that night, sitting in his office, trying to get his head around the enormity of it all, a figure had appeared at the door, tapping gently.

Henry stood up. 'Boss.'

It was Bernard Ellison, the acting chief constable, and from the expression on his face, Henry gleaned he was not the bearer of good news . . .

Henry downed half of the Stella in one. He could easily have necked the whole pint, but he wanted to savour some of it. He sipped a little of the JD, wanting to save some of that, too. He knew he would be foolish to drink any more on an empty stomach and then drive all the way back to Kendleton.

'Fuck,' he mouthed despondently. He took out his warrant card and looked at it; the photo on it had been taken almost five years before, when he had been promoted to superintendent. He did not look that much younger, still had an air of weariness about him. 'Fuck,' he said again and tossed the laminated card on to the bar top, where it flopped on to a blob of spilled beer.

Henry glanced along the bar and saw someone he recognized – who, at the same moment, glanced his way. Their eyes met.

After Anna had gone, Jake sat hunched over in the waiting area for several very long minutes before re-entering the station and getting showered and changed.

167

Ten minutes later he was knocking on the door of Kirsten's flat in the Marton area of Blackpool.

It took her a very long time to answer, and when she came to the door she looked tired and drawn, her hair pulled tightly back, a cigarette dangling from the fingers of her right hand, which also gripped a wine glass. He knew she had been off-duty that day, but she'd clearly heard about the robbery and Dave Morton.

'Hi,' he said.

She glanced down tiredly at the small suitcase at his feet and rolled her eyes.

He tried to smile. 'I take it you know?'

'About Dave, yeah.'

'Can I come in?'

'I don't think so.'

'I've nowhere else to go.' His stomach had already done a nauseating flip at her reaction.

'Jake, your life's going to be complicated enough, and I don't want to get drawn into it – not under these circumstances. I was . . .' she began, then hesitated.

'Was what?'

He saw her swallow. 'I was going to call it quits, anyway . . . I'm not ready for this or anything like it. And to be honest it's not really like you were going to leave your wife, was it?'

'So that's it?'

She nodded, shrugged helplessly. 'Guess so.'

'You mentioned love,' he accused her.

'Nah.' She stepped back and closed the door softly in his face.

Five minutes later, purely by chance, Jake

168

walked into the Tram and Tower and spotted Henry Christie propping up the bar.

'May I join you?' the acting chief constable had asked Henry Christie from his office door.

'Absolutely,' Henry replied awkwardly. *You can go where you want*, he thought. *It's all yours.* He gestured to the chair on the opposite side of his desk.

The acting chief sat. Bernard Ellison, a man with just over twenty years' service, had reached this rank shortly after his forty-first birthday, a very quick rise to the top in police career terms. Henry didn't know much about him, other than that he had begun his career in Lancashire, transferred early to West Yorkshire, then had come back into Lancashire as an assistant chief constable and ended up first deputy chief, and then acting chief because of FB's death. It was more than likely he would become the actual chief, with which Henry had no problem. Ellison seemed a decent enough fellow.

Henry had not spoken to him since their conversation that Saturday after FB's funeral, but it wasn't a surprise to see him here, in Blackpool, after the day's events. A cop getting shot was always certain to rouse the chief from his office.

'Thanks,' Ellison said. He sat, gave Henry a smile with compressed lips. 'How are you doing?'

'OK.' Henry nodded, sitting slowly back down. He sensed some tension from Ellison.

'This shooting this morning – all very messy and tragic . . . Another police officer doing his job, shot dead by desperate villains. Awful scenario, even if there is a hero in there.'

169

'Jake Niven.'

The chief nodded. 'Although PC Morton was a hero, too.'

'Yeah,' Henry agreed gravely. 'But Jake Niven did well – and for that his life has changed for the worse. I haven't had chance to speak to him as yet, but I hear he's being put through the ringer.'

'Name of the game.'

Oh, that fucking useless saying, Henry wanted to blurt. Some game. But he nodded: he'd been there, done that, got the badge, survived more or less intact. 'Have you been to see Dave Morton's family?'

'Yes, been a very full-on day . . . Your DCI, Rik Dean? He's pretty much kept it all together . . . Good man.'

'Yes, he is.'

'And your day hasn't been plain sailing?'

'Nope.'

The chief paused and licked his lips.

Henry regarded him, thinking he knew what was coming next . . . He had that nasty little feeling he was about to be whacked by the proverbial wrecking ball.

'Henry,' the chief said at last, 'I've been keeping an eye on you since we last . . . chatted.'

Here it comes. Henry braced himself, but decided to say nothing – but then he had no choice but to speak because, in the way of a true manager, Ellison asked an open question. 'How do you think you've been going on?'

'In what way?' Henry responded in the manner of the trapped employee who knew he was being gunned for.

170

'Every way.'

'Fine.' What was the acronym? Fucked-up. Insecure . . .? Henry could not quite remember.

'Mm, OK.' Ellison's mouth twisted in disbelief. 'On the day we spoke, you landed that investigation into the missing policewoman, Laura Marshall . . .'

'The search for whom still continues to this day,' Henry interjected.

'But no breakthrough?' It was a question, but also a statement of fact.

'No,' Henry whispered.

'In a high-profile case that is worrying this organization massively . . . How does a cop and a car disappear without trace in this day and age?'

Henry swallowed, making a dry clicking sound in his mouth. He almost countered, 'How does an airliner full of passengers disappear in this day and age?' but thought it might have been seen as a tad defensive.

The chief arched his eyebrows, waiting. Henry said nothing and Ellison went on, 'You also ended up with the tragic shooting of that young lad at Blackpool.'

'Yep.'

'Good result on that?'

'It was.'

'But . . . pretty straightforward stuff, wouldn't you say?'

'A job any competent jack could have bottomed,' Henry agreed, then wished he hadn't.

'Yeah, I'd say that, too.' The chief hesitated slightly then said, 'Now – up to date. Three cops shot at in a surveillance van, a defendant in court

171

stabbed to death by an irate relative, and another cop shot down during a jewel robbery . . . all these things linked in some way.'

Henry clamped his mouth tight shut, definitely not daring to speak or hardly even breathe. *Fucked-up. Insecure . . .*

The chief pursed his lips. 'I am right in thinking you were after Fraser Worthington?'

'Yes.'

'And he was linked to the guns found in Wayne Oxford's possession?'

'Kind of.'

'So, you put on a surveillance operation with the hopeful intention of catching Worthington when he showed up to collect them?'

Henry nodded, feeling the heat working his way up his collar, so boiling hot that his head was going to start whistling like a steam kettle. *So this is what it looks like when an axe is falling,* he thought.

'Was it risk assessed properly? I only ask because the three cops cooped up in the back of a van almost lost their lives, Henry.'

'It was a fast-moving investigation. I risk assessed on the hoof. It happens.'

'Where is the assessment now?' the chief asked. 'You know – written down?'

'I haven't done it.'

'OK . . . Wayne Oxford appeared in court this morning and was fatally attacked. What measures were in place to protect him and others?'

'None,' Henry admitted, his lips tight.

'Was he considered to be a risk or at risk?'

'On reflection—'

'So were any measures put in place, or did he just get produced for court like any other run of the mill prisoner?'

'I think you know the answer to that, sir.'

'Tell me the answer, Henry.'

'He was produced like any other prisoner . . . and no, I didn't do a risk assessment.'

'Clearly.' During the course of this interchange the chief's whole demeanour had altered: gone from warm to very chilly indeed. 'Am I also right in thinking you did an unsuccessful surveillance operation of Fraser Worthington in amongst all this – and that when you briefed officers you showed them a fairly recent surveillance photo of Worthington walking along the main street in Lytham? Not a million miles from the jeweller's shop he and his gang attempted to rob today?'

'You're going to pin that on me, too? There was no way I could have known he was going to rob a shop in Lytham today. I'm not Mystic Meg,' he said, showing his age. 'I don't have a crystal ball.'

Ellison watched him, bubbling. 'I know that, but he could have been disrupted, could he not?'

Henry shook his head. 'That was on my to-do list for today – disrupt Fraser Worthington, a tête-à-tête to scare the crap out of him – but it didn't happen because I got diverted.' Henry's voice had started to rise, but then fell away to nothing on the last few syllables.

'Thing is, Henry, you're too gung-ho. You don't think things through . . . You've lost the plot, lost your grip on things, and people are getting hurt ever since FB died. Your judgement is flawed, and I cannot afford to have any officer, particularly at your level, making mistakes like this—'

'Oh, no, no, no,' Henry cut in.

Ellison raised a finger. 'Let me finish. I've decided that I'm going to relieve you of all your present caseload . . . I really do think that FB's death has had a major effect on you and, as I said, your judgement is flawed because of it . . . In fact, your head is way up your arse.'

'I'm not retiring for a month,' Henry blurted.

'I'm appointing someone else to take charge of Laura Marshall's disappearance and the whole Wayne Oxford/Fraser Worthington debacle . . . and as regards your retirement, you *are* retiring. I have received your report in this matter and have accepted it, so until you actually reach retirement date, you will be transferred to the Human Resources department, or if you don't like that, I'll turn a blind eye to you not turning in for work for the next few weeks.'

'Who's taking over?' Henry said, hardly having heard all those words spewing out of Ellison's mouth.

The chief stood up, went over to the office door and opened it.

At that point Henry remembered it all: *Fucked-up. Insecure. Neurotic. Emotional.*

Henry nodded at Jake Niven who, after having got his pint in his hand, had slid along the bar next to him. 'Mind if I join you, boss?'

'Not at all,' Henry said. He glanced around the pub and said, 'Fancy taking a seat?'

They moved over to a deserted alcove and sat across from each other, divided by a small wobbly table. 'How are you doing?' Henry asked. After a shooting there was always a lot of touchy-feely questions, often more than necessary.

'Well, seeing as how a guy who was my friend was shot dead in front of me, I killed someone, wounded another – who is critically injured – found my wife in the middle of all that shit, who then kicked me out for having an affair . . .' Jake curled his lip. 'Pretty good, I'd say . . . Oh, in addition to all that, the woman I was seeing has also told me to sling my hook, and I've been interviewed by two members of the Gestapo. Yeah,' he said, nodding appreciatively, 'pretty good . . . You, boss?'

Henry considered the question for a moment and in the same vein replied, 'Well, seeing as I was too late to save a prisoner's life and now my professional competence has been severely questioned, if not damned to hell and back, and I've been put out to grass like an old dray horse, and then usurped by someone too close to home for comfort, pretty good too. Cheers.' Henry raised his glass, clinked it with Jake's, and both sank their beers.

'Are we in for a sesh here?' Jake asked. 'I could do with one.'

Henry scratched his head. 'Sounds a good idea, but I've nowhere to roll home to around here any more, and you sound homeless too . . .' Something clicked in Henry's brain. 'But I have an idea on that point . . . Let me make a call.' He rooted out his mobile phone and minutes later he and

175

Jake were leaving the Tram and Tower, passing Rik Dean as he walked to the pub across the car park.

'Henry, I thought I'd find you here.'

Henry simply walked past him, his head rotating as he gave Rik the dirtiest, most contemptible expression he could muster and said simply, 'Back-stabber, Acting Detective Superintendent Dean.' He knew it was ridiculous, but could not stop himself jerking his middle finger up at Rik.

Colin Gorst stood in the muddy farmyard looking fearfully at the two dogs circling him. They were pit-bull terriers; their evil eyes fixed on him as they moved around him, deep growls emanating from their throats. For the moment, they were controlled as they listened to the soft commands of their owner, who stood facing Gorst.

It was a huge effort for Gorst to remain upright on legs that felt as squishy as raw calamari, and of course he was also deeply regretting his decision to do what he'd thought was the right thing.

'So the cops came,' the man said, 'and you drove off?'

Gorst swallowed some lumpy bile in his throat. He could hardly say the word, 'Yeah.'

'You were the getaway driver, but as soon as a cop car showed up, you left your colleagues to their fate? Have I got that right?' the man said softly.

Gorse's body twitched in fear. He jumped as one of the circling devil beasts got a tad too excited and let out a sharp yelp.

'Which means that Big Mack is in police

custody, Saul Dyer was shot and critically wounded, and Fraser Worthington was killed – shot by a fucking John Wayne cop. That is what I'm getting here.'

'Yuh.'

The man – the accuser – took a step forward. The dogs tightened their circle around Gorst. 'And you came here to tell me this?'

'I thought you would want to know . . . I thought . . .'

'I thought, I thought,' the man said, mimicking him cruelly. 'You chickened out and gave none of them the chance to escape because of your cowardice.'

'But the cops . . .'

The man's right hand slashed down through the air like an axe. The dogs stopped moving. They were standing on either side of Gorst now. 'You ran – and my brother died.'

'I'm sorry, Arlow,' Gorst sobbed. 'Fuck, if only I could . . .'

'Go back in time?' Arlow demanded.

'Yeah, yeah.'

'But you can't, can you? Because time travel doesn't exist. You ran, one man got arrested, another wounded and my brother killed. You can't change that, Colin.'

'I'm sorry,' Gorst said weakly. He could hear the dogs breathing and the slightly sickening flapping of their pink tongues in their mouths.

Arlow Worthington nodded. 'And now I have to take revenge, because that's the only option for a grieving man in these circumstances.' Arlow was wearing an old army surplus jacket. From the right hand pocket he extracted a small pistol.

'I could've just fucked off,' Gorst pleaded. 'Not come to see you, to tell you . . . I could've gone, done a runner.'

'In which case I would have hunted you down sooner rather than later, Colin.' He raised the pistol, aimed it at Gorst's face.

'I don't fucking deserve this! C'mon, I don't,' he pleaded, tears streaming down his face.

'Nor did Fraser.'

With a sudden surge of energy, a mix of the last fluid ounce of adrenalin and the flight factor, Gorst spun and ran.

Arlow raised the gun and fired twice, quickly. The pistol recoiled in his grip. The first round hit Gorst in the left side of his neck, tearing out a meaty chunk as it passed through and ripped out his windpipe.

The second smashed into him slightly higher, just at the back of his left ear, skewering into his skull, into his brain, mushrooming and exiting through his left eye, making a hole the size of a coaster. Gorst dropped, dead before he hit the ground.

At a flick of Arlow Worthington's hand, the two dogs attacked him, tearing him to pieces with ferocious, blood-crazed glee.

Twelve

Henry awoke with his head feeling like a boiled egg must feel when someone is smashing it open with a teaspoon. He groaned, not daring to open his eyes.

Then he heard a derisive laugh.

He exhaled and shaded his eyes with a hand just in case the brightness would destroy his eyeballs like daylight disintegrates vampires. It wasn't so bad. The curtains were still drawn, but when he squinted at the person hovering over him, an arc of shocking pain tore into his cranium behind his eyes.

'Now that *was* a bender,' Alison said. She was standing by the bed, arms folded, looking down at Henry with delight twinkling in her eyes.

Henry groaned again and wondered how pickled his liver was. It felt like a house brick tucked under his rib cage. 'Time is it?'

'Just gone nine.'

'In the evening? Have I slept for eighteen hours?'

'Morning, silly arse.'

Painfully, he propped himself up into a sitting position. 'Late for work.'

'From what you said last night, you have no work to go to.'

'Oh yeah,' he said, rubbing his bloodshot eyes. 'Long time since I've drunk that much.'

'And all on the house.'

'I'll pay for it.'

'Course you will,' she said sarcastically.

'Seen anything of Jake?'

'Yep – he's up, been for a run, showered, now eating a full English. The booze doesn't seem to have affected him.'

'He's a young colt . . . I'm an ageing dray horse,' Henry argued, using the metaphor he had been bandying about last night. 'How does he seem?'

'For someone who shot and killed another person, then got booted out of home by his missus? Shit, basically.'

'I'll go and motivate him.'

'And who will motivate you?'

Henry clacked his tongue in an effort to induce some moisture into his dry mouth, then tried to give Alison his best lascivious look, using his apparently permanently squinting eyes. 'You?' He let the duvet slip down to expose the flaccid mess that were his genitals.

'Think again, bud,' Alison groaned as she reared away with a look of horror. Then she relented, gave him a quick kiss on the cheek and left.

He slumped back, feeling a desperate need for more sleep, but then rolled off the bed on to all fours and in this position crawled to the shower room. Before he reached his destination, the bedroom door opened and Alison looked in.

'Henry! What the hell are you doing?'

'Going for a shower,' he said innocently from his hands and knees. 'Seemed the easiest option.'

180

'Whatever.' She shook her head. 'Forgot to tell you – Rik's been on the phone for you.'

'Well, you can tell that little back-stabbin' shit-fuck to—'

She slammed the door shut before hearing the final words of Henry's foul-mouthed rant.

Normally, Henry was pretty quick in the shower. In – shampoo – swill – out, but that morning he took it long and slow, lathering up repeatedly and washing off. Partly, he was savouring the decision not to rush into work, allowing himself a wicked chuckle when he thought about Rik Dean who would, hopefully, be floundering at that very moment. And partly he was still washing Wayne Oxford's blood off himself.

Henry actually liked Rik. He had championed him for many years, getting an enthusiastic thief-taking PC on to CID and up through the ranks, although it had never been Henry's intention that Rik would step into his shoes quite this way. Rik was also on the verge of marrying Lisa, Henry's flaky, younger sister, so he would have Rik as a brother-in-law soon: the bastard who had pinched his job.

As he stood under the powerful jets of hot water, Henry knew he could not stay mad with Rik for too long. It wasn't Rik's fault he'd been chosen to take on Henry's workload, and it really wasn't in Henry's nature to be too obstructive, though the devil in him knew that he would be for a tiny while.

This was because Henry knew his first respon-sibility was towards the missing, probably, undoubtedly, murdered policewoman and the dead schoolboy Jamie Turner and his family, who would now be in a very special form of hell. As much as Jamie's father had killed Wayne Oxford, Henry knew there was still a lot of work to do with the family to help them get through the horrible mess they were now in. He did not want the police to abandon them.

So perhaps he would tease Rik for a while and get some pleasure from seeing him squirm.

He dried off, dressed casually and went along to the kitchen of the Tawny Owl where Alison and her stepdaughter, Ginny, were busy prepping breakfasts for the paying guests.

Alison smiled. 'My, you look almost human now,' she said, appraising him. 'Not like that grotesque creature from *Alien* that woke up in my bed.'

'From the cocoon comes the butterfly,' Henry said with a twirl.

'Bap?' she asked.

Henry sidestepped the double entendre and graciously took the proffered Cumberland sausage bap and a mug of steaming coffee. 'Is he still in the dining room?'

'Yes . . . Er,' Alison said awkwardly.

'What?'

'How long will he be staying? We're not running a waifs and strays charity here, you know.'

'Don't know . . . Probably be gone today. I guess I just wanted to offer him a safe harbour for the night.'

'Fair enough,' she said.

182

He walked out of the kitchen into the pub itself: the main bar area to his left and the dining room through a door to his right. Glancing through, he saw Jake sitting alone at a table in the bay window. Two couples sat at other tables, everyone devouring their breakfasts, which had developed a good reputation in the area, as had the Tawny Owl as a whole, having been resurrected from oblivion when Alison took it over several years before. It was now a thriving business, popular with locals and travellers alike.

Henry decided not to interrupt Jake for the moment; instead, he stepped out on to the front steps and perched his bum on the stone wall that formed the perimeter of the car park. Armed with his brew and sausage bap, he took in the morning whilst hoping his headache would subside.

'Morning, boss.'

Henry half-turned as he bit into his sandwich. 'Morning, Jake, how are you? Been for a run, I hear?'

'Yeah . . . My running kit was in the suitcase. Very thoughtful, my missus.'

'I'm impressed.'

'It was a grind, especially after last night – which I'd like to thank you for. It was a good idea to come here.'

'Pleasure. I'd like to say you can stay for as long as you like, but . . .'

'Nah, I get it. Maybe one more night if possible, for which I'll gladly pay.'

'We'll charge you cost price, but just to reiterate, last night was free.'

'Appreciated.'

'What's happening today, then?'

'Need to get into work. There's a debrief at eleven a.m., then I'm booked in to see the force counsellor.' He shrugged. 'Then I need to go and see Dave Morton's wife, if the powers that be will let me.'

'I'm sure they will.'

'Then, I don't know. Maybe get home to see the kids if Anna will allow it. She's pretty shaken and very angry.' Jake had brought a mug of coffee out with him. He sat alongside Henry. 'Nice spot.'

'Very nice,' Henry agreed. 'Sometimes I see deer on the green.'

'And you're going to retire here?'

Henry nodded.

'I ran up past the police house,' Jake said. 'It's empty.'

'Yeah . . . It's one of the last rural-beat houses still owned by the constabulary, but they want to sell it. It's hanging on because the locals are campaigning to get a bobby back on the beat here. The local MP's on their side, but—' Henry shrugged. 'It's all about money. Decision time soon, I think. Anyway.' He stood up and drank the last of his coffee. 'In the hope that my blood-alcohol levels are under the legal limit, I'm going to drive into work and clear my desk, then begin my new career in Human Resources. For a month or so, anyway.'

Henry walked along the corridor towards his office on the first floor of the FMIT block at headquarters – formerly student accommodation for the training centre, but snaffled by what was the SIO team a few years ago and refurbished as their offices, the block now belonged to FMIT, which is what the SIO team had become.

He had often wondered what the last walk would be like, even though he knew this probably wasn't his last one as such, but he tried to imagine it was.

Curiously, he felt nothing. Thirty-plus years and he felt nothing.

He had expected to be overcome by emotion, to be sobbing uncontrollably, but there was hardly anything other than the taste of bitter resentment and the notion that he had been unfairly ousted before he'd finished what he'd started.

The organization, he thought, could be cruel if it wanted, and in his case, that seemed to be true.

He stopped at the closed door of his office.

It was at that moment he did begin to feel something.

Rage.

It rippled through him. The brass nameplate bearing his name had been unscrewed and removed. All that was left were four screw holes and a rectangular patch of wood that was darker than the faded door.

He swallowed. They had already started to erase him from their memory banks.

'Bastards,' he whispered. 'They don't fuck about.'

He tried the door: locked. He searched for his key and inserted it into the Yale lock.

Which did not turn.

He tried twisting it in both directions, then withdrew it and peered at the key. The right key.

He slid it back in, turned it, and it was only at that point that the realization dawned on him: nameplate removed, lock changed. Some other bastard cuckoo had taken over his nest.

Dumbfounded, he withdrew the key and stared at the door, blinking away the tears.

He made his way to the dining room at the training centre where he bought himself a coffee from the machine, then sat at a table as far away from anyone else as he could.

Brooding, frustrated, suddenly feeling isolated and vulnerable.

'Henry,' came a wary voice behind him.

He did not turn to look or acknowledge, just sipped his coffee.

Rik Dean sat down beside him at the table. 'Henry,' he said again.

Henry's eyes turned to him with the malevolence of the devil.

'I didn't ask for this.'

'And your point is?'

'And nothing . . . I didn't ask for this. I was approached, asked a lot of questions, and what the hell was I supposed to do or say? No, thanks, I don't want to be a detective super, even if it's temporary?'

'Who approached you?'

'The chief.'

'And what exactly did he ask you?'

'If I'd be prepared to take on your caseload when you retired. At that moment I didn't even know you'd put your ticket in, Henry, so I just said yes. I had no idea it was to be, like, now.'

186

'I've basically been binned, Rik. Yeah, I was going to retire, but on my own terms, not with a boot up my backside.'

'I'm sorry. I didn't realize.'

'I can only assume you did your part in shafting me, Rik. Cheers, mate.'

'You know what I think of you, Henry – as a colleague and as a friend,' Rik said genuinely. 'And as a prospective brother-in-law.'

Henry snorted. 'You'll be shagging me next.'

Jake spent his day in a haze, being debriefed and wheeled into various offices to be spoken to by a series of high-ranking officers and support staff, before being told to go home and wait to be contacted whilst 'decisions were made'. He knew this was the start of not knowing what was going to happen to him. He knew he had lost his place on the firearms unit, was being investigated by the IPCC and was probably starting a period of limbo in which he would be shunned by the force. He would not hear anything for months, nor be kept updated with any developments. One thing was certain: he would be kept at arm's-length until it all resolved itself. But even then, when he was found to have acted lawfully (of which he was certain), the force would probably still not know what to do with him.

It didn't help he had no home to go to: a bolt hole where he could lick his wounds, surrounded by people he loved.

That side of it, of course, was his own doing.

He was hugely grateful to Henry Christie for last night, taking him under his wing and giving him a bed for the night – and getting riotously drunk. Jake had needed that, but he also knew he could not stay at the Tawny Owl, as great as it might be. He needed a cushion of one more night there, just to give him time to sort out his immediate life, but that was all.

Throughout the morning his mind whirled, continuously thinking about Anna and his family and how he'd made a right royal screw-up of things just because he'd been weak and fallen into bed with a younger colleague who'd seemed to be everything that Anna wasn't.

He now knew that was complete tosh.

He desperately tried to think of how he could get back with Anna who, apart from the infidelity, must have been suffering terribly from the other events she'd been part of the day before.

After a gruelling hour with the superintendent in charge of operations, Jake wandered into the training-centre dining room about three p.m. and saw Henry Christie sitting alone at one of the tables. He walked over and asked him if he could buy him a coffee, which seemed to startle Henry, who had been in a bit of a trance.

'That would be good,' Henry said, slurping the last dregs of his current brew.

Jake brought two new cups back to the table, and Henry raised his eyebrows at him questioningly.

'Not going well,' Jake said. 'The whirlwind of interviews has kept me going, but now I've been told I can go, I don't quite know what to do . . . How about you?'

'Similar. No office to go to; they've done a

handover to my *successor*,' he said, almost choking over that last word. 'Went over to HR, who looked at me like I was Shrek . . . Apparently, the head of HR had not been told I was going to be with them for a few weeks, so I just spun out and left 'em to it. I'm having this brew, then heading north. Will you be there tonight? You're most welcome.'

'I think I will be, and thanks again.' Jake sipped his coffee. 'Just one more night. I think I might have somewhere to go after that: a divorced mate of mine said I can crash with him, however long it takes. Can't wait for all that fast food, TV and the Xbox,' he lied. 'All because I couldn't keep my pants up.'

'Been there,' Henry said with a smirk. 'Took me a long time to realize that family is where it's at.' He thought about Kate and how she had been taken from him before there was time for him to make real amends for his past misdemeanours.

'But you've got Alison.'

'And I won't let that go wrong this time,' he said. 'My daughters are both behind me now. Ginny – Alison's stepdaughter – is all for us, too. I'm determined to make it work – so maybe this is all to the good, me getting booted out. I could easily have let it all drag on.'

'I can see Alison adores you.'

'And I can see you know you've made a mistake, and if Anna loves you – I mean, you don't just stop loving someone like that—' Henry clicked his fingers. 'So my advice, not drunken this time, is: go and prostrate yourself at her feet,

189

beg forgiveness. She'll do it . . . and then you make things good again.'

Jake nodded as Henry spoke.

'There is one thing,' Henry said hesitantly. 'Whilst I was hanging about in the corridor at HR while they were panicking about what to do with me . . . and I don't know if it's of interest . . . I saw a notice on the board that the rural beat at Kendleton is to be reopened. They've found funding from somewhere for a PC for three years. The house is rent-free with an option to buy at market value. Just a thought.' Henry shrugged.

'Oh, it's you.'

Jackie Powers glared balefully at Jake on the doorstep of his own house. She had answered the door on his knock.

'Yeah. Can I come in?'

'Anna doesn't want to see you.'

'She's my wife. This is my house.'

Jackie laughed harshly. 'Really?'

'Just let me in, eh?' Jake said, deflated.

'Tell you what.' Jackie looked down her nose at him. 'I'll ask her, shall I?'

She reversed back in and closed the front door gently but firmly in his face – the second time such a thing had happened to him in the last few hours.

He stood waiting, feeling stupid and embarrassed, thinking that all the neighbours' eyes were on him, peeking from behind the curtains, sneering and chortling: adulterer and killer. A parallel, silly part of him wondered what those words would look like on his tombstone.

The door opened again. Jackie rocked her head and stood aside for him to enter. As he came alongside her she hissed, 'I'll be outside having a fag. If you upset her in any way, shape or form, I'll kick your sorry arse out of here myself, and don't think I won't.'

'I'm sure you will.' Jake made to move on, then stopped. 'By the way, I'm sorry about the accusation – the custody record thing.'

Jackie's face remained impassive, and she said nothing.

Jake turned into the living room and looked across at Anna, who was sitting on one of the armchairs in her housecoat, hands clasped on her lap, a tissue scrunched up. He gasped at her appearance: drawn, exhausted, bags under her eyes, her hair unkempt, the dressings still on her face . . . but yet, beyond that he could see her beauty, maybe for the first time in two years, that trait he'd been idiotic enough to miss because he had been such a fool.

'Hi,' he said.

'Hi.'

'Can I sit?'

She nodded.

He sat on the settee. 'How are you?'

'Not good. Jackie's been great.'

'Yes.' He bit his tongue, not wanting to say something he would regret. 'Tough day yesterday.'

'In so many ways.'

Jake picked his thumbnail. 'I've been binned from the ARV.'

'No surprise there.'

'Suppose not. Look, I haven't come here with any prepared speech or anything . . . I just want to speak from the heart.'

Anna waited.

'I want to say I am truly sorry. I forgot the meaning of love and the importance of family. I forgot all about loyalty and commitment, sticking together through hard times . . . But I do know that I love you and the kids, and you are my world. You mean everything to me, and I'll do anything to get you back. I know things will never be as they were, but they can be better.'

'You mean once I get over the fact you've been shagging some slag behind my back?' she said. 'You know how much that hurts me even just to think about that, to imagine?' Tears formed in her eyes.

'I know.'

'I blame myself,' she declared then.

'Eh? No.'

'For letting it get that way, for letting us get that way . . . for letting me get like this.' She pointed at her face. 'Dowdy, boring . . . a fucking housewife! I—'

'No, no,' Jake cut in. 'You're wrong. I was the idiot.'

'We're in a rut.'

'Yeah, maybe, but that doesn't excuse me cheating on you. I'm so sorry. I don't want us to split up. I know it'll be tough . . . I know,' he stressed weakly. 'But if that's what you want, then I'll go with it.'

'I don't. I don't want that, but you've hurt me so much, Jake, and I don't know if I'll ever be able to trust you again.' One of her tears rolled down her cheek into the dressing.

'I know it sounds corny, but I want to hold you.'

She shook her head. 'If only it was that easy.'

'I'll never let you down again, never ever,' he promised.

'But I don't think we can go back to how it was, even if we stay together.'

'Then let's get out of the rut.'

'How?'

'I have an idea on that.'

'This is your idea?' Anna moaned.

It was an hour later. At Jake's suggestion, Anna had taken a quick shower to freshen up, dressed in her jeans and a top, and packed an overnight bag, and then the two of them had got into Jake's car. Without a further word, Jake had driven on to and up the M6, coming off at Lancaster up the Lune Valley, then sprung off towards Kendleton and parked up on the driveway of the empty, detached police house.

He had got Anna out and was standing alongside her in front of the building. 'Look . . . the beat is going to reopen again. Apparently, there's funding for three years. The house is rent-free with an option to buy . . . We could move out here, make a fresh start . . . What d'you think?'

'Jake, it looks a complete mess,' she said truthfully.

She was not wrong. Although structurally sound, and despite signs of some major repairs to the front of the house, it had an air of neglect and possibly damp. But it was a substantial property, brick built, definitely large enough to accommodate the family and more. Plus, it had an attached garage on one side and an integral ground-floor office on the other. What was more, it was in a superb position on one of the roads rising out of Kendleton and had a huge garden, which Anna's heart frequently panged for.

'Could we afford it?' she asked. 'We would have to buy it because we don't want chucking out on our ears after three years. A place like this, even if it is in shit order . . . Bet it would cost more than we could make from selling ours. I don't know, Jake. I don't know.'

'We need an adventure . . . and somewhere where we can fall in love again.'

Thirteen

Three months later

'Nothing fucking works.'

The gas boiler made a dangerous, belching, gurgling sound, shook dramatically, and then, reluctantly, fired up with a loud bang as the gas ignited. Jake and Anna had watched the process, realizing that if it exploded they would be blown to smithereens.

'Well, at least it got going,' Jake said. 'And by the way, I love it when you talk dirty.'

Anna sighed, and they backed out of the garage in which the boiler was situated, turned and stood side by side to look at the day. It was cold and frosty, winter beginning to creep in as the days grew shorter. Their breath came in visible clouds, and Jake tried to blow smoke rings. He slipped his arm around Anna's waist, then hugged her tightly as a red deer stag appeared from the trees opposite, shook its head and fine set of antlers and simply trotted regally up the road in front of them, its breath hissing like a steam locomotive down its wide nostrils.

The two humans stood stock still and watched in fascinated awe as the beast clipped past, seemingly oblivious to their presence, then dived back into the woodland further up. Both then let out their breath and laughed delightedly.

'Apparently, they come down off the moors into the valleys during cold weather,' Jake said knowledgeably. He looked at Anna, and their eyes locked. 'I'll get an engineer to look at the boiler and price up a new one,' he promised. 'It'll need replacing before winter really kicks in.'

'Please do that,' she said.

They walked into the chilly house to the kitchen at the back that Jake had refurbished bit by bit over the last few weeks. It was starting to look good, but as for the rest of the property, that was still a problem. Windows that did not close properly, a leaking roof that was proving hard to repair, and damp from another source in the living room that seemed to be creeping up from the foundations.

The children were at the breakfast bar in the kitchen, sullenly devouring their first meal of the day.

'Hi, guys,' Jake said.

They looked at him with just as much sullenness as they ate and said nothing.

'Taxi'll be here in five minutes,' Anna warned them.

Danny shrugged. Emma kept a straight face.

'Just seen a deer walk up the road,' Jake said with enthusiasm.

'Wow,' Danny said, underwhelmed. 'That supposed to make us feel great, back to nature? Fact is, I don't want to be here. I want to be back where we were, with friends I know, not these stuck-up nobs in Lancaster.'

'Danny, sweetie,' Anna cooed. She crossed the room and held his head to her bosom. 'It's early days, and this is a new start.'

'For you two,' he said. 'I didn't need a new start. I was fine where I was . . . It was you who screwed up.' He glared fierily at Jake, who started to redden with annoyance.

'We're a family,' he said, 'and we move as a family.'

'Giving us no say in anything. A family led by a fascist,' Danny said.

'Oi,' Jake said. 'We have to go where my work takes me.'

'You mean you couldn't have transferred to Fleetwood?'

It was just the latest in a long line of face-offs he and Jake had been having since the move to Kendleton three months earlier: a move that was very unpopular with Danny and Emma and almost as unpopular with Anna, who was struggling with it, but trying.

A horn tooted outside – the taxi that took them on their school run – and it broke the tension.

'It's tough for us all, Dan,' Jake said softly.

Danny simply looked at him bitterly as he collected his school gear. 'On top of which we get taken to school by Mr Creepy, the taxi driver.'

'I know, I know.'

Danny shouldered past Jake, but Emma stopped and pecked his cheek. 'He'll be OK, Dad,' she assured him. 'We all will . . . and I still love you.'

'Thanks, babe,' he said and hugged her.

'And good luck today, you guys,' Emma said to both of them. 'Big day?'

'Very big day, but we should hopefully be home before you,' Jake said.

Jake and Anna followed them to the front door, where Danny picked up his rugby kit – he was playing for his new school that afternoon – and then they watched them pile into the back of the KountryKabs taxi waiting for them. They waved them off.

Emma waved back; Danny just slid down into his seat and stared forwards.

'Do you think we've done the right thing?' Anna asked Jake.

'I think if we've done the right thing for us, then ultimately we've done the right thing for the family . . . Has to be . . . Maybe.' His voice trailed off uncertainly.

She sighed deeply.

Jake pulled her to him. 'I'm sorry for hurting you.'

'Tell you what, Jake – stop saying it now, eh? I get the message, and I'm learning to live with it and, actually, I think it'll be great here once everything else has settled down and this week is over.'

'OK. How're you feeling?'

'About today?'

'Uh-huh.'

'OK, I suppose. I saw what I saw . . . It's not nice, but I'm not the one who pulled the trigger, so it's *you* who needs asking how *you* feel.'

'I feel OK.'

'Then let's get ready to rock. Time to get into best bib and tucker.'

Henry emerged from the cellar of the Tawny Owl through the door behind the main bar, having just wrestled with a barrel of Guinness which he had then connected to the taps. He pulled a pint – for test purposes only – and practised making the shape of a shamrock in the foam, but with little success. He was not arty, and it more resembled an ejaculating cock and balls rather than the proud emblem of a country. He tipped it away, frustrated, but at least the beer was flowing OK.

'New barrel for tonight,' he announced to Alison, who had just served up a couple of breakfasts to some last-minute guests who had rolled in from the moors the night before.

'Well done, barman,' she said, looking harassed, and disappeared into the kitchen for more breakfasts for the pre-booked guests who had just come down from their rooms.

Henry surveyed the bar proudly. Spick 'n' span. It had become 'his' little area of responsibility and was fantastically clean, the glasses all extra sparkly, the bar top shining lustrously from his repeated polishing.

All he had to do now was learn how to draw in Guinness foam.

He glanced up as two people entered the pub, Jake and Anna Niven, both looking very smart.

Jake had been keeping Henry up to date with the progress of the inquest into the sudden, violent deaths of PC Dave Morton, Fraser Worthington and the other member of the robbery gang, Saul Dyer, who Jake had been forced to shoot and who had, unfortunately, later died from his wounds.

Since retiring, Henry had kept his distance from that inquest, but had been involved in the inquest into Wayne Oxford's and Sophie Leader's deaths, which had started but been adjourned for various reasons.

'Morning, folks,' Henry greeted the couple, who he liked immensely. And not only that, Jake was turning out to be a popular and effective rural-beat bobby, whilst Anna was working a few evenings a week at the Tawny Owl.

They walked up to Henry's bar. 'Two pints, two whiskey chasers,' Jake said.

'Coming up.'

'Or just two very strong coffees.'

'Also coming up . . . Americanos?' Henry asked. They both nodded, and Henry turned to the newly installed coffee machine, a gleaming monstrosity Henry had insisted on buying. He had even gone on a two-day Barista course to master it. It was his pride and joy and did make wonderful coffee – something he never tired of pointing out to Alison.

'Big day,' Jake said.

Henry detected a slight tremor in those two words. 'It'll be fine; you'll see,' he reassured Jake.

Even though it was against all the rules of Human Resources and their personnel transfer policies, as a superintendent in HR, Henry had ruthlessly steered Jake's application to become the new cop on the beat in Kendleton and the surrounding area through the system. The selection process should have been open to all, but Henry was having none of that. He pleaded a special case to the head of HR – a lady who actually seemed to despise him – and won.

Jake's application was turned around within days of receipt, and the new cop on the block was in place less than a month later.

Henry had retired after that, quietly and without fanfare. His leaving 'do' had consisted of a dinner for a few selected friends and colleagues at a very posh hotel in Blackpool, at which Henry got royally drunk, made an embarrassing speech slagging off the constabulary, and then fell over. Alison had dragged him bodily to bed, and it had taken three days before his very nasty, lingering hangover had departed.

He retired on half-pension with a hefty lump sum in the bank, thank you very much, a couple of grand of which went on the fancy coffee machine – money well spent.

He did not have much time to mope around, though, because he immediately began working at the Tawny Owl and sank another chunk of his money into the refurbishment of the wedding function room upstairs, much against Alison's wishes. Not that the work wasn't necessary, just that she was very wary of him investing in the business and then regretting it. And she was at pains to point out that she wasn't after him for his money, but then she got extremely cross with him when he gave her a knowing look.

He knew he would never regret the investment, and eventually she accepted the money with good grace.

There were plans for a long holiday, but they were put on hold until the inquest into the deaths was over and the trial of Charlie Wilder came to court, as Henry knew he would be required to attend both to be cross-examined minutely.

Neither worried him.

He was, of course, following the progress of the Fraser Worthington inquest via daily updates from Jake, who was a vital witness and player in the game.

Even though an inquest is not a criminal trial, it does establish a cause of death and can have a big influence on subsequent criminal proceedings. Henry knew Jake had gone through a torrid time at the hands of a barrister representing the Worthington family – this despite it being obvious to all that Jake had acted lawfully and bravely in an intense, dangerous confrontation, and all witness testimony backed this up.

Jake was a hero, there was no doubt about that, but he would never carry a firearm again as a police officer, and his whole life would never be the same again – even though he was allowed to give his evidence from behind a screen and not be identified because of possible repercussions from the criminal underworld.

The inquest had lasted over three weeks, and today was the last day. The jury had been deliberating for two days, and now the coroner was ready to hear their verdicts.

'We don't have to be there until eleven a.m.,' Jake said as the coffee dripped from the machine into two large cups. 'Hence the brew.'

Henry placed a cup in front of Anna, who smiled at him. He vaguely remembered her being a policewoman some years back, but he had not known her, as such. He'd come to like her a lot over the last couple of months. He asked her how she was feeling.

'Jittery.'

'Yeah, I get that,' he said, placing the second cup in front of Jake. 'How's the house progressing?' he asked, changing the subject.

'It's damp, cold and quite windy,' Anna said, grinning. 'But y'know . . .'

'You're going to love it, ain't ya, babe?' Jake said.

'You know something,' she said, pondering, 'I think I am.'

Danny and Emma Niven sat morosely in the back of the taxi, not speaking or even acknowledging the presence of each other, as per brothers and sisters the world over. It was a longish haul, a tedious journey, for them to be deposited at their new schools in Lancaster, and their earphones were plugged firmly into place; each inhabited their own little musical world.

It was the usual taxi, an eight-year-old Skoda, driven by the usual driver. Not that either teenager was remotely interested in who drove them or in what car, and they certainly had no interest in chatting to the country-bumpkin behind the wheel.

With the tunes of Eminem thudding into his brain, Danny wedged his elbow on the door and supported his head on his hand as he watched the countryside whizz by. His mind churned with annoyance at his whole fucking family and the way in which his whole fucking life had been turned around just because his stupid fucking dad couldn't keep his cock in his pants.

Danny thought he hated Jake now, but he was trapped: living in a freezing house in the countryside – which bored the living shit out of him – unable to mix with his mates or see his girlfriend (who he knew was now seeing someone else).

He swore under his breath and caught the eye of the taxi driver, who was watching him in the rear-view mirror. He tried to shake the negative thoughts from his mind and looked around the taxi, which had seen much better days. It was a mucky, unimpressive heap. He sighed.

The taxi passed under the motorway bridge into Lancaster. Danny was first to be dropped off, and he reminded the driver he was playing rugby that afternoon and would not need picking up at the usual time and place. He would get a lift back to Kendleton.

'But I will,' Emma piped up.

The taxi driver nodded.

Danny slammed his car door as he got out and walked towards his new school without a backwards glance at Emma.

The move to Kendleton had been a culture shock to all the Niven family.

Jake had always been a town cop; he'd spent his service in and around Preston and Blackpool first on uniformed patrol, and then in firearms. He was used to turning up at work and being pitched into a maelstrom, job to job, incident to incident, emerging bleary eyed, eight hours later, from the lake of human existence.

Anna had got used to being a busy mum with two fast growing kids; she had a part time job and adored looking after the home, providing a bolt-hole for her family. She had a small but thriving social circle and was completely happy until Jake had spoiled it all. She'd realized then, too, that they were in a rut of their own making and needed to do something drastic to get out of it.

Running away to the back of beyond was not the adventure she had anticipated.

On the day Jake had driven her to Kendleton for the first time, and they'd stood looking at the battered old police house, her heart had sunk. But then Jake had wooed her, slowly and skilfully, and glimpses of the way their relationship had once been began to appear again.

Firstly by his words, then his actions.

On that day he had asked her to bring an overnight bag, so after viewing the house (which did not go that well), he drove her into the village and pulled up outside the Tawny Owl, where he made an announcement.

'Look, you don't have to do this, but do you fancy a night here?' He pointed at the pub. 'I can get my mum to look after the kids, and I thought maybe you and me could have some time together, talk, walk, sleep. I mean, y'know,' he stuttered, 'we don't have to "do" anything . . . I won't force you to do anything you don't want to. I know what's going on is massive, but a bit of me 'n' you time might not go amiss.'

She sighed, deeply troubled.

'If nothing else, we could just get legless

– without consequences. No driving, no kids . . . What d'you think?'

She closed her eyes and shook her head as she considered this. Then: 'OK.'

It had been a lovely night, and the owner of the Owl had been amazing and welcoming, and Anna had been surprised to discover that Henry Christie lived there too. Not a man she knew well, but one whose reputation she had been well aware of during her time in the police.

The meal was superb, and in the bar afterwards they were looked after by Henry and Alison and also met a few of the locals, who all seemed to be drunk and larger than life.

There was one point in the night when Anna was sitting alone at a table and Jake was at the bar ordering drinks. She watched him, scrutinizing him and thinking, 'You utter bastard . . . but I still love you,' and at that exact moment he glanced her way and smiled. There was still a lot to get over, to work out, but, putting all that aside for a while, she did something she hadn't done for a long, long time. When they retired to bed that night, she fucked his brains out.

And now after many deep conversations and pledges, they were living in Kendleton and maybe just about starting to get a grip of their lives.

The move had not been easy for Jake, either. The shootings were still hanging over him, and the pace of life as a rural beat officer was much less frenetic than in town. It was a very different job. He found himself simply getting to know the locals, and he was welcomed warmly into a community desperate for their own cop.

'Good luck – you won't need it,' Henry said to Jake and Anna, then stood back from their car as it drove off. He gave a wave and went back into the Tawny Owl, where it was time to grab breakfast.

He had been sensible enough to wean himself off anything fried, so he had two slices of wholemeal toast and a coffee from his new toy, which, as usual, he took outside and settled on the wall. The early morning had been chilly and misty, but now a weak sun had cleared all that and the bright sky seemed to foretell a beautiful early winter's day.

Henry crunched his toast and sipped his coffee, amazed at how lucky he was: retired, debt-free, living in a superb location with a beautiful lady who he was definitely going to marry (no more excuses), and running a healthy business.

He blinked sadly as he thought of Kate, but though she would always be there inside him, her memory was becoming more distant. That was just a fact of life.

He sniffed, drank his coffee, watched the village creak into life.

The local doctor drove past in an old Rover, waving at Henry, then swerving dramatically to avoid the immense four-wheel drive monstrosity driven by a farmer coming the opposite way. Both shook their fists angrily at each other, even though they were good drinking buddies. Both had been in the Tawny Owl the evening before, drunk. Henry suspected their blood-alcohol levels were still over the limit.

Then they were gone, and the next vehicle to come along was Spencer Bartle's animal transporter from Thornwell, packed with maybe a hundred sheep. Henry stiffened, put his coffee slowly to his mouth and watched the vehicle trundle noisily past.

Spencer Bartle was at the wheel.

Henry found himself grinding his teeth. The missing policewoman and her car still had not been found, and Henry remained convinced that Bartle was the one in the frame for it. Henry knew from bitter experience that running a murder/missing person enquiry from a room in Lancaster, fifteen miles away, was not the way in which this case would be solved. It was totally impractical.

That was one of the selfish reasons why he had ensured that Jake got the job in Kendleton. He knew Jake was a decent cop and would be good for the community. He also knew that having a cop in the heart of this area could be the key to cracking the case, because folk opened up when they trusted the local bobby.

Plus, now that he himself also lived and worked full-time in Kendleton, he could keep his ear to the ground. Even though he was retired now, he had made a promise to himself that one way or another he would crack the job, and if it meant getting the locals to talk to him over a pint of Guinness, then so be it.

Henry gave Bartle a little wave and a cheeky smile. 'I'll get you, you fucker,' he whispered, then returned to the bar to have another go at drawing a shamrock in the top of a pint of the black stuff.

* * *

It was a day of waiting, killing time.

The inquest was being held at Blackpool Magistrates' Court, across from the police station. When Jake and Anna arrived, expecting the inquest jury to have reached their verdicts, they and other key witnesses were told there had been a delay – the reason for which was not explained – and to return to court at two p.m.

The message had been passed by a court usher to Jake and Anna, who had been waiting in a secure witness room, separate from the other room, in order that Jake could maintain his anonymity. They strolled out through a side door and walked into Blackpool to have a look around the shops and get lunch.

Even though the delay was a pain – Jake's nerves were shot enough – the enforced time spent doing nothing was quite nice, and they looked around for possible Christmas presents for the kids.

Anna also texted them both to say they might be home later than expected, but promised them a meal at the Tawny Owl that evening.

Emma replied with a smiley face. There was nothing back from Danny.

Henry's Guinness-decorating was only partially successful. Before he could reach perfection he was chased out of the bar by Alison to help clean and change the bedding in a couple of the guest bedrooms, which he found hard graft, bending and twisting and lifting heavy mattresses, forcing himself to use muscles he had not even known existed. After these daily chores he

209

usually had a little bit of free time, in which he went for a run, often as far as Thornwell and back. It took him the best part of an hour at a steady pace.

That morning he trotted to the next village along, having at one point to stand aside on the descent into Thornwell to allow one of the KountryKabs taxis, a Skoda, to pass. He arrived in the village and caught his breath outside the Swan's Neck, then walked around to the back car park where he had found Laura Marshall's hat under the hedge. The bushes had been ripped up and replaced by a low wall, and the gravel surface of the car park was now covered by a thin layer of cheap tarmac.

Standing there, hands on hips, he re-imagined the visit he had made, squinting as he tried to visualize what might have happened to her here, because it was 'here' that whatever it was had taken place. Forensic and DNA analysis of the hat confirmed it did belong to Laura and that the broken glass in the gravel was from the window of a car of similar make and model to the police car she had been driving that night. Some minute specks of blood had also been discovered on the glass that also matched Laura's DNA profile.

Henry sighed in frustration, then braced himself for the run back to Kendleton, setting off at his usual slow pace. He was now determined to swallow some of his pride and call Rik Dean to see how the investigation was progressing.

'Have you reached your verdicts?' the coroner asked the jury spokeswoman.

'Yes, sir, we have.'

'Are they unanimous on all three counts?'

'Yes, sir, they are,' she said.

'Could you read them to the court, please?'

The middle-aged woman looked nervously at the sheet of paper shaking in her hands. 'With regards to the death of PC David Ian Morton – unlawful killing.'

Jake and Anna were sitting behind the screen, still masked from the rest of the courtroom. Jake was tense. His teeth clamped together, and his face was rigid.

Anna slid a hand over his. He gripped her thumb tightly. The rest of his life was now about to be revealed.

'And in regard to Saul Dyer?' the coroner asked.

The juror glanced at the paper. 'Lawful killing.'

'And in regard to Fraser Aldous Worthington?'

Jake's grip on Anna's thumb grew even tighter.

'Lawful killing.'

A little gasp hissed out through Jake's lips, then he closed his eyes and drooped his head.

As much as Henry had no desire whatsoever to set foot inside a police station or police head-quarters again, his curiosity made him follow several Twitter accounts related to the police and police activity. He was looking at his Twitter feed on his laptop when he picked up the phone and dialled Rik Dean's mobile number.

'Detective Superintendent Dean,' came the terse voice.

'I see you've dropped the "acting" bit,' Henry said.

211

'Too much of a mouthful . . . Henry, do you want to come back into this madhouse?'

'Not for all the tea in wherever tea comes from,' he said. 'How's it going?'

The two men had not been in contact for almost two months, but Henry knew Rik was at the inquest in Blackpool concerning Dave Morton, Fraser Worthington and Saul Dyer. The outcome would be crucial to any criminal proceedings that followed.

'Good result for Jake just in: lawful killings.'

Henry breathed out. 'Thank God.'

'Yeah, you could say that . . . I'll be speaking to him in greater detail, probably tomorrow.'

'And everything else?'

'Manic,' Rik said. 'Nightmare.'

'You're welcome to it.'

'I don't know how you did it, Henry. I have a shed collapse at least twice a day,' Rik said, meaning a nervous breakdown.

Henry laughed cruelly. 'Now all I'm bothered about is drawing shamrocks in Guinness froth.'

'Don't,' Rik said enviously.

Henry smiled, watching his Twitter feed scroll down the computer monitor.

'So what can I do for you? Long time, no see.'

'Uh-huh . . . Laura Marshall?' Henry asked.

'Getting absolutely nowhere. She disappeared, Henry.'

'Mm,' Henry said doubtfully. 'I seriously doubt that.'

'Well, you didn't exactly . . .' Rik's voice trailed off, and the line went silent. He didn't dare add the words 'find her'.

Henry scowled. He knew what he 'didn't

'exactly' do and wasn't proud of it. 'So, nothing new?'

'Nope.'

'Bye.' Henry hung up rudely and watched his Twitter feed, something he had only just got familiar with. He was a dinosaur where technology was involved, and it took him a long time to embrace new things, but for some reason he quite liked Twitter. Not that he himself had any presence on it (he had three followers, one of whom claimed to be Darth Vader's brother), but it kept him abreast of news and police issues, of some of the idiotic things people were up to, and, of course, of what The Rolling Stones were doing.

As he scrolled down, his eyes caught a tweet from North Yorkshire Police who were concerned about a teenager who had been reported missing in Skipton a couple of weeks earlier. There were now grave concerns for her safety. Henry clicked on to a link taking him to the local BBC site, showing an interview with a uniformed chief inspector. Henry watched it, grimaced, then skipped back to his Twitter feed.

After a few more minutes he got bored, stood up and made his way out to the bar to relieve Ginny, where a few hardy locals had begun to assemble in the mid-afternoon, including the farmer and doctor who had almost wiped each other out earlier in a head-on vehicle collision outside the Tawny Owl.

Henry joined in the conversation, but something was playing at the back of his mind, gnawing away. He wasn't completely sure what it was.

'What d'you think, Henry?' Doctor Lott asked him.

'About what, Doc?'

'Horse meat in pies and burgers.'

'That old chestnut?'

'Well?' the farmer, whose name was Don Singleton, demanded of him.

'I thought it had all been sorted,' Henry said. It was a heated subject that reared its ugly head from time to time in the pub: the scandal of horse meat being passed off as beef and finding its way into pies and burgers. It was one of those stories that had kept the nation enthralled a while back, but now seemed to have been resolved by the government, meat suppliers and supermarkets, who'd all promised to do better.

'Still going on if you ask me,' Lott said.

'Around here?' Henry asked.

'Oh, aye.'

'Tell me more.' He feigned interest.

'Bartle . . . Still at it,' the farmer chipped in knowingly over his pint of Guinness.

'Really?' Henry said – now interested. 'I thought he was horrible but honest.'

'Cunt, if you ask me,' Lott said, reverting to more old-fashioned medical terms.

'Yuh – twat,' the farmer concurred. He downed his Guinness and handed his glass to Henry. 'Fill her up . . . I hear you bin practising shamrocks.'

Henry took the glass and refilled a clean one, displaying his artistry, then handed it to the farmer, who peered at the image in the froth. 'More like a cock and balls,' he declared and showed Dr Lott.

214

'And jizz,' Lott added.

The farmer tipped it into his mouth and guzzled about half a pint.

'Bartle kills a lot of horses at his abattoir,' Lott told Henry.

'I thought he dealt in livestock – cows and pigs and sheep?'

'He does – and horses. He buys old ones, zaps 'em, butchers 'em and sells 'em into the animal food trade, or so he would have you believe.' Lott tapped his nose. 'He got half-looked at by the health inspectors, but I think he pulled a fast one . . . Anyway, he didn't get done cos he's sneaky.' Lott finished his drink and held it out for Henry, who was now feeling troubled. He had never explicitly discussed Bartle with the locals in the Owl, always going for subtlety; now he was kicking himself. Maybe he should have done. 'You think Spencer could be a killer?' he said, tossing it out there.

'Could very well be,' they said in chorus, then each took a long gulp of their drinks.

Henry was back at his laptop after Ginny took over again at the bar, re-watching the chief inspector talking to the BBC about the missing teenage girl from Skipton, North Yorkshire. Henry was still not certain why this was beginning to intrigue him, but as he sat at the desk in Alison's office, his arsehole was doing a little bit of a dance: the 'half-crown-thruppence' as he called it, using old monetary terms to describe the way it reacted – contracting and expanding – when he thought he was on to something.

After a further search with the computer, he dialled Rik Dean's mobile again.

'Acting Detective Superintendent Dean?' Henry said quickly, before Rik could answer. 'You're right, it is a mouthful.'

'Ahh – ex-Detective Superintendent Christie,' Rik riposted wearily.

'Sorry about hanging up on you before.'

'What d'you want, Henry?' He now sounded exhausted and not a little pissed off; Henry grinned. 'I don't really have time to chat to ex-coppers who can't quite let go.'

'Oh, OK, see you then.'

'NO!' Rik shrieked. 'Sorry. What do you want?'

'To share a hypothesis.'

'That'll be a first.'

'And a last. Laura Marshall.'

'Go on.'

'Spencer Bartle.'

'What about them, him?'

'Just for argument's sake, let's theorize that he did abduct and kill Laura, even though we can't prove it.'

'Gee, never thought of that.'

'Shall I go on or not?'

'Go on, go on.'

'And then suppose . . . hang in there,' Henry said when he heard Rik groan, 'that she wasn't the first or the last girl – stroke – woman he has abducted – stroke – killed.'

'There's no one else missing that could be attributed to him,' Rik said. 'So what are you getting at?'

'Just suggesting a line of inquiry to follow . . .

216

There's a girl missing from North Yorkshire who the cops over there are concerned about.'

'And?'

'She went missing about two weeks ago, and they're fearing for her life . . . Rebecca Merryweather, she's called.'

'And why are you putting two and two together? It doesn't even sound like the same MO.'

'I know that,' Henry snapped. 'It's just that she went missing close to the cattle market in Skipton, and Bartle attends these sorts of places regularly.' Henry found himself shrugging and wincing to himself because, as usual, when thoughts became the reality of speech they often lost their clout. 'And,' he added, 'another girl went missing about a year ago in Richmond – last seen near to the auction mart.'

'You sure of that?'

'Uncle Google tells me that. Check her out . . . Grace Greenwood, not seen since.' It was a little lie, because when Henry had found this on his Google search, there was no mention of a cattle market. He knew there was one there, though, and he'd put it in to spice up his theory. 'Another thing that might be worth checking—' He heard Rik groan, but kept on going. 'There could be other patterns, too . . . Like, Bartle had been arrested for violent conduct quite a few times, sometimes hitting females. Might be worth seeing if his arrests coincide with any disappearances: y'know, psychopaths, moons, a build-up of tensions and all that shit.'

'OK, Henry, I'll look into it, just because it's you.'

* * *

After the verdicts, all Jake wanted to do was sneak out of the court room by the back door and head home. Behind the screen, he and Anna waited impatiently for the court to empty, his heart still pounding, head light, fingers dithery. He knew it was not all over, that there was a criminal trial to come – that of the armed robber who had surrendered. He also knew that the getaway driver, identified as a crim called Colin Gorst, had also been circulated as wanted. So there were still bridges to cross, but at least he was over the first one cleanly. It very much helped his cause that, in his summing up, the coroner had referred to 'Policeman X' (as Jake had been called throughout the inquest) as a 'brave, committed officer who had acted with both restraint and decisiveness which had saved other lives'. He had added that X was 'a credit to Lancashire Constabulary'.

When the court was clear, Jake said, 'Let's go,' to Anna. They exited via a side door, into the secure witness room, then left the court by a further side door, out on to the concourse between the court and the police station.

'Constable,' someone called to Jake as he walked towards the nick.

Jake stopped and turned, recognizing the man approaching as the barrister who had been acting on behalf of Fraser Worthington's relatives. He came towards Jake with his right hand extended.

'What?' Jake said warily. This man had been allowed to see Jake during the proceedings.

'Nothing to worry about,' the man said. 'I just

wanted to say I think the jury was correct in its findings.'

'OK,' Jake said. He did not extend his own hand. Jake had no desire to shake the hand of the man who had put him under severe pressure in the inquest.

The barrister kept his hand out until he realized there would be no reciprocation. 'Whatever,' he said. He turned his handshake gesture into a pointed finger, then a wave, and walked away from Jake, who was uncomfortable about the incident.

'What was that about?' Anna asked.

'You know as much as I do,' Jake said. 'Come on. Let's head home, maybe stop for a brew on the way. I'm parched.'

Emma Niven quite enjoyed school that day, maybe for the first time. It had been a laugh – a bit of teenage girlie stuff with a few new mates and a few half-decent lessons. Unlike Danny, who was at a different school, Emma had decided to try and settle in. After a few false starts, it seemed to be working.

School finished at 3.30 p.m., and fifteen minutes later she was standing at the usual taxi pick-up point.

It was late, and she was getting infuriated enough to think about calling the taxi firm to gee them up when she saw the same taxi that had dropped her off that morning coming towards her. It stopped, and she jumped in the back. As the vehicle set off she noticed it wasn't the usual driver, but that didn't bother her too much. Occasionally, there were different ones.

'My brother's playing rugby,' she reminded him. 'I presume you know that?'

'Yep.'The driver checked over his right shoulder and pulled into traffic.

Emma could not help notice the size of the driver: a huge, broad shouldered man with long, ape-like arms and fingers as thick as sausages. 'Where's the usual guy?' she asked.

'Busy.'

'You work for him?'

'Now and then. When he's short.'

'What's your name, then?'

The taxi driver slightly adjusted the rear view mirror so that he could see Emma's face clearly, and she could see his eyes in the reflection.

'Spencer,' he said.

Fourteen

Even Danny Niven had a good day, particularly enjoying the rugby match after school. He was getting into a game he was unfamiliar with but was growing to like. He managed to cadge a lift back to Kendleton with one of his team mates, whose parents were minted and lived on the outskirts of the village. He even enjoyed the chat with the other lad, sitting in the back of a huge Mercedes 4x4, before getting dropped off outside the police house, where his dad's police Land Rover was on the drive.

He stood outside and frowned at the house, but not for the usual reason.

Evening was fast approaching, but there were no lights on in the house as he would have expected because Emma should have been home by now. Even though her bedroom was at the back of the house, the other lights would have been on because Emma was a lights-on monster. He knew his mum and dad were going to be late back – he'd got the text earlier – but Em should be here now.

He frowned as he walked up the drive. Thinking about his parents made him screw up his face: not in regards to them, but in admonishment of himself. He realized he had been a little bastard for the last few months, and yet they had never given him any real pain in response, in spite of their own problems. Maybe it was time to ease up on them, chill, and see if the move out here into the wild wasn't perhaps as awful as he made it out to be.

He inserted the key, opened the front door into the dark hallway.

'Em . . . Emma,' he called. No reply.

He stepped into the chilly house and turned on the hall light. She usually dumped her school gear in the hallway and kicked off her shoes under the stairs, but there was no sign of her having come home.

Danny sighed irritably, fished out his iPhone, found a signal (*for a change*, he thought) and called her as he walked through the house into the half-completed kitchen. Her phone went straight to voicemail, and he said tersely, 'Call me.'

Next he checked the downstairs room before going up to her bedroom, but it was empty, with no sign of her having been home at all.

'Silly cow,' he said under his breath, but felt uncomfortable. She was ditzy, but also a creature of habit and routine. 'Don't like this.'

He sent her a text, also asking her to call him, then got out of his school gear into jeans and a T-shirt.

There was no reply to his text.

More from frustration than anything, he decided to call his dad, who might know something he didn't. This call was immediately answered.

'Hey!' Jake sounded inordinately pleased to get a call from his son. 'How was rugby?'

'Yeah, good . . . Dad?'

'Yep?'

'I'm home, but Emma isn't here. Was she doing something?'

'What d'you mean?'

'Did she have anything on after school?'

'Not that I know of . . . Hang on, I'll ask your mum.'

Danny heard the half-muffled sound of his dad talking to his mum, then Jake came back on the line. 'Your mum doesn't know anything . . . Er, it's probably nothing to worry about. Tell you what – hang fire a moment and I'll call the taxi firm. They should have picked her up, usual time and place.'

'OK, Dad . . . Oh, Dad?'

'Yep?'

'How did it go today?'

'It went well, Dan, very well.'

A surge of relief went through Danny at this news. 'That's great, Dad.'

'Thanks, mate.'

'And Dad?'

'Yeh?'

'Sorry for being a plonker.'

'Hey . . .' Jake's voice cracked. 'It's OK.'

'No, it isn't.'

'Well, anyway, love you.'

'Love you, too.'

'Now let me call the taxi people, and I'll get back to you.'

Jake turned to Anna. They'd got partway home up the M6, but had then detoured on to the motorway services at Forton, south of Lancaster, where they'd sat for a long time in the café overlooking the motorway, with coffee and cakes, and had a long talk about the future. Ultimately, they'd decided to give Kendleton a proper try, even though the children were not happy with it.

Talk, somehow, had then moved on to Jake's infidelity.

That was an uncomfortable half-hour for him, but he thought he'd come out of it well, a bit like a job interview, saying – and meaning – all the right things.

Danny had called at that point and interrupted.

Hanging up, Jake said, 'Good and bad. Danny says sorry for being an idiot, but Emma isn't home yet.'

'I gathered that much. I'll try and call her; you call the taxi guy.' She fished out her mobile phone and called Emma whilst Jake called KountryKabs.

They finished their calls at the same time and said, 'No reply,' in unison.

Jake tapped his head and thought. 'I'm sure it's nothing to worry about.'

'I'll call the school.'

'I'll call Danny back after you do.'

'Danny, it's me . . . Has Em landed yet?'

'No.'

'Right, your mum's talked to the school, and they say she left on time, wasn't doing any extra-curricular activity . . . Look, mate, I'm sure it's nothing, but I can't seem to get through to the taxi place in Thornwell to see if they picked her

224

up, or whatever . . .' Jake wracked his brains. 'Tell you what – make your way down to the Tawny Owl and see Henry Christie, yeah?'

'Right,' Danny drawled dubiously.

'I'll call him now and tell him to expect you. We'll see if he'll be good enough to drive across to Thornwell with you and knock on the taxi office there . . . In the meantime, we'll keep trying Emma's phone. I'm sure it's nothing; she's probably just gone into town with a few mates and completely forgotten to let us know. She's reaching that age, you know?'

'So, Henry Christie?' Danny asked, seeking confirmation.

'Yeah . . . He won't bite your head off.'

'OK, whatever.'

As Jake made that call, Anna had been trying Emma again, but without success.

Jake suggested, 'Let's go to the pick-up point in Lancaster, just in case she's still there . . . I know,' he said, seeing Anna's 'as if' expression. 'But just in case. If she isn't there, we'll head home.' Anna nodded, and Jake said, 'Be nothing, just a teenage thing.'

They stood up, collected their belongings, then hurried out to the car park, not noticing the man in the café, who had arrived only moments after them, stand up and follow them.

Before leaving the house, Danny had the good sense to find a piece of A4 paper and scrawl on it in big, fat, felt tip letters: 'EM – CALL ME OR MUM URGENTLY.' He signed it and Sellotaped it to the front door, before pulling on his zip-up jacket and trainers to jog down to the Tawny Owl to see Henry Christie, who was already hovering at the front door of the pub, waiting for him.

'I've spoken to your dad,' Henry said quickly, pulling on his jacket. 'He's put me in the picture . . . I'm sure it'll be fine, usually is . . . So I'm going over to Thornwell, and I take it you're coming with me?'

'If you don't mind.'

Henry led him to his battered Audi coupé. 'Hop in.'

'Didn't realize this was yours,' Danny said, folding himself in. 'What happened?'

'It got assaulted,' Henry explained mysteriously. 'Long story, but it still works, and I've fixed all the leaks.' He fired it up, skidded off the car park and turned towards Thornwell.

'She always answers me.'

'I know,' Jake said.

'Could she have had an accident?'

'I don't know, love.'

'It's not like her.' Panic was starting to make Anna's voice tremble.

'I know, but you and I both also know from experience that when kids go missing, the parents always say, "It's not like our Johnny," because they simply don't know the half of little Johnny's life. And kids can be very, very secretive. She might have a boyfriend we don't know about.' Jake sighed. 'It happens.'

Anna nodded, but was not convinced. She was certain she knew all the ins and outs of Emma's

226

life, and even if she didn't and Emma was starting to lead some sort of double life, her daughter wouldn't be stupid enough to not answer the phone, arousing suspicions.

Jake came off the motorway at Junction 34 and turned towards Lancaster. To make it as easy as possible in the traffic snarl-up that was the city, the usual arrangement was that Danny and Emma walked from their respective schools down to Parliament Street. This meant the taxi driver did not have to battle the one-way system, but could simply loop around and pick them up, then head back along the A683 towards their home.

So far that plan had worked.

As Jake approached the north of the city along the A683, the road forked, and at the first set of proper traffic lights he bore right, so he was effectively coming back on himself on Parliament Street, where Emma was supposed to have been waiting.

There was no sign of her as Jake stopped. Neither of them spoke, and they could not prevent that horrid sensation of parental dread – normal, they knew, when children were unaccounted for – from engulfing them.

'She'll be OK,' Jake said hopefully.

Anna's face creased worriedly. 'It's just not like her.'

'I know, I know,' he conceded as that pit-of-the-guts feeling started to shred his insides. It was an almost indescribable terror.

He tried to control his breathing and the dithering shake of his hands.

'Call her again,' he said to Anna.

'I just have done.'

'Do it again.'

Anna's thumb did a little dance on the face of her iPhone and redialled Emma's number.

It went instantly to voicemail. Anna looked at Jake just as a text landed. She looked at the screen. 'Oh, thank God,' she said, breathing a sigh of relief. 'It's from her.'

She slid a fingertip across the screen to open the message, which she read, and then could not stop an animal-like utterance escaping from her mouth. She clasped a hand over her mouth and said, muffled, 'Oh my God,' into the palm of her hand.

'What?' Jake snatched the phone from her, read the text.

There were just two words:

Help me.

Henry drove quickly over to Thornwell with Danny alongside him, lost in worried thoughts about his sister. Henry wanted to make small talk, but decided against it. One of the most irritating things a person can do to another when they're fretting about something is chatter away.

The journey took about eight minutes, and he soon was driving past the Swan's Neck and on to the road beyond, where KountryKabs had their office. It was actually on a small, fairly decrepit industrial estate, the office being in a small unit in a row of similar ones. There was a roller door, next to which was an office door with a sign over it bearing the name of the firm. From his previous dealings with the firm when Laura Marshall had gone missing, Henry knew that, inside, the unit was set up as a garage/repair shop for the taxi cabs owned by the firm, of which there were about six in operation, Henry seemed to recall. The firm, run by a creepy guy called Owen Overwall, seemed to have cornered the rural market for taxi rides. Overwall also ran a couple of coaches and minibuses from the unit.

The place was in darkness as Henry drew up on the forecourt.

Henry also knew that around the back end of this industrial estate was the abattoir owned by Spencer Bartle – behind which was Bartle's farm, although Bartle himself lived in a house in Thornwell. Henry had visited the abattoir and Bartle's home a few times, and had even searched the places, whilst investigating Laura's disappearance. He had not been happy with Overwall backing up Bartle's alibi for the night in question. Overwall had said that he'd picked up Bartle in a taxi from outside the Swan's Neck and that they had actually passed Laura's police car on their way to Lancaster. Because of Overwall's evidence, Henry hadn't been able to break Bartle's alibi.

'Bugger,' Henry said, sighing when he saw the office was obviously closed. Nevertheless, he got out of his car and went to the office door, rapping on it loudly. The sound of the knocking echoed beyond. Danny was behind him. 'No one home.'

Henry got out his phone and called the taxicab number, which was still on his contact list. It was a mobile number and went straight through to voicemail, which, he thought, was not great practise for a taxi-firm.

229

'Must be busy, out and about,' Henry mused. He tried the office door, through force of habit. It was locked, as was the roller-shutter door which he also rattled and tried to drag up.

'We need to speak to them, to see if Emma was at the pick-up point,' Danny said.

'Yep,' Henry said, thinking. 'Let's head back, Dan. I'll drop you off at home, then I'll come back here and sit outside the place until something happens one way or the other.'

'Why should I go back?' Danny asked as they got back into the Audi and set off.

'Just in case Emma does turn up. I think it would be better if someone was there.'

Danny shrugged. 'Whatever.'

'Your mum and dad might be home now, anyway, and if they are, we can work out what to do for the best,' Henry said as his mobile phone rang. It was back in his jeans pocket, and he had to contort to fish it out and answer it.

'Henry, it's Jake.'

'Yeah, you got any news?'

'Yeah . . . got a text from Emma.'

'Thank God,' Henry said, glancing at Danny and giving him a smile and a nod, but at the same time he could hear the tension in Jake's voice. 'I take it she's OK?'

'No . . . no, I don't think so. The text said, "Help me." We called her back, but couldn't get through.'

'Right – where are you now?'

'Halfway between Lancaster and Kendleton.'

'OK, I'm more or less back in Kendleton with Dan. There was no sign of life at the cab firm . . .

230

I'm thinking of dropping Dan off at your house then heading back to Thornwell and sitting outside KountryKabs until someone shows or I hear anything different. I think getting the taxi firm's story is the key to this, the starting point, and then we can take it from there.'

'Yeah,' Jake agreed. 'If they went to pick her up and she wasn't there, why haven't they told us? And where the hell is she?'

'Exactly.'

There was a pause, then Jake asked Henry, 'D'you think we're reading too much into this? Overreacting?'

Henry didn't have to think for one second about his response. 'No. If it's all OK and she turns up safe and well, bollock her . . . If it's otherwise,' he said bleakly, 'let's not be playing catch-up.'

'I'm glad you think that,' Jake said with relief.

'I'm at yours now,' Henry said, pulling up outside the police house.

'And?'

'Still in darkness.'

The man had easily followed Jake and Anna from the motorway services. He was curious as to why they had come off the motorway, driven to the outskirts of Lancaster and looped around, before heading back under the motorway, going first towards Caton, and then, when they were beyond that village, cutting right towards Kendleton.

Curious, but not concerned. All he had to do was keep up with them until they arrived home, wherever that was.

As soon as they were there, he would allow them to settle before moving in for the kill.

Henry went into Jake's house with Danny just to have a quick check, even though it seemed obvious that Emma wasn't home. He did a few cursory searches, watched by a slightly bemused Danny.

With Danny's permission, he looked in Emma's wardrobe and under her bed, and repeated the process in Danny's bedroom, then Jake and Anna's. Anywhere a slim teenage girl might fit.

'What are you looking for?' Danny asked.

'Emma,' Henry said. From experience he knew that any missing person inquiry, if this was going to be that, had to start at home. He had known too many instances where a police officer taking an initial report of a misper had circulated details countrywide only to find the person had been hiding at home. As a uniformed PC, Henry had once attended the report of an eight-year-old girl missing, and before he'd even begun to fill out any forms he had insisted on looking around the house. He found her playing with her dolls in the garden shed, the door of which had somehow slammed shut and locked her inside. She had not noticed because she'd been too engrossed in serving tea to Barbie. 'Bread and butter basic,' Henry had said.

He looked in the shed too now, but Emma wasn't in there playing with dolls. 'You have to check these places,' he explained.

'I get it,' Danny said.

'OK, Dan, I'm going back to Thornwell. You stay here, and if she turns up, be nice to her.'

'Can't promise that.'

'I know. You're her brother. Brothers are nasty to sisters.'

'And the other way round.'

Henry left him on the threshold at the front door and drove away.

The roller-shutter doors were descending the last few inches when Henry drove on to the forecourt of the taxi unit on the industrial estate.

He heard the door clatter on the ground as he got out of his car and could see a line of light along the bottom. He slammed his car door and walked to the shutter, slapping it with the palm of his hand, making it rattle loudly.

The light inside went off.

Henry stood back, then kicked the door, making it rattle even more loudly.

He heard footsteps from inside.

He banged again, then walked along to the office door and rang the doorbell and kicked that door also at the same time.

He heard the door being unlocked, a bolt being slid back, a chain being released, then the door opened a fraction.

'What?' came the voice from inside.

'Need a word,' Henry said to the one eye he could see.

'Sorry, closed.'

Henry jammed his foot in the door just in case. 'Need a word, I said.' His tone of voice dropped an octave.

There was an audible sigh, then the door opened to reveal the man Henry recognized as Owen Overwall, proprietor of the taxi firm.

'What do you want?' he asked Henry wearily, adjusting his rimless glasses.

'Remember me, Mr Overwall . . .?'

'No.'

'Henry Christie. I spoke to you with regard to the disappearance of PC Laura Marshall, if you recall?'

Overwall gave a non-caring shrug.

'Need to speak to you again.'

'As I said, we're closed.'

'And as I said, I need to talk to you.' Henry smiled at him, enjoying himself in spite of the scenario. 'And isn't it a bit odd being closed? I thought you were a taxi firm . . . It's still only just after tea time.'

'My business is out on the road, not in here.'

'Let me come in, and let's have a chat,' Henry insisted fairly politely. He was now getting annoyed by this man who, when he had interviewed him previously, had not impressed him. He placed a hand on the door, and that, plus the foot in the door, made his intentions clear.

'No, I don't have time,' Overwall insisted.

'You need to make time . . . I want to talk to you about another missing girl.' Henry looked at Overwall's face, but saw nothing flinch.

'I thought we'd already had that discussion?'

'Like I said . . . a different one,' Henry said.

With great reluctance, Overwall stood back and opened the door.

Henry's 'thank you' was sarcastic.

234

They stood in the corridor. To the right was the door for the taxi office; next along was a door to a toilet; then at the far end was the door leading into the garage/workshop. Next to Henry, on his left, was a large window that looked into the garage. Henry could see four cars parked up, fairly tightly packed, but with some space available, including the white Skoda which Overwall must just have driven in. Henry recognized it as the same vehicle Overwall had allegedly picked up Spencer Bartle with and then driven him into Lancaster on the night Laura disappeared.

'So what can I do for you?' Overwall asked dully and without interest.

'You were due to pick up Emma Niven from Lancaster this afternoon, three forty-five p.m. in Parliament Street. Part of an ongoing contract.'

Overwall nodded to this statement. Henry shrugged to encourage a response, which, when it came, was: 'Yuh.'

Overwall was small, rodent-like, with a pinched face and harsh features, his eyes like black holes.

'And?' Henry said. 'Look, don't mess me around, just answer the question. It's not exactly hard.'

'She wasn't there.'

'And – again?' Henry pumped him.

'And what? She wasn't there. What am I supposed to do about it?'

Henry nodded thoughtfully. 'Can I have a look at the car?' He pointed through the window at the white Skoda. Overwall shrugged, and Henry took that as a yes. He walked along the corridor into the garage, followed by the taxi owner, who was close behind him as he walked around the car. Henry said, 'You are contracted to pick her up from home, take her to school, pick her up from school, drop her at home. Am I right?'

Overwall said nothing, did not blink, but Henry could see his mind working.

'She's fourteen and she wasn't there, is that what you're saying, even though you're not saying very much?' Henry asked.

'That's exactly what I'm saying.'

'Did you try to contact her or her parents?'

'No, why should I?'

'Because she's fourteen,' Henry said, starting to sound dangerous as his patience began to grow thin.

'Look, I haven't got the time or the money to chase up fares who don't turn up. I just haven't.'

Henry heard another car draw up outside the unit, saw the flash of headlights under the roller-shutter, probably parking alongside his Audi. He half-assumed it might be Jake.

'Can I have a look, then?' Henry said, indicating the Skoda he was prowling around.

'Help yourself.'

They were two words that made Henry think Overwall believed himself to be on solid ground here and that there was nothing of interest in the car. He opened the rear door, leaned in over the back seat, pushed the seat cushion down and ran his fingers into the gap, found nothing. He looked in the magazine racks on the back of the front seats, both clear, as were the trays in each door.

He pulled himself up and glanced at Overwall, whose rat features were impassive. 'So she wasn't there and you didn't give a flying fuck?' Henry accused him.

'Long and short of it. Maybe I should've, but I didn't.'

Henry stared with disbelief at the man as these words exited his mouth, wondering if he believed them or if he just did not want to believe them.

'OK,' Henry said at length.

'That it, then?'

'For the time being.'

Henry stalked back into the corridor, noticing that the office door was closed and there was a light on inside. He stepped out on to the forecourt.

'Hang on a minute,' Overwall said.

Henry stopped and turned, but at the same time saw that the car that had pulled up next to his Audi was another KountryKabs taxi, a white Skoda, same model as the one in the garage, the one he'd just looked through.

'I've just remembered something,' Overwall went on. 'You're not a cop any more, are you? You fuckin' live at the Owl with that slag of a landlady . . . So what're you up to, pretending to be a cop?'

'I never said I was a cop,' Henry informed him. 'You just made the assumption.'

'You sneaky turd.'

'Hey, if the cap fits,' Henry said, and pointed accusingly at Overwall. 'That said, I don't think you've seen the last of me, or the real cops.' He spun, intending to go to his car, but stopped short, and a feeling of terrible dread flooded through him as he eyed the Skoda on the forecourt.

He walked to it, checking the registration plate, peered in through the windows, shading his eyes with his hand, edging along the car until he was looking into the back seats. Squinting, he saw something in the footwell, square and white. An iPhone.

'Fuck,' he said, stood upright and turned back to Overwall.

At that exact moment, something very long, hard and heavy struck him on the side of the head, just between his left eye socket and ear. Although the effect was almost instantaneous – the jellying of his legs – in the nanosecond before he became unconscious and crumpled to the floor like a parachutist hitting the ground, the last thing he saw was Spencer Bartle's face screwed up with the effort of having just smashed Henry across the head with a crowbar.

Fifteen

Even though Rik Dean's field promotion (albeit to an acting rank) into Henry Christie's still-warm shoes had not been something he had purposely engineered, and although Henry had 'sort of' forgiven him, the relationship between the two men remained strained. Henry had not even invited Rik to his little retirement soirée, which had wounded the younger man.

Henry had looked after Rik's career since he'd been a PC, and it must have hurt Henry badly to have lost his job to him; it was the ultimate irony. Henry had tried to keep a fairly objective perspective on it – mostly – but behind his eyes, Rik could see pain.

Obviously, Rik dreamed of becoming a detective superintendent, which was probably the ultimate job for any ambitious jack – to be a Senior Investigating Officer in charge of what essentially was a murder squad. However, Rik found himself unprepared for the role and soon began to sink, at the same time as being amazed at how Henry had coped with it all.

As well as the disappearance of Laura Marshall, he had inherited what remained of the Jamie Turner murder case, the Wayne Oxford courtroom murder, and the Fraser Worthington shooting, with all the baggage that came with that, including Dave Morton's death. If that was not enough, a new murder had come in, a serious robbery had been committed and he was also expected to assume Henry's role on two national CID forums, as well as deliver daily briefings to the chief constable, plus everything else that came with the rank. All stuff that Henry seemed to have strolled through, but now Rik realized it was probably the 'duck on water' syndrome.

He was wallowing in the mire with no one at his shoulder to guide him, as pathetic as that sounded. To cap it all, he didn't seem to be faring much better than Henry in regards to Laura Marshall's disappearance, and if Rik had thought he could pick Henry's brain, he had been way off the mark.

Henry had simply withdrawn to the Tawny Owl to pull pints, shag the landlady and generally ignore Rik, who, although realizing that pride came before a fall, could not bring himself to pick up the phone, call Henry and say, 'Pretty please.'

So Henry's call out of the blue had been welcome, even if the conversation had been stilted and tinged with bitterness.

Rik looked now at the names Henry had given him: Rebecca Merryweather and Grace Greenwood. Two teenage girls missing from North Yorkshire.

'How the hell have you pulled these two out of the hat?' Rik muttered as he searched for the number of North Yorkshire Police and asked to be put in contact with the officer leading the search for the first girl.

Twenty minutes after that, Rik was then

speaking to the OIC of the investigation into Grace Greenwood's disappearance – still in North Yorkshire, but in a different division.

Not long after that he plunged into the National Missing From Home Database. As he trawled through the results chucked up by his search criteria, a cold chill pervaded his body and he said, 'You brilliant bastard, Henry.'

This utterance was because of the fact that both of the officers Rik had spoken to had run their fingers down a list of people, witnesses or otherwise, who had been interviewed by the police on the other side of the Pennines, and whilst there were names that cropped up on both lists because they were farmers, legitimately going about their business, buying and selling livestock, one name stood out like a shining beacon.

Spencer Bartle.

He wasn't on a suspect list; he'd just been in the vicinity on or around the actual dates the girls went missing.

Rik tried to keep calm as he logged into Lancashire Constabulary's Intel database and searched for the dates and times that Bartle had been arrested.

It was a fairly busy list. He had been arrested eight times over the last twelve months, resulting in six court appearances for drunken behaviour or breach of the peace, none of which had landed him with anything another than fines or conditional discharges.

Rik printed off the list and compared the dates of the arrests to the disappearances of the teenagers.

He swore again, snatched up his phone and called Henry's mobile. There was no reply, so he called the landline at the Tawny Owl, which was answered by Alison.

'Henry there?' he asked after the preliminaries.

'No, he's out and about. You know Jake Niven, our new Bobby?' she asked, and Rik said yes (how could he not know?). 'Apparently, his daughter's gone missing, so Henry's just making a few enquiries.'

'How d'you mean, missing?'

'I'm not sure, Rik . . . She didn't get the taxi back from school in Lancaster, or something.'

'So where is Henry?'

'Gone to Thornwell, I think.'

'Uh . . .' Rik had a thought. 'Which taxi firm?'

'Our local KountryKabs.'

That was a name that rang a suspicious bell with Rik. 'Right, thanks,' he said dubiously and hung up. His eyes fell back to the lists in front of him: Bartle's arrests, and the dates the young women or girls had gone missing. He saw that Bartle's most recent arrest was just three days ago; he was locked up in Lancaster for being fighting drunk and had been fined at court the next day. 'Surely not,' he said, thinking about what he'd just heard concerning Emma Niven.

He grabbed his PR, coat and mobile phone and dashed to his car.

Jake swerved into the driveway, the family car rocking as he slammed the brakes on, and parked next to the police Land Rover. He and Anna were inside the house moments later, Jake calling for Danny as they burst through the front door.

Danny appeared at the living room door, looking pale.

'Is she back?' Jake demanded.

Danny shook his head.

Anna pushed past Jake and hugged her son.

'How did you get on with Henry?' Jake asked over Anna's shoulder.

'Went across to the taxi firm, but it was closed up,' Danny said with a release of breath when Anna let go of him. 'He dropped me off, and he's gone back over. He also searched the house.'

Jake took this in, then asked Danny if he had the phone numbers for any of Emma's friends.

Danny scrunched up his face and shook his head.

'I know some from Blackpool,' Anna said. 'I could probably find their number and call them, check if she's met up with any of them or spoken to them and told them she was up to something.' Anna lowered her eyes and looked at Danny. 'Is she up to anything? Has she got a boyfriend or something?'

'Not that I know of.'

Jake's mind was on the verge of exploding. 'OK,' he said fairly decisively. 'Are you staying here? I'm going to leap into the Land Rover and get over to Thornwell, too. I really need to speak face-to-face with that taxi guy.'

'We'll be OK here,' Anna said, taking Jake's hand and squeezing it. 'I'll start phoning.'

Jake exhaled. His eyes criss-crossed from Anna to Danny: two of the three most important people in his life. His family – something he would never forget again. 'Let's just put this into perspective,' he said as calmly as he could. 'It's only a couple of hours down the line. Chances are, it's just a teenage kid thing, so let's keep our heads and not panic. We do what we have to . . . She'll be fine.'

Anna nodded, but her maternal instinct told her otherwise.

Jake hugged her tightly for a moment, patted Danny on the shoulder, left the house and, still wearing his best suit and shoes, got into the short-wheelbase Land Rover that came with the job. The constabulary had found it in some forgotten corner of a garage at headquarters and provided it for the beat, as opposed to giving Jake a car allowance, which would have let him use his own car for the job. The powers that be had decided that giving him a battered old Land Rover with over 100,000 miles on the clock was the cheaper option. It was a pig to drive, uncomfortable and as chilly as the Arctic, but it was liveried with an old-style constabulary crest on each door and was still great for going places he would never have attempted to take a normal car.

He fired up and reversed out of the driveway, hurtled down to Kendleton and stopped at the Tawny Owl. He could not see Henry's Audi in the front car park where it was usually kept. All the same, Jake popped in to check. Alison confirmed Henry was not back yet, and without any further conversation, Jake got back into the Land Rover and set off towards Thornwell.

He was at the taxi office ten minutes later,

finding it in darkness, no vehicles outside, not even Henry's, which made him scowl worriedly. On the way across from Kendleton he had not seen any other cars on the road, so he was puzzled as to Henry's location.

He called the taxi firm from his mobile – no reply; then he tried Henry – and got no reply either. He slid out of the Land Rover and knocked on the office door, pounded hard on the roller-shutters. Another no reply, causing his frustration to mount. He was about to get into the Land Rover when a car swung into the industrial estate and pulled on to the forecourt, its headlight beam sweeping across, briefly lighting up a dark shadow of something in the surface of the concrete that looked like a diesel spill.

The car lights were turned off. Jake waited for the driver to get out.

It was Rik Dean.

'Jake.'

'Hello, sir.'

'Call me Rik, please.'

Jake gave a little shrug, not really caring what he wanted to be called. 'Sir' was good enough for Jake, who tended to keep his distance from senior officers if at all possible. He'd had some dealings with Rik over the last few months in connection with Oxford and Worthington and thought he was an OK boss, though nothing outstanding. He certainly didn't fill Henry Christie's shoes. But Jake didn't hold that one against him. He wasn't sure anyone could.

'What's the latest?' Rik asked him.

'On which bit?'

245

'Your daughter? Henry?' Rik said.

'Both missing now,' Jake stated. 'My daughter should've been picked up by this shower of a taxi firm in Lancaster after school, but wasn't, and I haven't been able to speak to the firm. Henry came across from the Owl to speak to the owner, but he isn't here now. No one's here. Er . . . what are *you* doing here, by the way?'

'It's a circuitous story, and I'm not sure if the dots are connected yet.'

Jake stared blankly at him, baffled by the words.

Rik caught the look and said, 'Anyway, I'm here, and I need to speak to Henry urgently about . . .' He was going to say 'the disappearance of girls', but stopped short because Jake was clearly not listening.

Jake had had a quick thought. He reached into the cab of the Land Rover for his torch, turned it on and flashed the beam across the concrete forecourt on to the dark stain he had seen when Rik arrived.

Initially, he'd thought it was oil or diesel. Nothing unusual in that – there were several dark patches of both on the concrete – but there was also another patch of liquid, and it was neither of those two. He walked over to it and bounced on to his haunches with Rik at his shoulder, curious.

'Fuck,' Rik said.

'Yeah,' Jake agreed, standing stiffly back up.

The two men looked at each other. Both knew what bloodstains looked like.

'Could mean nothing,' Rik said.

Jake shook his head. 'Too much of it *not* to mean something. Someone's been hurt here.'

246

'Let's kick off with the premise that it does mean something,' Rik said.

Rik shuffled out his mobile phone and called Henry's number. It went straight to voicemail again, so he called Alison at the Tawny Owl, and she told him Henry still was not back.

'Right,' Rik said decisively, 'let's kick a door in.'

Jake attempted to force up the roller-shutter door, but it was impossible to move. Whilst he did this, Rik put his shoulder to the front door of the taxi office and found that it, too, was well locked and resolute.

They looked at each other. Jake indicated for Rik to stand aside whilst he braced himself, raised his right foot and flat-footed the door hard, just under the lock. It rattled slightly at the frame, but, essentially, did not budge.

He did the same again and got the same result.

This door was not going to succumb to human strength.

Jake paused, got his breath back, then looked sideways at the Land Rover, which had a towing ball fitted to the back bumper, protruding maybe eight or ten inches from the rear of the vehicle. He got in, reversed off the forecourt and swung it round to face away from the door, then lined it up, selected reverse and rammed his foot down. He wanted to hit the door with the tow-ball, but not cause damage to the building or the Land Rover.

Rik watched, wondering – as superintendents do – how much this was going to cost. He winced as the tow bar connected with the door. Fortunately, it had the desired effect first time, and the door flew open.

Jake pulled away, stopped and alighted, and the two cops entered the unlit unit.

Rik found a bank of light switches and ran the side of his hand down them. The interior lights flickered on, one by one, lighting first the corridor, and then the garage on the other side of the viewing window, illuminating all the cars parked up therein.

Both men stood at this window, looking into the garage from the corridor, made speechless by what they saw.

The last car to have been driven in was a silver-grey Audi coupé which bore the marks, dents and scratches of having been 'assaulted'.

Henry's car.

Sixteen

Henry Christie regained consciousness slowly and painfully. His skull was a cracked-up concoction of disorientation and swirling blackness, and for a fleeting moment he thought he was back in a deep, flooded tunnel. Yet, from somewhere, he could hear the sound of voices – two men – arguing.

As his senses returned, the side of his head throbbing and pulsing from the blow delivered by the crowbar, he could feel the deep gouge of the cut it had caused, and even in the haze of nausea, he realized he was lucky to have survived such an assault. He had dealt with people who had died from receiving a single blow from such an instrument.

He kept his eyes tightly closed. His head was as heavy as if it was filled with lead, and he could taste his own salty blood on his tongue. He tried to make sense of what was happening and what had happened.

At that moment he knew only the answer to that last question.

He recalled seeing the taxi parked on the forecourt, looking inside and seeing what looked like an iPhone in the rear footwell, then looking at the number plate and turning accusingly back to Overwall.

Except Overwall was not there.

249

It was Spencer Bartle, and his arm was elevated and arcing down towards Henry's head with the crowbar in his hand. Henry did not even have time to raise his own forearm in defence to try and deflect the blow. Clearly, he hadn't, because Bartle had smashed the crowbar across Henry's head in a truly stunning blow that had sent a shock wave through him and poleaxed him into oblivion, from which he was now surfacing.

Although he tried not to, he emitted a groan.

The two voices stopped instantly. They knew he was awake.

More clarity returned to Henry's head, and he opened his eyes, which were crusted over with his own blood, but there was nothing to see. He realized that he had a hood or a sack pulled over his head and he was actually hanging upside down like a bat.

He tried to squirm to free himself, but as even more clarity came back, he realized his legs had been taped tight together at the knees and ankles, and his hands were fastened behind his back; he was trussed up like a rolled carpet.

He stopped moving, knowing he did not have the strength to break free, and sensed someone standing close to him. He strained to listen, but his ears were blocked, he assumed, with his own coagulated blood, and they hissed like bad tinnitus.

Something touched him, then with a flourish the hood was whipped from his head.

And Henry screamed as the steaming-hot head of a dead horse swung towards him, with its massive purple tongue lolling obscenely out of

250

its mouth, fresh blood dribbling from his wide nostrils.

Henry tried to writhe out of the way, but the horse's head crashed into his face, hard, smearing him with its thick blood and other disgusting fluids. He screamed again in horror as the huge, brown head swung away, then back into his face again, crashing into him, causing him to cringe with revulsion. It swung away again, and Henry steeled himself for another contact, but this time the head was replaced by Spencer Bartle's face as he squatted down in front of Henry with a cruel, terrible expression on his face and placed the muzzle of a captive bolt gun against Henry's forehead.

'What the hell have you done that for?' Owen Overwall had demanded of Spencer Bartle as he stared numbly down at the prone, unmoving body of Henry Christie on the forecourt of the unit, blood gushing out of the massive cut Bartle had inflicted in Henry's temple. 'I had it under control, you freaking idiot.'

Bartle's face was engorged with his own pulsating blood pounding through his body as he towered over Henry's prostrate form, the crowbar dangling from his right hand. He panted with the exertion of delivering the blow; he'd put everything he had into it.

'Had it coming,' Bartle gasped and turned malevolently to Overwall, who shied away slightly. 'Bastard was harassin' me.'

'He's not even a fucking cop any more.'

'And that's the beauty of it . . . No one'll be

looking for him; not for a while . . . Gives us time to sort him.'

'Is he still alive?' Overwall stared at the amount of blood collecting under Henry's head.

Bartle knelt down and inspected Henry. 'Yeah, still breathing, sort of.' He grimaced, hearing Henry's snorting breaths. He turned slowly to Overwall, his face evil. 'Shall I just kill him? I could. I could do that.' He flaunted the crowbar. 'Just smash his head to nothing? I could.'

'I know you could, but no. Not here, at least . . . Someone might spot blood and brains all over the place.'

'Yeah, you're right.' Bartle sounded disappointed, then flashed a smile – although 'flashed' was pushing it slightly. His mouth was crammed with brown and black misshapen teeth. 'I wanna have some fun with him first, anyway.'

'Get him in the boot. We'll stick his car in the garage for the time being,' Overwall said.

Bartle clicked the remote unlock for the boot of the Skoda, then picked up Henry's legs between his armpits and dragged him to the back of the taxi, scraping his head along the concrete. He dropped the legs before heaving Henry into a ragdoll sitting position, then scooped him up, arms under his armpits, lifted him and rocked his body over so the top portion of Henry's torso overbalanced into the empty boot. He completed the task by pulling up Henry's legs and shoving them in next.

'I need his car keys,' Overwall said.

Bartle went through Henry's pockets, found the keys for the Audi and tossed them to Overwall, who was already opening the shutter door. There was just enough space in the garage behind the other Skoda to squeeze in the Audi and close the shutter.

By the time Overwall had done this, switched off all the lights and locked up the unit, Bartle was in the driving seat of the taxi, the engine ticking over.

Overwall slid into the passenger seat and noticed Henry's blood staining the front of Bartle's jacket. 'You'll need to get rid of that.' Overwall pointed at the jacket.

'Yup – but we're good at that, aren't we?'

Then, with Henry out cold in the boot, Bartle reversed off the forecourt, spun the car around and floored the accelerator.

There wasn't far to go.

He drove to the far, bleak, back corner of the industrial estate, through the gates of Bartle's abattoir, and pulled up by the unloading bay. Bartle whizzed the car around with a flourish and drove backwards to the door. He yanked on the handbrake, stopping the car with a rocking lurch, and laughed hysterically at the thudding noise made by Henry's body rolling sloppily around in the boot. He climbed out, opened the boot and dragged the loose-limbed form of his victim out by grabbing the front of his jacket. With Henry under one arm he half carried, half dragged him through the front door of the abattoir – similar to Overwall's taxi unit, but much larger – and along the corridor through to the abattoir itself. He then went further into the building, to a huge, cold storage room where dozens of animal

253

carcases hung down from sliding rails on meat hooks: sheep, pigs and horses.

Without requiring any assistance from Overwall, the big, strong Bartle trussed Henry up with duct tape, fastening his legs together and pulling and securing his arms behind his back. Then he fitted a sack over his head with a tie at the throat, and hung him head down from one of the hooks, so that Henry swung there next to a dead horse.

Other than the fact he was dealing with a human being, this was the sort of work Bartle did almost every day, without effort.

Satisfied, he looked at Overwall, who had watched the process, and smiled. 'Every time I see this guy, he waves at me.'

'And that's harassment?'

'Good as.'

Overwall considered Bartle, then asked plaintively, 'What exactly have you done?'

Bartle grinned widely, and although he knew what Overwall meant, he replied, 'What d'you mean?'

'I mean, where is she?'

'Where is who?' he teased.

'You know . . . I asked you to step in and help me out cos my regular driver didn't show and I was busy . . . then when this bastard came snooping and asking awkward questions it became bloody obvious, bloody quickly, that you'd taken the girl you were supposed to pick up and drop off at home. A cop's daughter, for fuck's sake. I had to ad-lib like mad . . . I can put two and two together!' Overwall's voice started to rise.

'So what? I'd got to that point again,' Bartle

said mournfully. He bunched his fists and held them against his chest, over his heart. 'When I needed to do something.'

'You can't just take who you want, when you want, Spence, just because you're starting to feel it.' Overwall mimicked him by crossing his arms over his own chest and bunching his fists. 'And especially not my customers. These things have to be thought out.'

'You haven't complained before.' Bartle smirked knowingly.

'We don't shit on our own doorstep.'

'What about the cop-woman?'

'Again, risky . . . Cops're still sniffing around. They will be forever, mate . . . Jeez, you got to control yourself.'

'Sometimes I can't.'

Overwall shook his head and closed his eyes. 'We've been lucky so far.'

'Like I said, you didn't complain,' Bartle said with his nostrils flaring. 'She was too good to miss today, and so what if she's a cop's kid? What did you tell him?' Bartle thumbed at Henry's upside-down body. 'Not that it matters; he isn't going to tell anyone, not going to get the chance.'

Bartle picked up a captive bolt gun from the floor. It was dirty, blood caked, animal hairs bristling around the muzzle.

'This has gone too far, Spencer,' Overwall whined.

'Stop moaning. You—' Bartle shoved the barrel of the gun into Overwall's chest – 'have had your fun. It'll be right . . . No one'll ever find him

. . . You know how good I am at disposing of bodies.'

That was the moment at which Henry groaned and regained consciousness. They turned to look, and Bartle pulled the hood off Henry's head and cruelly swung the horse's head into his face; the hanging man screamed like a baby as the bloodied head of the dead beast smashed disgustingly into his face twice, then was replaced by Bartle staring at him and the captive bolt gun being skewered into his forehead.

'Mr Christie,' Bartle said.

Henry glared at the upside-down face. 'You need to let me go.'

Bartle guffawed. 'Nah.'

'People know I'm here.'

'What? Here? In my slaughterhouse? I don't think so.'

'They know I went to see your mate.' Henry's eyes shifted to Overwall.

'So what? Let me tell you this.' Bartle removed the muzzle from Henry's head. 'By the time anyone figures anything out, you won't even exist, Mr Christie. You'll have been dismembered – professionally, obviously – and minced, your flesh ground up and your bones gone to dust,' he said, relishing every word, 'and in about a week's time, some poor fucker is going to buy a meat pie from their local butcher, thinking it's beef, but it won't be. It'll be horse meat and human flesh – yours. Yummy!' He held the captive bolt gun in front of Henry's eyes. 'Know what this is?'

Henry did an upside-down nod.

'I've been using one of these since I was twelve.'

'Congratulations.'

'This is a penetrating one.'

'OK.'

Henry knew about captive bolt guns: a device used to stun animals prior to their slaughter, though he always thought the use of the word 'stun' was arguable. The one that Bartle had in his hand used a bolt that penetrated the skull of the animal, into the cranium, and smashed into the brain, basically destroying that organ – hence Henry's dispute with 'stun'. The animal was essentially dead, but the brain stem remained intact, so the heart could continue to beat during the bleeding process to make it flow out easier.

This piece of usually useless information was confirmed by Bartle.

'It'll smash the fuck out of your brain, then when I cut your throat you'll bleed out like a stuck pig.'

'OK,' Henry said again. 'Is that what you did with Laura Marshall?'

'Who? Her from today?'

'The policewoman.'

'Nah, why would I do that? Not yet, anyway.'

It didn't help Henry that his soon to be destroyed brain was already a mush from being whacked with a length of iron, so he was puzzled. 'She's still alive?'

'My harem,' Bartle said proudly and winked at Henry, then glanced at Overwall. 'Our harem.'

'And the one from today?' Henry asked.

'Too good to miss, that one. Little girl, all alone,

in the back of my taxi . . . She's on tonight's menu.'

'I don't believe you haven't killed her,' Henry challenged him. 'You've killed them both, haven't you?'

'Nah, why should I? Not yet, anyway,' Bartle said, as though offended.

'Show me,' Henry demanded. 'Before you kill me, show me.'

Bartle considered the request. 'OK.'

'Jeez, Spencer, what you playin' at?' Overwall asked. 'He's just tryin' to waste time . . . If you're going to kill him, get it done. The longer he stays alive, the more chance there is of us getting caught.'

'Show me,' Henry pleaded, seeing the possibility of Bartle changing his mind under pressure from his running mate. 'Like you said, why should anybody know I'm here? I'm tied up, can't go anywhere . . . I just want to know they're alive, that's all.' Truth was he was playing for time, even if it only meant delaying the inevitable, and he was purposely pandering to Bartle's obvious power trip. Bartle was a psychopath and proud of his achievements, however sick they were. Henry could only speculate, but he knew he had stumbled into something here that was very awful in the extreme. A *harem*? 'Show me,' he insisted again.

The two men looked at each other. Then Overwall said, 'I need to get his car. I can't leave it in the garage . . . If what he says is true and others know he went there, they'll come looking at some point. And I need to power wash that blood away.'

258

'You go, do that, then.' Bartle stood up. 'I'll give him a little display before I slit his throat and gut him.'

Rik and Jake stood by the open shutter door of the taxi unit. Jake was speaking into his PR, calling the comms room at Lancaster, trying to tell them concisely what had happened – his daughter had gone missing, and now Henry Christie had also disappeared, and though the incidents may or may not be connected, there was a genuine reason to be concerned for the welfare of both. He was requesting uniform to attend and for other bosses further up the chain of command to be informed.

As he was talking, trying to keep coherent and sensible despite his rising panic, he noticed a car approaching slowly from the rear of the industrial estate, headlights on. For a moment, Jake did not really focus on it; he was concentrating on getting what could be a vitally important radio message right, until he saw the small plastic sign on the roof. It was a taxi. Even though it was dark now, he recognized the car to be a Skoda and did the sums.

'Stand by,' he said into his radio. He stepped off the forecourt into the road, raised his right hand and flashed his torch at the car, which stopped twenty metres away from him.

Rik, who had watched this, started to walk diagonally towards it from the front door of the taxi unit, but Jake held back a shade, cautious.

'Out of the car,' Rik shouted on his approach. He was waving his mini-Maglite torch in one hand; in the other, he flashed his warrant card. 'Police officers! Out of the car,' he repeated.

When he was five metres from the car, the engine revved, and it shot past Rik and sped towards Jake, driving hard at him. He pirouetted out of its path like a bull fighter, managing to avoid its last moment swerve at him. The car missed him by inches. He caught a glimpse of a very grim faced Owen Overwall, gripping the steering wheel, with his body hunched tightly forwards.

Using the momentum of his spin, Jake sprinted back to the Land Rover and leapt in behind the wheel, restarting the old engine, which was fitted into a vehicle not designed to chase anything, let alone other cars. He crunched it into first and put his foot down, going after the Skoda.

The vehicle set off with a kangaroo jump, then Jake took it as far as it could go in first, making the engine scream horribly in protest, before he dropped into second, lurching sickeningly as the gears synchromeshed – just.

By this time the Skoda was swinging out of the industrial estate, heading towards Thornwell village, less than a quarter of a mile away.

Jake followed. The Land Rover skittered and rolled as he negotiated a tight bend into a narrow, dark road. Ahead, he saw the brake lights on the Skoda come on, then go off.

He forced his foot down on the accelerator, and it seemed to take a long time before the message to speed up was passed to, then received and acted upon by, the engine. Jake even had time to smack the steering wheel in frustration, but he also had the chance to call up comms and make them aware of the situation – which was about all he could do, because any back-up to help out was over twenty minutes away at best, by which time a wide variety of things could have happened.

Comms said they were going to call out the helicopter, India99, but Jake just shrugged at that. He guessed that might be fifteen minutes away at best.

On the outskirts of Thornwell, with the Swan's Neck on Jake's left, the Skoda had pulled well ahead. Jake was glad to see that Overwall had stuck to the road and gone all the way around the village green; Jake himself could go diagonally across it, even though he knew that the thick Land Rover tyres would leave deep ruts on the well-tended grass. He made up some distance by doing this, but was only halfway across the green by the time Overwall reached the Kendleton Road on the opposite side and was powering the Skoda up the hill and away.

Jake swore and tried to coax something more out of his vehicle. 'Come on, you crusty old git,' he yelled at it, then saw a red warning light pop up on the dashboard. He winced, chose to ignore it.

He bounced off the far side of the green on to Kendleton Road, having to select second for the hill ahead, knowing he had closed the gap a little on the taxi.

The road wound up – tight on some bends, unlit and not really suitable for any great speeds, particularly at night. It was a road that demanded skill and concentration. He rolled the Land Rover around the next bend, which unfurled into a long, straight stretch of road, bounded by sloping farmland on the left and a rising, stone-strewn banking on the right, from which rocks and boulders often rolled on to the carriageway.

He could see the rear lights of the Skoda about two hundred metres ahead and knew that Overwall was outgunning him. He almost gave the chase up at that point, believing it to be futile. It was only a transitory thought, though, and he jammed his foot down again, forcing, willing the lumbering square box on wheels to dig deep.

He flicked on the roof spotlights to illuminate the road ahead just as it dipped and fell, and he lost sight of the Skoda as it careened around a hairpin bend, with maybe a quarter of a mile to go before hitting Kendleton.

At the village boundary, Jake had a good open view of the centre with the Tawny Owl on the left, just a little further on than the butcher and general store, the only two shops.

The Skoda sped past the pub, and Jake used the incline to wheedle just a tad more speed out of the Land Rover, and to be on the safe side he flipped on the blue light.

Fortunately, the main street of Kendleton was just as deserted as Thornwell when the two vehicles screamed through.

Overwall chose the road that would take him up past Jake's police house, beyond which Jake knew that he would have little or no hope of catching Overwall, who, he guessed, would know all the ins and outs, highways and byways, whereas Jake was still pretty much a stranger to the area.

It wasn't that Overwall would not be caught and arrested at some time in the future – but that was no good to Jake.

He needed to speak to Overwall now. Later might be too late.

Henry hung upside down, swaying slightly, with his head about two inches from the floor, looking into the huge eyes of the dead horse. He raised his head and tried to look around the big, cold room. There were rows and rows of animal carcases, mostly gutted, skinned and prepared for sale. Others were not so far advanced. They were just gutted, their bellies hanging open, probably waiting their turn. He saw two deer carcases and knew they would have been poached from private land, probably from the Duke of Westminster's estate, which covered thousands of acres around this part of the world.

He struggled against his bonds, but they were tight and immovable. He quickly tired himself, and his vision swam with the effort and the pain in his head.

As soon as Overwall had gone, Bartle had said, 'You want to see, eh? OK, Mr Christie, I'll show you . . . You just hang on there.' He cackled mirthlessly at his own joke and left Henry straining to see where he went. He walked to the far end of the cold room, and Henry saw his feet disappear through a door.

He was back a short time later.

'Come on, ladies, do as you're told,' Henry heard him say.

There was a scraping noise, like chains being dragged. Twisting his head, Henry saw feet appear back through the same door.

There were four pairs of feet.

He recognized Bartle's boots.

And behind these were three pairs of naked, dirty, blood-caked feet.

Seventeen

Jake almost lost control of the Land Rover while hurtling around the right-hand bend just beyond the Tawny Owl. The vehicle skittered across the greasy road surface, but he wrestled with the heavy steering and righted it with a dramatic fishtail.

Overwall was still ahead, drawing easily away as he passed the police house.

Out of the corner of his eye Jake saw the lights in the house, the front door open, and Anna standing there, silhouetted, obviously awaiting the arrival home of her daughter, keeping a vigil.

She ran down the front steps, confused as Jake flew by.

Beyond the house the road ascended, then dropped into a fairly long straight stretch before becoming a twisting, turning labyrinth in which Jake knew he would lose Overwall for certain.

He was way ahead of the police car now, maybe 250 metres, his own headlights on full beam.

Even from this distance, Jake clearly saw what happened next.

Seemingly from nowhere, a magnificent red deer stag leapt from the blackness on the right, directly in front of Overwall's car. The huge beast was captured in all its full masculine glory in the main beam, and it spun its head to look directly

265

into the headlights, causing its eyes to shine ruby red.

Overwall's brake lights came on as he slammed the brakes on.

The stag remained as still as a magnificent carved bronze statue, staring defiantly into the lights. Jake was convinced that the Skoda was going to ram into the animal.

Two things happened simultaneously.

Overwall swerved violently to the left, his Skoda leaving the road and plunging into the dyke by the roadside. And the stag shook its head in some haughty gesture and, with a surge of power and strength, leapt off the road into the darkness and was gone.

'Our stag,' Jake said. 'Thank you.'

They were in chains. They were handcuffed, and another chain was threaded through the link between the cuffs and was in Bartle's hands.

Bartle dragged them, like a slave master, between the hanging carcases until all three were standing in front of Henry.

'You wanted to see. Here they are, Mr Christie.'

Even in his own sorry state, Henry was shocked by what he was looking at.

Emma was one of the three females, the only one fully dressed, but even so, what remained of her school uniform were rags, as if the clothing had been purposely torn. All she had on was her shirt and tiny pencil skirt, her tights laddered and ripped. She looked cowed and terrified and dishevelled, her pretty face swollen and bruised, lips bust open and bleeding, hair a mess. Her head was bowed in defeat, but her eyes looked pleadingly at Henry as tears flowed down her face.

The other two had filthy bed sheets wrapped around them and were obviously naked underneath. Their faces were dirty, like Victorian urchins.

Henry instantly recognized one of them, even though her face seemed misshapen and out of line: Laura Marshall, the missing special constable.

He did not know the other girl.

Bartle yanked the chain, pulling the girls to their knees.

'Jesus,' Henry said, 'you sick bastard.'

Bartle leaned over in front of Henry. 'Now that I've given you a show, I'm going to give them one. They're going to love seeing your guts spilled – aren't you, girls?'

Henry heard Emma stifle a scream.

'Please don't be dead,' Jake said, swerving to a halt and stopping at the point where the Skoda had veered off the road. He could see the deep indentations of the tyres in the grass verge and the car itself just beyond, nose down in the ditch. Smoke and steam rose from its front end. The driver's door was flung open.

Overwall wasn't dead. He was out of the car and running across the field.

Jake swore, grabbed his torch, jumped down out of the Land Rover and went after him.

He slithered down the banking into the wet, evil-smelling ditch, the dirty water at the bottom of the dyke coming up over his ankles, his shoes slurping in the glutinous mud. He had to drag his feet out of the mud before scrambling up the opposite bank and vaulting the barbed-wire fence into the field, ripping a huge hole in his suit jacket. This was all well and good, but Jake was still wearing the suit he'd had on for the inquest – his best one – and also his best shoes.

That did not deter him. Slithering in the mud, he came upright, got his balance and went after Overwall, who he picked up fifty metres ahead of him in the beam of the torch.

Jake set off at an easy trot. He knew Overwall slightly, had seen him most mornings picking up the kids, often lounging against the side of his taxi with a cigarette in his mouth and coughing disgustingly. He would be easy to hunt down, and the best way to do it would be like a hunting dog, going for the long game. This would ensure that when he grabbed him Jake would not be too exhausted himself to deal with him.

But Overwall had no pace at all, and Jake wondered if he'd been injured in the accident. He hoped so, but not too much, because Jake wanted to inflict some injuries on him. He was staggering and limping when Jake caught up with him, and with a push in the back, Overwall dropped on to his knees and raised his arms wide in submission.

Bartle dragged the young women down, then wrapped the chain around the head of a hanging deer.

'You don't move,' he warned them. None of

them dared to look him directly in the face. 'I'm going to keep you entertained now,' he said.

'Where's the police car?' Henry blurted. It was something that had bothered him from the word go, and before he was sliced open, he needed to know. How could it have disappeared so completely, without trace?

'Eh?'

'PC Marshall had a police car . . . It was never found.'

'Ah,' Bartle said, getting it. 'Covered in shit.'

In his rage and with his momentum, Jake could not prevent himself from smashing into Overwall and flattening him into the soft, muddy ground, then pushing and kneading his face into it, before hauling it out and screaming into Overwall's ear, 'Where's my daughter? Where is she? And where's Henry Christie?'

Overwall spat out mud and wet grass and spluttered, 'I've got my rights! You can't treat me like this.'

Jake's response to this was to force his weasel face back down into the mud and hold it there, half-suffocating him, before lifting his head back out by his hair.

'No rules here, you bastard. I'm searching for my daughter, and I'll do what I have to do and face the consequences . . . Just me and you here,' he growled into Overwall's ear. Just to prove this statement, he pulled back Overwall's head, then rubbed his face back in the mud. He pulled it out again and demanded, 'Where is she?'

Overwall coughed and choked. 'Oh God, oh God, I'm sorry.'

Henry tried to writhe and turn and watch Bartle as he walked towards a table on the opposite side of the room, where he picked up a huge gutting knife in one hand and a slightly smaller carving knife in the other.

Bartle inspected both knives under the light cast by the fluorescent tubes overhead, running his fingertips down the blades, holding them up to catch the light. Satisfied, he turned and smiled at Henry. The blades flashed.

'Fuck,' Henry muttered desperately, his fear rising so far that he was sure he was about to burst.

The big, lumbering man walked slowly across and stood in front of Henry's dangling body, weighing him up, casting his professional slaughterer's eyes over him.

He squatted down, placed the knives on the floor and reached for the captive bolt gun he had left there.

'In some ways, it's tempting not to use this,' he said of the gun. 'Part of me just wants to gut you, pull out your innards, let them hang down over your face so you can see and smell them, watch them steam, while you're still alive. I mean, I can do that . . . easy . . . then slit your throat and watch the life pump out of you. Trouble is, I love using this baby.' He shook the gun.

He rotated slightly on the balls of his feet, in order to be directly in front of Henry. He placed the open palm of his left hand gently on the right side of Henry's face. Henry could feel the

270

rough callouses and harsh skin and recoiled as terror like he had never known coursed through him.

'Ah, ah, ah, just holding you steady,' Bartle explained.

'Fuck you,' Henry growled darkly.

Bartle smirked, held Henry's head firmly and placed the muzzle of the gun into the side of his head on the hairline between his left ear and eye, then screwed the barrel hard.

'It's a bit like a nail gun. It only fires into a hard surface. That's why I have to keep your head still or it won't work properly and you'll suffer unnecessary pain.'

Henry swore at him again.

'Just thinking of your welfare,' Bartle started to say. 'I'm a—'

Whatever he was going to say was cut short when Bartle screamed ear piercingly like a demented devil, dropped the gun and at the same time pitched forwards on to the cold concrete floor, then rolled, moaning, clutching his groin. Henry jerked and saw Emma Niven standing there, having somehow extracted her petite wrists from Bartle's old-style handcuffs and chain and sneaked up behind him as he was crouching in front of Henry. She had delivered a ferocious kick between his legs with as much force as possible.

Bartle rolled away in agony, but was quickly up on his knees again, red faced, hissing like a steam train, with both hands clasped over his balls.

'Bitch,' he said, starting to rise, 'you're gonna die now.'

Emma spun towards him like a ballerina, but Henry realized her movements were more like a ninja than a dancer as she flipped her body around like a top, lashing out with her right foot and kicking Bartle in the face, sending him sprawling underneath several hanging carcases.

Henry saw the moment of impact – the way Bartle's face distorted, the saliva whipping out of his mouth like a slavering dog.

'Cut me down,' he screamed at Emma.

She ran to him, picked up the smaller of the two knives, reached up above Henry's feet and sliced through the cord around his ankles which was looped over the meat hook. Henry thudded down awkwardly on the side of his head and shoulder, banging hard even though the drop was only a few inches.

'The tape, the tape,' he encouraged her.

Bartle was already rising, shaking his head like a grizzly bear, pure malevolence in his eyes as he scrambled to his feet whilst Emma sliced at the tape that bound Henry's wrists. Feeling it give, he began to strain his wrists against it to speed up the process and help to tear it apart.

Bartle lumbered towards them, his arms swinging like a speed skater. One of Henry's hands jerked free, but it seemed too little, too late. Bartle barged into Emma. The knife flew out of her grip, and then he had his huge arms wrapped tightly around her slim frame. He lifted her away from Henry and ran her hard against the side wall of the abattoir.

She screamed, kicked and punched at him, fighting wildly.

With a swell of strength, Henry broke his second hand free from the tape, ripping the hairs out of the back of his wrist with a grimace. With his legs still strapped up, he writhed across the floor like a mermaid to reach the knife, sat up and hacked at the tape to release his feet.

Seeing this happening, Bartle roared, hurled Emma to one side and ran for Henry, who sliced the last thread of tape to free his legs and scuttled on his hands and knees behind a huge carcase of beef.

Bartle sidestepped and went for Henry, who had managed to get to his feet, still with the knife in his hand.

Henry screamed a warning. 'I'll use this.' He brandished the blade menacingly.

Bartle stopped abruptly and dropped into a wrestler's stance, wiping blood off his face with the back of his hand. Henry saw that Emma's karate kick had broken the man's nose.

'You're finished, Spencer,' Henry taunted him, backing away. 'This – whatever it is – is all over now.'

'Not yet.' He spat blood, wiped his face again, then charged, moving more quickly than a man of his size should have been able.

Henry brought up the knife, his mind blank but desperate, knowing he was fighting for his and other people's lives here, and if it meant plunging the blade deep into Bartle's heart, he would do it – and then give it a twist.

But Bartle was very fast, coming at him in a blur, and suddenly the knife was spinning out of his hand and Bartle was on him. His huge, muscled arms surrounded him, forcing Henry backwards and crushing the air out of his lungs, squeezing the life out of him.

The pair of them crashed against a side of beef. They ricocheted off that into the dead horse, off that into another side of beef, until their balance went in this terrible macabre ballroom dance and they toppled over, Bartle on top, Henry underneath, struggling and fighting.

Henry managed to pull one arm free and clattered his open hand across Bartle's face, but the man simply flicked the pathetic blow off with contempt and continued to hold Henry down, then sat upright, straddling Henry, moving himself up Henry's body, pinning his shoulders to the cold floor; then, adjusting himself, he carefully wrapped the fat fingers of his left hand around Henry's throat. He dug his calloused-tipped fingers in, rooting for the windpipe, which Henry was certain would be ripped out.

Henry's eyes bulged, and his tongue started to swell. Bartle squeezed slowly, looking down, starting to laugh.

Then – abruptly – the laugh stopped. Bartle went rigid. His whole body jerked upright. His expression turned to one of horror. His mouth contorted, and he heaved up a mouthful of blood and screamed silently, before pitching heavily on to Henry, crushing him with his weight.

Laura Marshall stood behind him. She was a thin, wasted figure, her eyes sunk deep into their sockets, her frame withered and weak.

But she had found enough strength in her to

plunge the knife that Henry had dropped deep into Bartle's back, just by his left shoulder blade and into his chest cavity, driving the full length of it in.

She stood back, horror-struck, as Henry disentangled himself and pushed Bartle off him at the same moment Rik Dean and Jake Niven ran into the abattoir.

The man watched the house, not caring how long this would take. He saw the police Land Rover pull up outside, saw Jake Niven get out and go around to the passenger side and help out his daughter. He carried her in his arms towards the front door, which opened, and Anna Niven rushed out, their son Danny behind her.

As a family they entered the house.

'How very touching,' the man whispered cynically to himself. He did not know for sure what was going on, but that did not matter.

A couple of minutes later, the door opened again, and Jake came out and got back into the Land Rover, reversed off the drive and sped off. The man watched, not too concerned, because Jake would be coming back sooner or later.

The man got slowly out of his car and walked up to the front of the house, knocked gently on the door. It opened after a few seconds. Anna Niven stood there, drying her eyes, clearly having some sort of hyper-emotional time.

'Yes?' she said.

'Mrs Niven?'

'Yes.'

The man put a finger to his pursed lips and said, 'Shh. My name is Arlow Worthington . . . You might know of my brother, Fraser Worthington.' He then drove his fist into Anna's face.

Eighteen

'There.'

The nurse took a step back and proudly surveyed her handiwork: Henry Christie's head.

She had done all the dirty work on the deep gash caused by the crowbar. She had shaved his head and cleaned it carefully, making the patient wince and gasp as she dabbed and swabbed, causing him to go, 'Ooh, ooh, ooh' (in a slightly disconnected thought, Henry reminded himself of the 'monkey' joke, the one about a chimp getting into a hot bath); then she gently eased each side of the wound together and began the painful process of stitching him up, because it had been medically decided that butterfly strips would not be strong enough to hold it together.

Henry's eyes were tight shut as she did this; she then applied a plaster and dressing.

'Done,' she added. 'A work of art.'

'Even if you say so yourself.'

'Even that.'

Henry had been at the Accident and Emergency unit at Lancaster Infirmary for four hours. He'd had his head, literally, examined by the on-duty consultant (who looked about nineteen, Henry thought) and an X-ray machine that confirmed nothing was broken. Though the blow had been hard and heavy and had floored him into unconsciousness, it had glanced off his head at an angle like a tennis player's slice, as opposed to a straight down smash. Had it been the latter, the doctor assured him, he might well be on a mortuary slab now. He had been lucky.

He sat up on the edge of the bed in the cubicle. His head was still swimming under water.

The nurse said, 'Really, we should keep you here for twenty-four hours' observation with a wound like that.'

'I know.'

'But we have no bed space, so . . .' She handed him a leaflet. 'If you have any of the symptoms listed in this, you must come back. You know – nausea, vomiting, dizziness, that sort of thing.'

'Got ya.' He smiled at her. 'Thank you, you've been great.'

'Just one last thing.'

Henry hoped for a kiss – just to make him feel extra better – but instead she fitted a crêpe bandage skull cap over the dressing for extra protection and said, 'That's a nice look.'

'Thanks again.'

The cubicle curtain rustled, and Jake Niven's face appeared in a gap. 'Can I come in?'

'Yes, I think we've finished here.' The nurse left, giving Jake an appreciative glance of the type Henry rarely got from members of the opposite sex these days.

Jake stepped in, and Henry looked at him. His suit and shoes had been ruined, and it looked doubtful that any type of cleaning would rescue them. The trousers were torn and filthy, and his shoes were sodden.

'How are you doing?' Jake asked Henry.

278

'Unless the X-ray missed a fractured skull, I think I'm OK.'

'Good.' Jake perched next to Henry on the bed and looked sincerely at him. 'Haven't had a chance to say this properly, Henry – but thank you.'

Henry frowned, and his stitches constricted painfully.

Jake, seeing that expression, said, 'For doing what you did – going over to see Overwall with Danny, then going back after you dropped him off. You didn't have to.'

'I never liked Overwall, something sleazy about him; always thought he was lying about the night Laura went missing, but just couldn't prove anything . . . and Emma *was* missing, Jake. Anyone would have done what I did.'

'No, they wouldn't,' Jake said. 'And because of what you did, two very dangerous men have been caught.'

'And by the way, your girl packs a punch,' Henry said with admiration. 'She can kick ass.'

'I know . . . Her karate lessons came good,' Jake said.

Henry nodded. 'What's happening with Overwall?'

'He's in custody down the road at Lancaster nick. I've done all the initial processing, and he'll be interviewed by detectives in an hour or two. From what I've heard from him so far, they won't be able to shut him up.'

Henry sighed. 'Things that go on under your nose.' He shook his head in disbelief, though the truth was that over the span of his career Henry had often found out what went on under people's noses, and nothing surprised him any more. This worried him slightly, because sometimes he wanted to be surprised.

'I thought Kendleton and district was supposed to be a quiet backwater?'

'Don't you believe it.' Henry slid off the bed on to his feet, staggering slightly as he put his zip-up jacket back on, threading his arms stiffly into the sleeves with Jake's assistance. The front of the jacket was a bloody, snotty mess: a combination of fluids from a dead horse and Spencer Bartle and his own blood.

They stepped out of the cubicle and made their way along the A&E ward to another cubicle with the curtain drawn across, containing Laura Marshall. Both men stopped and hesitated here. A uniformed cop sat twiddling his thumbs in the empty cubicle, opposite.

Further down the ward, in another cubicle, was the other young woman who had been one of Bartle's prisoners. She was being spoken to by a detective, and her family had just arrived at the hospital. She had been identified as Rebecca Merryweather.

The curtain opened, and the young-looking consultant who had treated Henry emerged, clipboard in hand, stethoscope dangling from a pocket in his housecoat, his hair a tousled mess.

'How is she?' Henry asked.

The consultant did a quick calculation. 'Exhausted, emaciated, damaged in so many ways . . . a victim of rape, abuse – psychological and physical – torture. To be honest, I'm amazed she is still alive, but, having said that, she is still very, very strong inside herself, and although I'm no psychiatrist, I'd say she will do well. Eventually.'

'Can we see her?'

'One second.'

The doctor disappeared back into the cubicle. There was a muted conversation, then he stuck his head out a moment later. 'She'll see you, but only for a few minutes. At this moment in time she needs rest, recuperation and to feel very safe.'

Henry nodded. He knew her family were on their way, which would be a great help for her.

The doctor stood aside, as did the nurse who was still inside the cubicle, and Henry looked at the tired, haggard, beaten face of Laura Marshall. An X-ray had confirmed her jaw had been broken and had meshed back together crookedly. It would need to be broken again and reset surgically.

'Hiya, Laura.'

'Sir,' she said, through unmoving lips. She was able to talk – just.

'It's Henry,' he said, correcting her gently, and sat down on the chair next to the bed. Jake stood back. 'How're you feeling?'

She gave a short laugh, and Henry could see a twinkle in her eye. 'Glad to be out of that, thank you.'

Henry swallowed. He still did not have a full idea of what she and the other young women had been through in the last few months – and others, maybe, over years . . . Laura would be interviewed by highly trained detectives, and he would not find out anything, anyway, because he was

281

out of it now. But he did have an imagination, and the thought of her imprisonment, torture and abuse sent a cold shiver of revulsion rippling down his backbone.

'I thought he was going to kill me on the night he took me,' she whispered. 'He held one of those captive bolt guns to my head . . . I thought I was dead then. I spent the next six months wishing he had killed me . . . and he would've done eventually . . . He killed all the others after he'd finished with them.' She said, sobbing, 'When I saw the young girl he brought in today, I knew it was only a matter of time before he killed me, and you know what? I was glad.' A tear rolled slowly down her face. 'It felt so good sticking that knife into him . . . Will I get done for that?'

Henry shook his head. 'No . . . and you're safe now, Laura, and you saved my life, so I thank you for that.'

'Thank you for finding me,' she said quietly.

Henry blinked away his own tears.

'Gents? Time's up,' the consultant interrupted. 'Can we call it quits for now?'

'Yeah, sure . . . There is just one more question,' Henry said to Laura, 'if you don't mind?'

'It amazes me how she managed to miss every vital organ,' Jake said, getting into the Land Rover.

Henry eased himself up and into the passenger side, wheezing with effort and pain. 'People like him often have luck on their side, and I've known people get skewered through the skull with a sword and survive. It happens.'

282

'One lucky bastard.'

'But the beauty of it,' Henry said, 'is that he gets to face the ignominy of going through the justice system . . . I quite like that phrase, you know? Killing's too good for 'em, because it is. I'm glad he'll survive, actually. If nothing else, his life in prison will be hell.'

'You really believe in the system, don't you?' Jake queried.

'Are you mocking me?'

'No, not at all.'

'Actually, I think the system stinks – it's as flawed as hell, there's too many loopholes for the bad guys to climb through – but nothing gives me greater pleasure than seeing someone like Spencer Bartle never see the light of day again.'

Jake nodded and started the beast that was the ageing Land Rover, which had done him proud that night.

He and Henry were discussing the fact that, unbelievably, Spencer Bartle was still alive – just – after having a very long, sharp knife thrust into his back and through his chest cavity. It had somehow missed his heart, spinal column and all major arteries and had just nicked a lung. It had caused a whole lot of bleeding, but had not killed him. He was presently undergoing emergency surgery to repair him, and two burly cops were waiting outside the operating theatre for him when he came out.

Henry knew that if he had died, his sordid story might have died with him, and a number of families would have remained in a terrible, emotional limbo, and possibly might never have learned what had happened to their loved ones. From his experience in dealing with grieving families, Henry knew they would rather have bad news than none at all, because as cruel as this was, it was 'better' than a lifetime of false hope.

'Shall we go back to the village?' Henry said.

Henry remained blank for the journey, sucked up in a swirl of his own thoughts, still wondering what it would have been like to bleed out, having his throat cut while his heart pumped away. Maybe he would have felt nothing if Bartle had stunned him first, but the thought made him feel sick.

About halfway back, his phone rang. It was Alison.

'On my way back from hospital,' he said immediately, pre-empting the question. 'Sewn-up, patched-up, head shaved, wearing a bob cap, sort of.'

'Henry . . .' she said, then hesitated.

He steadied himself for the tirade. The: 'You can't let go! You'll always be a cop!' lecture, which might well be the straw that broke the camel's back of their relationship.

Instead, he wilted internally when she said, 'I'm so proud of you.'

'Eh? Come again?'

'You heard, daft bloke.'

'Thanks,' he said. 'If it's OK, I just want to nip back over to Thornwell to get the Audi and see what's happening over there. Jake's driving me back.'

'That's OK. Can't wait to see you . . . I love you so much.'

He glanced self-consciously at Jake and said, 'Ditto.' The call ended, and Henry said, 'She still loves me,' with incredulity.

'Nice one.'

Henry slid the phone half into his jeans pocket.

Fifteen minutes later Jake drew up outside the gates of Bartle's abattoir in Thornwell, now a very busy hub of policing activity. There were marked cars, plain cars, CSI vans and major-incident vans with lighting rigs and – ominously, Henry thought – a very nice Jaguar belonging to the new chief constable of Lancashire Constabulary, one Bernard Ellison.

The big nobs are out, he thought.

He twisted stiffly and lowered himself from the Land Rover, hearing a dull thud as he did so, but thinking nothing of it because Jake was also getting out the opposite side and had caught his torch on the steering wheel. Henry winced as a result of two things as he placed his feet on the ground; firstly from the soreness, and secondly from the approach of the chief constable, even though he had nothing more to be worried about from the man who had 'eased' him out of his job. He could even call him by his first name, if he so wished – which is what he decided he would do, just to wind him up.

'Henry, Henry, Henry,' the chief said, beaming. He had recently been confirmed as the new chief, FB's successor. He was dressed in a heavy tweed overcoat and reminded Henry of a character from a fifties film, but without the trilby.

'Bernard,' he said, avoiding the outstretched hand.

'You've done incredibly well, Henry,' Ellison said, recoiling slightly at the sight of Henry's blood splattered frontage.

'You mean for somebody with their head up their arse?' Henry asked with a fake, impish smile.

'Mm,' Ellison muttered. 'That was then, and it was a justified comment.'

'One I would very much have liked to have seen on an appraisal form. "This employee has his head up his arse,"' Henry said. 'Very objective.'

Ellison gave him a steely look. 'That said, you've done a brilliant job here, uncovered a real lair. So, so nasty and perverted.'

Henry glanced at Jake, who was standing nearby but trying to keep his distance.

The chief turned to him and said, 'I'm so glad your daughter is safe.'

Beyond Ellison's shoulder, Henry spotted Rik Dean marching purposefully towards him, now garbed in a forensic suit and shoes.

'My replacement, if I'm not mistaken,' Henry said, like Stanley meeting Dr Livingstone.

Ellison glanced back, then turned to Henry. 'Someone had to replace you.'

'You could've let me get out of headquarters before you did the deed, though,' Henry bleated. 'There was no respect, and I think that is what pissed me off as much as having my brother-in-law-to-be as my replacement.'

'Your . . .?' Ellison said.

'Yep.'

Then he said sharply, 'Oh, fuck off whingeing, Henry. I came out all this way to congratulate you.'

'Well, you can stick your—' He stopped, realizing the road he was just about to go down was one from which neither man would come up smelling of roses. 'Well, you know what? Some words are better left unsaid . . .' Then he paused and said, 'No, changed my mind. Sometimes a cathartic release is absolutely necessary. Stick your congratulations up your arse . . . Bernard.'

He flounced past the open-mouthed Ellison, with Jake scurrying after him, and went to meet Rik.

'How are you, Henry? You look a mess.'

Henry winked at him. 'Cheers . . . How's it going? I've come to pick up my car and have a look around, if I may?'

'Oh . . . uh . . . we need to keep the Audi for forensics, actually.'

'OK,' Henry said. He turned to Jake. 'Can you take me back after I've had a nose round?'

Jake nodded.

'Er, look, mate, I see you've spoken to the chief, yeah?' Rik said awkwardly.

'I have.'

'Did he mention anything about the crime scene?'

'Our conversation did not quite get that far.' He looked suspiciously at Rik. 'Why?'

'He's not told you?'

'Rik, spit it out, or I'll kick your arse.'

Tight-lipped, Rik said, 'He said he doesn't want any civvies messing up the scene.'

Henry blinked. 'Meaning me?'

Rik jerked around with his hands and shoulders like a marionette, displaying his nervousness. His face was suddenly a mass of tics, as if an electrical current was being forced through it. 'Well, you know what it's like.'

'Too many big-footed cops trampling all over the scene . . . You don't get a second chance at a crime scene . . . All *that* shit?'

'Standard procedure,' Rik said defensively.

'Let me put a suit on, and you walk me through what you've got, once,' Henry said. 'Suited and booted, one walk through, and that's it. I won't touch a thing. Then I'll go home and practise making shamrocks in Guinness.'

'Eh?'

'It's the least I deserve, and you know it.'

'If the chief finds out, he'll eat my bollocks.'

'That,' Henry said, putting a patronizing hand on Rik's shoulder, 'is an everyday occurrence for a superintendent: get used to it.'

Rik closed his eyes, feeling the pressure. 'OK then, but we do it sneaky.'

They looked around and saw the chief had stalked off somewhere. Henry followed Rik to the back of the CSI van from which the forensic suits were dispensed. Rik signed one out for Henry, and he pulled it on over his clothing behind the van, slipping the paper shoes over his own and pulling the hood over his head. He pulled the hood's drawstring tight, and then covered his face, bar his eyes, with a surgical

288

mask. When he was ready, not even his eyebrows showed.

Rik watched him, as did Jake.

'Unrecognizable?' Henry asked, doing a twirl.

'Whatever,' Rik mumbled glumly.

'Let's go then.' To Jake, he said, 'You keep nix.'

Rik opened the gate in the fence surrounding the abattoir and walked Henry across to another gate that led into an outdoor animal enclosure. This was essentially a very large holding area, where livestock was unloaded from trucks. There was a system in place reminding Henry of a queue at Disneyland: a series of corridors formed by interlocking, flexible fencing, into which the unfortunate animals could be herded to form a line, one behind the other, which led into the killing area inside the abattoir itself.

This enclosure was also large enough to park several lorries, but at the moment there was only the one in there: the tractor and trailer unit belonging to Bartle that Henry had seen passing through Kendleton on a couple of occasions, driven by Bartle. The trailer had been crammed with pigs or sheep when Henry had seen it. The rear of the trailer was open, the ramp into it down. Henry saw two suited CSIs in the back of it and wondered what was of interest in there.

'Let me show you this first,' Rik said and steered Henry up the ramp into the foul smelling trailer. It was illuminated by a small, but powerful lighting rig, powered by a portable generator that hummed softly.

Henry stopped at the top of the ramp and looked in, his mouth popping open behind the mask.

He swore.

'Yeah,' Rik said, knowing Henry had worked it out. At the front of the trailer was a construction that looked similar to a garden shed, but quite narrow and small and made of steel. 'It's for garden storage . . . You can buy similar ones in any big garden centre or DIY store,' Rik explained.

Henry nodded.

'It's bolted to the front end of the trailer so it can't move . . . c'mon.' He touched Henry's shoulder, and they walked down the trailer, past the lighting rig. The two CSIs stood back, allowing them to see inside the small construction.

Henry's heart froze as he looked into the mini-shed. He could see the solid bolts that fixed it to the trailer, and the pair of manacles – two metal rings joined by a chain – secured to the roof of the shed, hanging down. He swallowed something very vile.

'I was right, wasn't I?' he whispered, but not with any degree of pride. 'It's barbaric.'

'Yeah,' Rik said, equally quietly. 'I checked after you called me, with North Yorkshire Police first. The two missing girls you gave me the names of . . .'

'Rebecca Merryweather and Grace Greenwood.' Henry remembered the names.

'Bartle was interviewed and eliminated from both enquiries.'

'Shit.'

'I've identified another eight missing girls, not just from North Yorkshire, but from all over the country, with the common denominator being farmers' auction markets.' Rik swallowed. 'There may be more, and some, not all, disappeared on dates close to when Bartle had been arrested.'

'When he howled at the moon.'

'Something like that.'

'When he couldn't control himself.'

'Maybe,' Rik said, 'but it looks like he's actually out of control now.'

Henry nodded. 'He kidnaps them and keeps them manacled in this tool shed thing like animals, brings them back here, surrounded by pigs or sheep or whatever, and then what?' He turned his face slowly, pulled off his mask and looked at Rik, the artificial light cast by the rig catching the contours of his face, the shadow, the light, in an eerily demonic way.

Rik led Henry through the abattoir itself, through to the cold storage room where not many hours before Henry had been hanging upside down, contemplating a violent death.

Rik was saying, 'Looks like Bartle has been putting horse meat back into the food chain and selling it on to unscrupulous burger manufacturers.' He pointed out the carcases of four horses, including the one that had licked Henry's face so gruesomely. 'Still possible to do, especially for someone like Bartle, a sole trader operating under the radar. The food health inspectors don't have the resources to keep a lid on it all.'

Henry grunted. 'He might have been putting

other products into the food chain, from what he told me.'

'Such as?'

'Human beings,' he said, finding his mind was beginning to fester with self-recrimination.

'That's yet to be established,' Rik said. 'He might just have been trying to scare the shit out of you.'

'He succeeded,' Henry admitted.

'There's a very long way to go with this,' Rik said.

Henry was becoming more and more furious with himself the more he learned about Bartle and Overwall, quickly coming to the conclusion that maybe Ellison had been right. Maybe his head had been so far up his arse that he'd believed he was operating as normal and, because of that, not doing the routine things he should have done. He stopped between two sides of beef and said, 'How the fuck did I miss him, Rik? I searched this place.'

'Because he's a sneaky, deceitful and careful operator – like most psychopaths – and he was in cahoots with Overwall, too, the straight man of the duo, the one without any funny lines.'

'The taxis,' Henry said. 'That's why I got smacked on the head, because Bartle pulled up in a taxi . . .'

'Seems he did some driving for Overwall.'

'And he was using exactly the same taxi . . .'

'Yep,' Rik confirmed.

It had been the taxi, the Skoda Octavia, that had stopped Henry in his tracks as he had been leaving Overwall's place. If it hadn't been on the forecourt,

292

he would have jumped in his own car, gone straight back to Kendleton and reported that, as obnoxious as he was, Overwall denied having picked up Emma that afternoon, saying she wasn't at the prearranged pickup point. It would have been virtually impossible to disprove. The focus of the investigation would then have shifted to Lancaster.

Not that a parked-up taxi would normally have stopped Henry, even if it was the same colour and model as the one he had just looked through inside the unit. It wasn't unusual for a taxi firm to buy the same make and model of car because it was like a recognizable brand. In Overwall's case, white Skodas with the same logo.

What stopped Henry was the registration plate. First he noticed it was an 05 registered vehicle, 2005. Even then it might not have clicked, except he then realized that the number plates were exactly the same. Each car displayed the same number, and in a ferocious churning of his mind, it slotted into place for Henry.

On the night Laura Marshall went missing after her visit to the Swan's Neck, Spencer Bartle had been taken into Lancaster by Overwall. Henry had the taxi that Overwall presented to him given a thorough going over by a forensic team, and there had been absolutely nothing in it linking Bartle to the disappearance. Not a tiny piece of glass from the police car window, which would have matched the glass found on the Swan's Neck car park. Nor any blood or hair that could have been matched to Laura Marshall. The car that Overwall said he had taken Bartle to Lancaster in was clean.

Because it was not the car.

Overwall was running two vehicles with the same registration number, and one thing Henry had not checked in his 'thorough' search of the vehicle was the Vehicle Identification Number, the VIN.

Overwall was running cloned vehicles, thereby saving a small fortune on tax and insurance by simply declaring he was just running one, effectively doubling his income. It was a common enough scam amongst disreputable transport firms, big and small.

Overwall and Bartle had tricked him and, because his head was where it was, he had fallen for it. He hadn't been concentrating.

Henry had also seen an iPhone in the rear footwell, which turned out to belong to Emma, and which Bartle had knocked out of her hand as she'd texted her mum and asked for help.

Henry and Rik faced each other.

'Still trying to put this together,' Henry mused. 'He must have attacked her on the car park behind the pub, then driven off with her in the police car . . . done whatever . . . then got Overwall to take him somewhere to dispose of his clothing – because we never found any evidence of anything on any of Bartle's clothing. Overwall then got into the second taxi and took him to Lancaster.' Henry's reasoning was slightly fuzzy, but his hypothesis seemed sound to him. 'Overwall presented me with the clean car and got away with it because he knew there would never be any chance of him cleaning up the first car, because that's impossible . . . I'll bet, even now, if you get a team on those cars, you'll find some trace in one of them. Be worth doing, even if it's been valeted.'

'But where is the cop car?'

Henry allowed himself a slight grin. 'I asked Laura that just now, because it was bugging me, and Bartle half-alluded to it just before he was going to cut me up. How does a car disappear? We checked all the scrap yards and regular car dumping grounds – nothing. Because it's closer to home than you might imagine. It's out back.' Henry pointed. 'Follow me.'

He and Rik threaded their way through the rows of hanging meat to the door at the far end of the cold room: the one through which Bartle had dragged the chained-up young women to display them proudly to Henry. They emerged into a concrete yard with large units built on three sides, including the one they had just stepped out from. Henry turned to the open side with Rik in tow and walked to the edge, up to a four-foot high fence that surrounded a circular concrete structure, about a hundred feet across and sunk deep into the ground like a huge pudding bowl. A putrid, awful smell wafted from it.

'That stinks,' Rik said, glad he was wearing a face mask.

'Slurry pit,' Henry said, 'containing animal waste, water from washing down the abattoir and other unusable stuff, which eventually breaks down into fertilizer.'

'Eh?' Rik was still puzzled.

'It's a hole, bigger and deeper than a swimming pool, and it's full of shit, a lethal place if you fall into it, or inhale some of the gases that come off it. And that's where you'll find the police car.'

'You reckon?'

'Bartle virtually said so, and Laura thinks so too.'

'Don't fancy that.'

'There'll be other stuff in it, too,' Henry predicted bleakly, but did not elaborate. He meant bodies, but unless they had been put in there recently, they would just be part of the slurry itself now. 'Great job for the underwater search unit.'

'I'll get on with it . . . Now then, follow me,' Rik said.

He took Henry into the unit opposite the abattoir, which was a huge garage filled with a selection of farm vehicles and equipment. They went all the way through this to a door at the far end and out through this into another, smaller yard, beyond which was a large field bordered by woodland.

A police traffic van with a portable lighting rig on its roof was parked by the gate to this field, and the light from the floodlight rig swathed the first ten metres of the field.

'He went to a lot of trouble, and to be honest, if he hadn't brought out the girls to show to you, we might still be none the wiser,' Rik said, gesturing across the field. Henry could see nothing, other than a JCB digger tucked away in one corner. His eyes roved until he gave up. 'OK, what am I looking for?'

'Bartle's harem.'

Henry looked across the field again, then said, 'Stop teasing me.'

'Follow me.' He led Henry into the field.

Rik peeled back a rectangle of turf, maybe three feet by four feet, and several inches thick – but it was not real grass; it was artificial turf that blended with the real grass surrounding it.

'If you park a tractor or a trailer over this, you'd never know,' Rik said, 'especially if real grass and muck is thrown over it to hide it.' Rik finished and stood back to reveal a trap door underneath the false grass, which was bolted shut.

He slid the bolt back, slid his fingers under a handle flush with the door and raised it on its hinges. It opened easily.

Henry remained silent as he looked down into the black hole, seeing a set of metal ladders similar to those used to gain access to lofts. They led down to whatever was there. It was like looking into a storm drain.

Rik said, 'You can climb down the steps and close the trap door over your head, so anyone who happened to be walking by would just see something that looked like a manhole cover. Not that anyone walks by here. *Nobody* comes by here. When you come back up, you just cover it with the artificial turf and, to all intents, it's just part of the field again.'

Henry really, really, really did not want to descend into the hell down there that his imagination was now painting vividly for him. He swallowed, found he could hardly breathe.

'An underground lair,' Rik said.

'I'm not sure I'm up for this,' Henry said.

'You just scammed your way past the chief constable,' Rik pointed out.

Henry nodded. 'Show me.'

Rik began to back down the ladder into the darkness. Henry watched him disappear, then as he looked into the hole a light came on, with Rik standing at the foot of the ladder, looking up. He beckoned Henry to follow.

Henry turned and placed his right foot on the ladder and lowered himself down. When he stepped off to look, he saw this was not just a hole he was in, but the inside of a corrugated steel container, the type usually found on a lorry trailer or a cargo ship. The lighting was poor, and there was a lot of shadow. There was a terrible stench of rotting flesh.

'Yeah, it's a container, and it's been buried underground,' Rik said, confirming Henry's analysis.

It was easily big enough for a tall man to stand inside without having to stoop. Henry guessed it was about eight and a half feet high, maybe twenty feet long and about eight feet wide.

'This is the first of three, all interconnected,' Rik said. 'Probably dug out with the JCB up top.' Rik turned on his torch and led Henry to the end of the container, where a panel had been cut out of the metal to form a door, leading into the next one along. Rik stopped here, then shone his torch on the side of the container and held the beam on a chain that had been screwed into the side, about halfway up the wall, on the end of which was a pair of manacles.

'It's medieval,' Henry said.

A dirty, torn blanket was spread on the floor.

'I think this is where Emma was held,' Rik said.

Henry stared at the chains, imagining. 'He takes them from the streets and brings them here,' he said. It was a statement and a question combined. 'An underground prison, a torture chamber. This took some planning.'

'Two more of these, with air vents in the roofs but disguised from above . . . It gets worse,' Rik said bleakly. 'There's a body in the furthest one along. Not sure, but it could be Grace Greenwood . . . Half rotted away. It's no wonder you didn't find all this, Henry.'

'But I should have done. I should have done my job and saved people's lives, Rik.' He paused, then decided abruptly, 'I've seen enough, seen enough for a lifetime.' He looked into Rik's eyes, but was disgusted with himself. 'Over to you, mate. I know I've been a shit with you about it, but you are the man for the job.'

'Thanks, Henry . . . that means a lot.'

Nineteen

Jake dawdled patiently in the Land Rover, waiting for Henry's return. At least, he was trying to appear to be patient, but he was on pins because all he wanted to do now was get home and hug his daughter and his family for a very long time, shed tears of relief, probably, and count his blessings. And get out of his dirty clothes.

Whilst waiting he had chatted to several people, detectives and CSIs, and although they were cagey about the whole scenario, coupled with his involvement so far and the knowledge he had pulled together, Jake began to realize just how fortunate he and his family had been.

Bartle was clearly a cunning, dangerous sexual predator and murderer. It seemed as if he had reached a point where his urges were beyond any sort of control, hence his opportunistic abductions of Laura Marshall and Emma. He had gone beyond planning offences and taking his victims from further afield. Now he was operating close to home.

But just because Bartle was committing offences on his own doorstep and taking more chances, it did not necessarily mean he would get caught. He had spent a great deal of time and effort burying containers in the ground and camouflaging their existence, so he could very easily have lied his way out of the situation again, and

Emma, quite possibly, would never have been seen again.

Jake shuddered at the thought. The prospect of never seeing his daughter again terrified him beyond belief.

His thoughts then turned to Henry. On the whole, Jake was pretty ambivalent as far as detectives were concerned; he could take or leave them and had no desire to be one. He had known 'of' Henry – the force had so few SIOs, and because they handled major investigations they were bound to be known – but he had never really met him before the Wayne Oxford operation.

Something about Henry had impressed him, even from that first briefing. Possibly because Henry led from the front. And then, subsequently, because he had shown an interest in Jake on a personal level when he did not have to. Henry owed Jake nothing, really, but had been there for him.

It was only now as he waited for Henry's return from the crime scene that he actually realized that the constabulary's loss, caused by Henry's retirement and the shameful, ignominious manner in which it had been brought about, was huge. OK, life would go on, the force would continue to operate, but it would be poorer for Henry's absence.

He sat tapping the steering wheel, wishing the heating system was better.

Henry appeared at the door of the slaughter-house, walked to the rear of the CSI van and removed his forensic suit, handing it to one of the investigators. He trudged tiredly back to the Land Rover and climbed in next to Jake.

'Sorted?' Jake asked.

'Yeah.'

'Not nice?'

'Awful,' Henry said and looked squarely at Jake. 'Time to get back to our loved ones, matey.'

'My thoughts exactly.'

Henry drew his seat belt across his chest and locked it into place, tilted his head back and sighed.

Jake reversed away, swung around and headed back to Kendleton, off the industrial estate, which looked ordinary and safe but housed horrible secrets that would be fully revealed in the days, weeks to come.

The short journey was done in silence, each man consumed by his own thoughts.

Eventually, Jake stopped outside the Tawny Owl. 'Thanks again, Henry. I owe you one.'

'No, you don't, Jake . . . That said, you can come down and buy me a pint in the very near future and we'll call it quits.'

'Done.' Jake reached across, and they shook hands. Henry stepped out of the car and watched Jake drive away, before turning to walk to the pub entrance, but stopped and patted his pockets and looked back over his shoulder at the disappearing rear lights of the police car.

'Bugger,' he exclaimed.

Jake pulled on to the driveway next to Anna's car, put on the handbrake, switched off and put the Land Rover into first, not trusting the brake. He climbed out and locked it before walking up to the front door of his house.

The lights were all on, all the curtains drawn,

making him stop for another moment of reflection.

It could easily have been so different. His foolishness and infidelity had almost destroyed his family, the people he cared most about in his life.

'You tosser,' he admonished himself, then, continuing under his breath said: 'You will never, ever be so stupid again.'

He continued up the front steps to the door, which, he was pleased to see, was open, on the latch. They were ready and waiting for his arrival.

He smiled, emotion welling up inside him.

'Be a strong daddy,' he told himself and pushed open the door.

It swung open with a creak that showed it needed oiling, revealing the hallway beyond, the stairs on the right, the entrance to the lounge/dining room to the left and, directly facing him, the kitchen at the far end of the hallway.

He was about to shout, 'Daddy's home,' and had opened his mouth to say the words, but the first syllable stuck in his throat when he noticed the splattered blood on the white-painted stair banister and the smear all the way down the hall carpet that disappeared under the living room door, as if someone had been dragged, bleeding.

His mouth snapped shut, his eyes widened, and he became instantly alert.

The living room door opened slowly.

Anna stood there with Arlow Worthington behind her – although at that moment Jake did not know or recognise who the man was – his left arm hooked around her neck, obviously squeezing her throat in the crook of his arm. In his right hand he held a Glock pistol with a titanium silencer up to the right side of her head. Duct tape had been wound around the lower part of her face and jaw, and Jake could see her face had been smashed almost flat, her nose distorted, cheekbones and eyes black and swollen. Blood had flowed from her nostrils and covered her blouse and matted her hair.

Sheer terror was in her eyes, but at the same time Jake saw she was having problems keeping them open because of the swellings.

Her hands were behind her back and, Jake assumed, taped there.

'What the . . .?' Jake started to demand, making a move and only really for the first time focusing on the man holding his wife.

'Don't do it, Jake,' Arlow warned him. 'Just close the door and step inside.' His voice was soft, controlled.

Jake hesitated, weighing up everything: angles, distances, speed.

'Just do it, Jake,' the man said with a grin, 'or I'll kill your wife.'

Anna's eyes pleaded with him.

Jake stepped inside on to the welcome mat. His mouth was now dry, his heart pounding remorselessly, but his senses were acute. He closed the door, but saw it was still on the latch, giving the appearance of being closed properly.

Arlow gestured with the pistol and the almost clumsy looking noise suppressor screwed into the end of the barrel. 'Come in. Don't do anything silly,' he ordered, then edged backwards into the lounge with Anna still hostage. 'Come on.'

Jake's initial shock had morphed into fury now.

Arlow retained his half-smile, as if he was reading Jake's mind. 'Just do what I say and your family won't be hurt any further, Jake . . . Can't promise the same for you.' He then wrenched Anna back and flung her away from him, like in some violent ballroom dance. She spun across the room, hit the wall by the fireplace and slithered to her knees.

Jake started to lunge.

'Oh, no.' Arlow was ready, keeping his distance. He gestured with the weapon again.

Jake stopped himself. With his eyes boring into Arlow's face, he stepped into the living room and was horrified by what he saw.

Anna was kneeling, doubled over like the intended victim of a death squad assassination. Danny was splayed out on the carpet in front of the fireplace, lying on his left-hand side in the recovery position, with his right leg brought up. There was a deep gash just over his ear, and his head was in a pool of blood on the carpet. His breathing sounded ragged and difficult. His hands had been taped in front of him. Emma knelt by his head, stroking his arm.

She was the only one not duct taped.

'You bastard,' Jake uttered chillingly. 'What the fuck's going on here? What have you done?'

'Get down on your knees, Jake – now, or I'll kill you where you stand. Put your hands on your head. Do it, Jake . . . I don't want to kill you in front of your family, but I will if necessary. Knees!'

Jake slowly interlinked his fingers across the

crown of his head and sank to his knees, with his eyes burning malevolently at the man. 'Who are you? What do you want?'

'You'll find out soon enough, Jake. You—' The man pointed his gun at Emma. 'Pick up the tape and tie your dad's hands behind his back, my love.'

Emma, still dressed in the rags that were the remains of her school uniform, stared at him, as if she didn't understand what he'd said.

Jake said, 'Do as he says.'

'Dad, he's really hurt Danny,' Emma said.

'Why did you have to do that?' Jake demanded.

'He had a go at me,' Arlow sneered. 'Shouldn't have. This isn't a game.'

Emma crawled away from Danny and picked up a roll of duct tape that was on the settee. She got unsteadily to her feet and came over to Jake.

'Put your hands behind your back very slowly, Jake.'

He complied, crossing his wrists.

'Dad, I don't understand,' Emma said.

'It'll be OK, sweetheart, just do what he says.'

She edged around him and started to wind the tape around his wrists, the man watching carefully, ready to react.

'I don't mean any harm to your family, Jake . . . just you,' he said conversationally, but Jake knew this to be a lie. Whatever happened, they had all seen his face, and that meant they were witnesses. They would all have to die.

'What have I done?' Jake asked.

'Soon, Jake, soon . . . Let's have a look-see,' the man said when Emma stood back. Her father's hands were now tied. 'Good. Now you back away, love. Kneel next to your brother.'

Emma went down on her knees next to Danny. His breathing was laboured and worrying.

'You've hurt my son.'

'He'll be fine.'

The man came up to Jake, testing the binding at his wrists, finding it adequate, then stepped back and flat-footed Jake in the back, smashing the sole of his boot somewhere between Jake's shoulder blades, sending him sprawling, face down into the floor.

Emma screamed.

Almost nonchalantly, but with extreme force, Arlow sideswiped Emma across the face with the barrel of the Glock, knocking her across Danny.

'Shut it.'

'You bastard,' Jake roared.

Arlow's rage erupted. He came over to Jake and stomped his foot repeatedly down on to his head, pounding him, distorting Jake's face with each blow until he lay almost senseless with his jaw broken and several teeth loosened. He spat blood on to the carpet.

Arlow withdrew a couple of steps, panting heavily with his chest rising and falling with the exertion of the assault. Emma and Anna watched in silent horror, and when he turned to them, they cowered away like beaten puppies.

'Stand up, girl,' he ordered Emma.

Somehow, she rose. Her whole body shook; having been released from one hell, she'd been thrown into another almost immediately.

'Stick your hands out together.' He tucked the

Glock into the waistband of his jeans, grabbed the tape and quickly bound her wrists. He ripped off another strip, which he stuck across her mouth, and pushed her roughly down next to Danny. He then wound the tape around her ankles, trussing her up. 'OK, Jake boy,' he said, 'up you get.'

He grabbed the waistband of Jake's trousers and hauled him up to his knees, then stepped back with the gun again in his hand. 'Up,' he ordered Jake, waving the weapon at him.

Jake's head lolled loosely from the assault, but he managed to respond slowly and get to his feet, one motion at a time, then stood swaying unsteadily like a drunk. The gunman spun him around and shoved him towards the door. He steered Jake into the kitchen, then out through the back door and on to the outside path. He pushed him through the rear garage door, which was open already.

With his hand gripping Jake's collar, he piloted him to the centre of the garage floor and forced him back down on to his knees.

Here, he began to circle Jake, who, though his brain now had the consistency of treacle, knew he was a dead man.

'My name is Arlow Worthington, Constable Niven,' the man said, prowling around Jake. The Glock hung down at his side. 'Or should I call you Constable X?'

Jake blinked. A wave of brain nausea enshrouded him for a moment, then cleared.

'Ah, you recognize the surname . . . Worthington, a name to conjure with.'

Jake shook his head. He was certain that his brain was loose and was slurping around in his cranium like porridge. He could hardly keep his head up.

'I recognize your name . . . Arlow,' Jake slurred. And he did. He recalled Henry Christie mentioning Fraser Worthington's brother at a briefing, which seemed so long ago now. Arlow was the brother suspected of handling the jewels his brother stole in robberies.

Arlow stopped directly in front of Jake. 'You killed my brother in cold blood.' He placed the muzzle of the silencer under the 'v' of Jake's jaw and tilted up his bloodied face, looking directly into his bleeding eyes.

More blood dribbled out of Jake's mouth. He could feel his jaw expanding as it swelled. Could feel the loose teeth in his gums and agonizing pain throughout his head.

'No, I didn't . . . Nothing cold about it,' Jake said to the accompaniment of blood and saliva bubbling out of his mouth.

Arlow's expression remained intact, but he moved with great speed and slammed the pistol across Jake's face, knocking him sideways on to the cold, concrete floor.

Arlow stood back, swiping the back of his hand across his mouth. 'I loved my brother . . . He didn't deserve to die that way.'

'Only way he was going to die,' Jake said. Although disorientated from the blows, his mind was still just about functioning, and he knew that somehow he had to find time, to delay the inevitable. The more time he spent arguing, winding him up, the more time his family had to survive, get free, call for help. 'I should've blown his fucking face off,' Jake added, although the swear word in that sentence came out more like 'frushting', as his pronunciation suffered because of the injuries to his mouth.

It bought him a few more valuable seconds.

Arlow could not resist kicking Jake in the ribs again and again, like they were in some grubby street fight. Jake tried to brace himself, but Arlow was wearing light, but steel toe-capped boots, and they hurt a lot. After the first impact Jake did not have the capability to steel himself for the next half-dozen frenzied kicks.

Eventually, Arlow stopped, gasping for breath. A sustained attack also takes it out of the aggressor, too. He doubled up, with his hands on his knees. 'Now what you got to say?' Arlow challenged Jake.

'Up yours,' Jake mumbled.

Arlow crouched down. 'You know what happened to the guy who left my brother to his fate? You know, the getaway driver who you wankers never found?'

'I guess you're going to tell me.'

'I fed him to my dogs. They tore him to pieces.'

'Good for them.'

'I'd love to put them on to you and watch that,' Arlow said dreamily.

'Take heart,' Jake said, still managing to chide him. 'They'll meet the same fate as Fraser when you get put away for this . . . They'll get put down, like dogs should.'

Arlow reared back, roaring with laughter, which

stopped instantly as he assaulted Jake again, kicking him hard.

After this, Jake had no voice, and his world came and went. He knew ribs had been broken, and the pain where his liver was situated was terrifying. He was certain that organ had burst open and he was now bleeding internally.

Arlow stood over Jake, controlling his breathing, getting his strength back again before bouncing back down on to his haunches by Jake's head and poking the gun into his face.

'This is what is called revenge.'

'How . . . how did you know where to find me?'

'You were pointed out to me outside the court, remember?'

Jake's mind wasn't really fit to recall anything, but then he did: Fraser Worthington's barrister trying to shake hands with him on the concourse outside Blackpool Magistrates' Court after the inquest. Pointing at him when Jake refused to shake hands.

'Then all I had to do was follow, but you have been so busy catching baddies today ever since that I thought I would just hang back and wait.'

'Nice of you,' Jake mumbled.

'Well, probably time to call this quits,' Arlow said. He brought Jake back up on to his knees again and balanced him.

'You're going to kill my family, aren't you?'

'Course I am, Jake . . . but I promise I'll make it quick for each of them . . . . Be over in seconds.'

'They've done you no harm.'

Worthington shrugged. 'Your point being?'
Jake's chin drooped on to his chest.

Henry sauntered up the road, no special hurry. He had been indecisive about whether he needed to make the journey at all, but in the end he thought it was probably for the best, just in case.

The night was chilly and cloudless; a good night in Kendleton, he thought, but ducked, cringing, as a bat zipped by his head. There were a lot of these ugly little creatures in the village, and he had no great affection for them, called them 'pissed up bird-mice', for some reason he could not fathom, but he accepted they were part of the rich tapestry of his new life in the country. To be honest, as recent as it was, his life in the cops was starting to recede, become just a memory.

He stuffed his hands in his pockets and took his time, feeling the need to restore his equilibrium after the events of the last few hours when he had met Danny outside the Tawny Owl and driven him over to Thornwell. He knew that not long ago, when the scar of leaving the police had been more of an open wound, he would have envied Rik Dean his task ahead. Henry instinctively knew that the long, complex investigation into Bartle and Overwall would uncover many unsavoury secrets, which, he guessed, could have serious repercussions around the villages. What if other people were involved? Or was it just Bartle and the taxi-man, feeding their perversions? One good thing that would come out of it, Henry realized, was that if other girls had been abducted and murdered, then at least some families might get closure, as painful as that might be.

He reached Jake's house. The Land Rover was parked on the steep drive next to the family car that Anna mostly drove. All the lights were still on, and Henry guessed that a lot of tears of relief were being shed at that very moment. He did not want to intrude if he could help it, so he peered into the Land Rover, shading his eyes with his hands, and saw what he was looking for – his mobile phone, which had slid out of his pocket, was by the gear stick. He had heard it drop, but thought it was Jake banging his torch on the steering wheel. He tried both doors, frustrated to find them locked. He cursed.

Maybe he would forget it, after all. He needed his bed and Alison to soothe him now more than his phone. He was very sore, stitched up, but the walk had cleared his head, and things would have to wait. It wasn't like he was an SIO any more, having to be at everyone's beck and call.

He looked at the house, lights on – even, he noticed, in the garage. He could see the slit of light along the bottom of the steel up-and-over door.

Thing was, maybe there was no harm in knocking. He went up the front steps and saw that the door was actually open, just pushed to, which he thought slightly odd.

He tapped on it gently, and then slowly pushed it open, about to call a quiet, 'Hello,' when he caught sight of the blood on the banister and down the hallway, at which moment the living

313

room door opened and Emma pitched out, rolling and ferociously ripping at the tape which bound her wrists with her teeth.

Swaying, Jake managed to remain upright on his knees as Arlow walked to stand behind him, placing the muzzle of the Glock at the base of his skull where his head balanced on his backbone. Both men faced the front of the garage, looking towards the inside of the door.

'Well, Jake, seems we've reached that moment,' Arlow said, leaning forward to whisper in his left ear. 'I imagine this will be pretty quick, but don't worry, because even if it isn't, I won't hang around. I'll put another in your brain straight away.'

'And I'll look forward to spitting into your brother's face, cos I'm going to make sure I go to hell and kill him all over again,' Jake mumbled almost incoherently through his shattered mouth, his words slurred with blood.

Arlow's left hand crept up to Jake's face and took hold of his jaw, squeezing and twisting the broken mandible, sending searing agony through Jake, who screamed terrifyingly as the broken shards of bone grated against each other in his skull. Jake tried to jerk away by instinct, but Worthington held on, his fingers digging in deep and probing and gouging the sheared bone. Jake tried to contort, but Arlow went with him, until at last he let go with a flick, and Jake toppled sideways, at which point Arlow bestrode him and pointed the Glock down.

Two things occurred simultaneously at that exact moment.

The old boiler on the back wall came to life with an ear-splitting boom as the gas ignited.

And Henry Christie kicked open the rear garage door.

Arlow reared up in surprise, distracted from Jake for a few seconds. He brought the Glock up and fired. Henry dived sideways along the rear path as the bullet splintered the door frame. Acting on instinct alone, Jake kicked upwards with his right foot as hard as he could between Arlow's splayed legs, hoping to connect with his balls. He missed and kicked him in the backside instead. Although this did not have the same effect, it did cause Arlow to stagger forwards and lose his balance, tumbling on to all fours like a kid in a playground. The gun came out of his grasp, spinning away across the garage floor like a top.

Jake writhed around, finding a surge of energy, and tried to get to his feet, but Arlow rolled and started to get up at the same time as Henry Christie appeared warily at the door, took in the situation and propelled himself at the rising figure of the gunman.

Henry went low, powering his right shoulder into the pit of Worthington's stomach and encircling him with his arms. The impact drove Arlow backwards, tripping over Jake, and he landed heavily with Henry still firmly attached, keeping his head low down as punches rained down on the back of his neck and back.

The two men grappled like wrestlers, each fighting for an advantage, rolling across the garage. Henry smacked his be-capped head

315

against something hard. His stitches split, and the two men came apart with the faster Arlow leaping to his feet, turning to Henry, who was also rising, and hitting him in the face.

Henry sagged down.

Arlow twisted back to Jake, who had managed to get on to one knee. He was over to him in two strides, gave Jake a double-fisted sideswipe that sent him over again, before turning to find the gun and stopping suddenly.

Emma stood there, pointing the weapon at him. The remnants of her bindings hung from her wrists, blood dripped from the blow Worthington had delivered to her face and she looked as desperate as anyone, but resolve and determination oozed from her. She had the Glock in her right hand, resting on the palm of her left, and was settled in a perfect combat stance.

The gun did not waver.

'Give that to me, you stupid little bitch,' Arlow barked. He made towards her, but she jerked the gun at his chest, and this movement halted him.

'You think I won't shoot you?' she said.

'I don't think you know how to,' Arlow retorted, smiling.

'My dad was a firearms officer,' she warned him. 'So don't tempt me . . . After the day I've had, shooting you will be the easiest thing I've ever done.'

'You give it to me now.'

'No, you get down on your knees and put your hands on your head, or I will shoot you.'

At the other end of the garage, Henry groaned

as he pushed himself to his feet. Jake lay still where he had fallen.

Henry's noise distracted Emma. She glanced in his direction, and Arlow launched himself at her.

Emma pulled the trigger four times, each bullet hitting him in the chest, stopping him.

'Bitch,' he gasped, looking down at his body, seeing four holes, one of which in particular pumped blood like a water feature. He crossed his arms over his chest, as if trying to hold the blood inside, to stay alive, but he dropped with agonizing slowness to his knees. His eyes looked into Emma's with pure hatred, but then they turned up in their sockets so that only the whites showed, and he slumped down at her feet.

Twenty

Eight months later

The couple were so newly-wed that the ink wasn't even dry on the marriage certificate when they stepped out into the glorious sunshine that bathed the village of Kendleton in a bright, golden glow and almost tropical warmth on the hottest day of the year.

As they appeared at the top of the steps outside the Tawny Owl, hosting its first ever wedding, they were doused by what seemed a blizzard of confetti that covered them and the whole area in white, pink and silver paper droplets.

Henry Christie blinked in the strong sunlight. Alison's arm was threaded through the crook of his, and they smiled delightedly at the proceedings, although Henry did scowl slightly at the sight of the confetti snowfall.

'I'm going to have to sweep that up,' he moaned through the side of his mouth into Alison's ear. 'I'll need one of those leaf blower/sucker things now.'

'To add to your growing list of gadgets?' she said with amused cynicism.

He and Alison were standing at the rear of the main wedding party, which had massed on the front steps of the Tawny Owl and was being directed into various poses and clusters by Dr

318

Lott, who also doubled as the wedding photographer. He had recently put himself through a course at a college near Lancaster and had ingratiated himself with the husband and wife to be, convincing them he was the man for the job, a claim yet to be proved.

'You two now, yes, you two,' Lott said, and like a sheepdog separating a pair of sheep from the flock he jostled the newly-weds to one side and set them up with the bride displaying her gartered leg across the groom's groin.

'They look happy,' Alison said. She tilted her head and rested it contentedly on Henry's shoulder.

'They were made for each other,' he agreed. 'Both completely mad as hatters.'

The newly-weds they were discussing were Rik Dean and Henry's sister, Lisa, who had eventually set the date and decided to get hitched at the Tawny Owl, which now had a license to hold ceremonies. There was a new annex of extra bedrooms, and the upstairs had been refurbished with a function suite. Alison and Henry had decided to concentrate on small but extremely expensive events. Henry, having developed a bit of a business edge, had enjoyed relieving Rik of several thousand pounds.

'Right, that's good,' Dr Lott said. Having finished the shots of Lisa's leg, he started to rearrange the other guests on the front steps for even more shots at strange, but, he assured everyone, artistic angles.

Henry and Alison held back, but were beckoned forward to join the ensemble for a final few

319

photographs before the party retreated inside for drinks and the wedding breakfast upstairs. Rik and Lisa were at the centre of the group, Henry and Alison at the end of the back line.

'Come on, guys, big smiles,' Lott said, encouraging them all like a children's entertainer.

Henry forced a very large, false smile on to his face, which he managed to keep in place when Alison sneakily said, 'Us next, darling?'

He could not prevent the rise and fall of his Adam's apple as he gulped.

He was 1,000 metres away, hidden in the trees that rose on the hill opposite the Tawny Owl. He had been there for two days, having settled into a tight but comfortable hollow beside an oak tree and behind a gorse thicket, just wide enough for his lithe, prone body. Two days had been easy in comparison to what he done in the past. The British weather was pleasant, and he had been shaded during the summer days, and at night the ground retained enough heat to keep him snug.

He had not been seen, other than by a nosy fox and a badger that came snuffling around the night before. He had let them, and they'd left.

He was armed with the same weapon he had learned to shoot and kill with: an Accuracy International Sniper Rifle .338 Lapua Magnum (which he still used, even though the model had been phased out). It gave him a killing range of 1,500 metres. It was fitted with a Zeiss telescopic sight, through which he was now looking at the wedding guests on the front steps of the pub.

He moved fractionally from one face to the

other, zeroing in each time until the cross hairs in his sights turned from a blur into tight focus. He did this on the forehead of each person with the ball of his forefinger resting on the trigger.

He guessed that, had he wanted to, he could have killed about seven of them before anyone realized what was happening. And then another six before the remainder started diving for cover. He knew he was that good.

Later, in the bar, Henry Christie found himself in a group consisting of the newly married Rik Dean, Jake Niven, and his old friend, Karl Donaldson.

Henry, Jake and Donaldson toasted Rik for the umpteenth time, and they all downed their Jack Daniel's in one, then held out their empty glasses for Henry to refill from the litre bottle he had unofficially liberated from the store. Henry complied, and all four of them gravitated to the fireplace in which a fire was still smouldering, the embers red. The fire was completely unnecessary, but it looked good as they sat down in a semicircle around it.

'So how are we doing?' Henry asked no one in particular.

Karl Donaldson was up from London with his wife. He looked as healthy and as good-looking as ever. 'It's going well,' Donaldson said, raising his glass. He was tall and broad, had a jawline like Superman, piercing blue eyes like a film star and was ageing far too well for Henry's comfort. Henry had always been just a bit envious of him and of the way in which ladies seemed to swoon as soon as he put in an appearance; even today, Henry had seen some of the female wedding guests stop with their champagne glasses to their lips and watch him in awe as he walked into the bar. It was a nice envy, though; he and Donaldson had been friends for almost twenty years. 'Still hunting down terrorists like there's no tomorrow,' the American said.

Henry looked at Rik, who he knew had been working at full tilt for the last eight months on the Bartle/Overwall case, as well as doing the tidying up of everything that concerned Fraser and Arlow Worthington – and several other murders that had come his way: some straight-forward, others more complex. 'Where are we up to with Spencer?' Henry asked.

'He'll be at court in September,' Rik said. 'With Overwall, who still cannot shut up, which is a good thing. We've definitely linked six more girls to them both, and our CSI and forensics teams have done awesome work with regards to it all. I doff my cap to them – going down drains, emptying that disgusting slurry pit . . . that police car will never go on patrol again . . . and finding stuff in those underground containers. Incidentally, we found a pair of Bartle's boots in the slurry, which had glass fragments from the car's broken window in the tread of the soles. Also found glass in the back of one of the cloned Skodas, too.' Rik stopped, then said sadly, 'Unfortunately, all the girls are dead.'

A real conversation-stopper if ever there was one.

They all took a reverential sip of their JDs.

Henry turned to Jake. His family had taken the brunt of almost everything, from Fraser Worthington to Spencer Bartle. Henry knew they had been through hell and back, as clichéd as this sounded, but it was as close to the truth as it could be. The beauty of it was that, even though these were still early days in the grand scheme of things eight months down the line – they seemed to have dragged themselves out the other side.

Emma had proved to be a tough young woman, and fortunately Bartle had not had a chance to harm her before Henry had lumbered on to the scene; however, she had been transferred from one horror straight into another, when Arlow Worthington knocked on the door on a revenge mission on behalf of his dead brother.

Arlow had brought about his own death at Emma's hands.

It had to be said that few tears were shed for him, but Emma was a different thing. But with care and a little professional counselling she showed an incredible resilience that wasn't just a brave front. She truly was an astonishing person.

It also helped that the Crown Prosecution Service decided very quickly she had no case to answer and that she had acted in self-defence – of herself and her family.

Her brother Danny had been badly assaulted by Arlow, who had cracked him across the head with his gun when the lad had bravely tried to intervene and protect his mother. He had fractured Danny's skull, and for a while there had been major concerns for him, but he'd pulled through and, like Emma, had shown himself to be an amazing young person.

Anna's physical injuries were more superficial, and she had been easily fixed by doctors, but as Henry looked at Jake now he could still see the remnants of Arlow's frenzied attack on him. Jake's liver had been ruptured, his ribs broken, cheekbone and jaw fractured, which meant two months of scaffolding on his face and another two virtually immobile, sucking up chicken soup through a straw.

He had just returned to work, and now, although not really supposed to drink, he was enjoying a few JDs.

It had been a tough time for the Nivens, and they could easily have left Kendleton, but then the village itself showed its true character by rallying around in all sorts of practical ways, demonstrating just how seriously 'community' was taken around these parts.

Jake smiled crookedly at Henry – he had yet to master his old smile – and raised his glass. 'I'm good,' he said. 'Thanks, mate, this has been the worst and best move I could have made.' He glanced over Henry's shoulder and caught sight of Anna, who was chatting to another of the wedding guests. Their eyes met, and they shared a smile.

It was a long summer night, one of those perfect nights for a wedding.

About eight p.m., Henry drifted out of the proceedings alone, on to the front steps of the pub. He had a glass of JD in one hand and the stolen bottle in the other, dangling loosely down by his side. He just fancied a moment or two of chilling.

He was joined, one by one, by Donaldson, Jake and Rik, all in a line, with their eyes narrowed as they looked across the village green over towards the rising bank of woodland opposite, the leaves of the taller trees dappling the light of the sun as the beautiful golden orb dropped slowly in the sky, burnishing everything with gold and casting long, lazy shadows. Each man took a moment to contemplate the meaning of life, as influenced by alcohol.

'Guys,' Henry said, feeling incredibly serene and warm to everyone and everything in the way only Jack Daniel's can bring about. 'Guys,' he repeated. He raised his glass and toasted: 'To the future.'

Each man lifted his own glass and they responded like a choir: 'To the future.'

'Whatever it may hold,' Henry concluded.

He had been a sniper in his previous life. Had been highly successful at it, particularly in the Middle East, with over 150 kills to his name.

But that had been life as a sniper, authorized and paid for by the state, when he had learned to be an expert in camouflage and concealment, stalking, observation and map reading – as well as firing a rifle with extreme precision.

He had transferred these skills, but now he thought of himself as a hunter, as opposed to just a sniper. In addition to the skills he had learned, he believed there was much more to being a hunter.

Being a hunter called for wider knowledge.

Now it was a given that he had to get to know his prey, whereas when he was 'just' a sniper, it was totally impersonal. He'd shot people he did not, would not, ever know – albeit that person was out to get him first if possible.

As a hunter, his prey was not out to get him, as such.

They may have been out to get someone else – quite possibly the individual who hired him – but they would never, ever know of his existence. They would never know they were being stalked or watched. They would never know that danger lurked, and they would be dead in an instant and still know nothing about it.

So now he considered himself a hunter, probably the best in the business, and he saw it as a requirement to get to know his target, their habits, their associates, their routines and the times when they felt they were safe, but were, in fact, at their most vulnerable. The times when they would be most easy to kill.

The hunter looked down the Carl Zeiss telescopic sight, which had the mil-dot reticle and a scale enabling him to see the dialled elevation setting without having to remove his eyes from the lens. He was prone, right leg drawn up, his face pressed against the stock's cheek-piece and the stock itself supported by a sandbag he had brought along for the purpose. He breathed deeply, but was not yet ready to fire, even though conditions were just about perfect: no wind, nice weather and clear visibility.

He looked at each man standing on the front

steps, knowing them all, all the members of the herd.

Firstly, Rik Dean, high ranking detective in the local force: of no interest.

Then PC Jake Niven, local cop: no interest.

After him, Karl Donaldson, former FBI field agent, now nothing more than an office bod working in the FBI Legat at the US embassy in London.

The hunter held Donaldson's head in his sights and tensed slightly as the Yank shaded his eyes and seemed to peer directly at him, right down the telescopic sights. Surely the guy had not spotted him? Had he made a mistake?

Then Donaldson put his hand down.

He was of no interest to the hunter, anyway.

Rik Dean stepped in front of Henry Christie, obscuring him from view. He shook Christie's hand, then walked into the pub.

Jake Niven did the same thing, patting Henry on the shoulder as he walked past and back inside.

Finally, Donaldson did the same.

It was as if the members of the pack were paying their respects to the leader.

The hunter inhaled, then exhaled long and slow as Henry Christie came into view and Donaldson walked away.

Christie stood there, JD bottle in one hand, glass in the other, tilting his head slightly just to get the last rays of the sun, but even so, the hunter was able to focus the cross hairs right in the centre of his forehead.

This man was the hunter's prey.

The hunter took off, then replaced the ball of

his right forefinger on the trigger. Inhaled, exhaled again, holding his lungs on empty. The barrel of the rifle was rock steady and would be even more so when he took the shot between his own heartbeats.